*As he gave her what she silently demanded, she heard his deep-throated chuckle of masculine satisfaction.*

She felt his hands skim her body. Then panic took her. Stunned, she thought, It's too soon! I'm not ready! She pulled away. "You must do this a lot," she managed.

He jerked as if she'd slapped him. "What the hell is that supposed to mean?"

She tried to keep her tone light. "You're so good at it. I'm sorry—I'm not."

"Aw—" Stony looked up and swore at the stars.

"After all, you've been single almost as long as I was married. I've only made love with one man in my life."

"I'm not going to tell you I've been a monk. But damn it, I'm not some kind of playboy. I'm pretty particular about who I kiss . . . and I like kissing you. But if you don't want me to, then tell me. Is that the problem? You don't want me to kiss you?"

"No," she whispered. "The trouble is, I want you to . . . too much."

Dear Reader:

February has a reputation for being a cold and dreary month, but not at Silhouette Intimate Moments. In fact, so many exciting things are happening this month that it's hard to know where to begin, so I'll start off with *Special Gifts* by Anne Stuart. Anne is no doubt familiar to many of you, but this is the first time she's done a novel for Silhouette Books, and it's a winner. I don't want to tell you too much, because this is definitely a must-read book. I'll say only that if you think you know everything there is to know about love and suspense and how they go together, you're in for a big surprise and a very special treat.

Another name that many of you will recognize is Linda Shaw. In *Case Dismissed* she makes her first appearance in the line in several years. If you've been reading her Silhouette Special Editions, you'll know why we're so glad to welcome her back. This is a book that literally has everything: passion and power struggles, dreams of vengeance and, most of all, characters who will jump off the page and into your heart. Don't miss it!

Award-winning writer Kathleen Creighton treats a serious subject with insight and tenderness in *Love and Other Surprises*, the story of two people who never expected to find love again—much less become parents!—but are more than capable of dealing with such unexpected happiness. Finally, welcome bestseller Naomi Horton to the line. In *Strangers No More* she gives us a whirlwind romance and a momentary marriage between a heroine you'll adore and a hero who is not at all what he seems. Figure this one out, if you can!

No matter what the weather's doing outside, February is hot at Silhouette Intimate Moments!

Leslie J. Wainger
Senior Editor
Silhouette Books

# Love and Other Surprises

## KATHLEEN CREIGHTON

*Silhouette Intimate Moments*

Published by Silhouette Books New York

**America's Publisher of Contemporary Romance**

SILHOUETTE BOOKS
300 East 42nd St., New York, N.Y. 10017

Copyright © 1990 by Kathleen Modrovich

ISBN: 0-373-07322-4

First Silhouette Books printing February 1990

Printed in the U.S.A.

---

## *KATHLEEN CREIGHTON*

has roots deep in the California soil and still lives in the valley where her mother and grandmother were born. As a child she enjoyed listening to old-timers' tales, and her fascination with the past only deepened as she grew older. Today, she says she is interested in everything—art, music, gardening, zoology, anthropology and history, but people are at the top of her list. She also has a lifelong passion for writing and recently began to combine her two loves into romance novels.

TO MY DAUGHTERS,
DAWN, LISI and ILDY,
with profound love and deepest respect,
for seeing me through my second adolescence
with patience, wisdom and laughter

# *Prologue*

It's gone? Everything?"

The judge nodded. "I'm afraid so."

"What you're saying is, I'm broke." The cultured voice was soft but steady. The woman was very pale, which the judge knew was in large part due to her own natural coloring; other than that, there was only the slightest ripple of her throat to betray her emotions.

The judge wished he could say the same for himself. As he gazed narrowly at the woman across his desk, he was mechanically rubbing at a spot just above his belt buckle, an old habit retained from a particularly stressful period in his life, one that usually resurfaced only when he was feeling especially frustrated and impotent. He lifted a hand and let it drop. "I'm sorry, Toby. I wish—"

"It's all right," she said quickly, and even managed a breathy laugh. "I'm all right. It's just . . . well, it's quite a surprise, you know."

An understatement if there ever was one. "Yes," the judge agreed dryly, "Arthur seems to have been full of surprises."

With thoughtful compassion, he studied the girl in the big green leather client's chair. Not really a girl, of course—how old would she be—good grief, nearly forty?—but there was something about her that made him think of her that way. Something...he searched for a word and finally settled with dissatisfaction on *untouched*. As if, he thought, she'd spent the past twenty years frozen in cryogenic sleep and had just awakened to an unfamiliar and puzzling world.

Damn Arthur Thomas. Even though Arthur had been his friend and one of the very first to occupy that green leather chair way back in the days of his private law practice, the judge bitterly wished him in hell. It was a pity, he thought, that he hadn't had charge of the man's financial as well as personal legal affairs. If he had, it was a sure bet his widow wouldn't be in the mess she was in now.

Although maybe not, the judge reflected ruefully. Arthur Thomas had been a stubborn man. Did things his own way. Hadn't the judge advised him in the first place against marrying Toby Delancy after her parents had been killed in that crash in San Juan? Well, of course he'd told Arthur it was crazy—a girl twenty years younger, a college kid, for Pete's sake! How were his daughters going to take to having a stepmother only a couple of years older than they were?

To which Arthur had bluntly replied that since his daughters lived back East somewhere with their mother and he seldom, if ever, heard from them, it wasn't any of their business who he married; and besides, the girl and that younger sister of hers needed taking care of.

Take care of her, yes, the judge had firmly countered. Marry her, no. But Arthur, as usual, had done as he pleased. And even the judge had to admit that it had worked out much better than he'd have thought possible. Toby had made Arthur a good wife. She seemed to have overcome her natural shyness and developed a quiet elegance that had balanced Arthur very well. They'd certainly always seemed like a happy couple, right up until the moment Arthur dropped dead of a heart attack one spring Sunday morning, while out jogging. There were some things, the judge reflected wryly, that not even Arthur Thomas could have his own way.

"I will pay them all," Arthur's widow announced with a proud lift of her chin. "All the debts, the back taxes—everything."

"Toby, there are things we can do. File Chapter—"

But she was shaking her head. "No. I will not declare bankruptcy." The judge covered an exasperated snort. It seemed Arthur's stubbornness had rubbed off on his wife. "I mean to settle *everything*. If I sell everything, it should just about take care of it, shouldn't it?"

"It should, just," the judge conceded, frowning. "But I think you ought to consider keeping one of the properties for your own use. You'll need a place to live."

"Yes, I suppose I will." Toby Thomas's smile was thin and wry. "Which property would you suggest I keep? The Bel-Air estate? The condo in Maui? Or perhaps the one in Aspen?" She wrinkled her nose. "My skin can't tolerate sun, and I don't even like to ski." Shaking her head and drawing in a resolute breath, she repeated firmly, "No. Sell everything. I want every debt paid, down to the last dime."

"All right, if that's what you want." The judge sighed and sat back in his chair. At least, thank God, she had no children to consider. He wondered briefly whether that was by mutual agreement or Arthur's dictates. He rather thought it would have been the latter; Arthur hadn't been much of a father to his own daughters. The last he'd heard, they were married and living in Europe. They hadn't even come back for the funeral.

After a moment he asked softly, "What will you do?"

"I'll get a job," she said readily, but for the first time looked uncertain.

"Any idea what kind? Do you have any work experience?"

She shook her head. Her soft gray eyes looked lost. "No—except for part-time jobs when I was in high school. I was still in college when I married Arthur, you know."

"Did you finish? Get your degree?"

"Oh yes, I have a B.S." She grimaced. "In psychology. I don't think that's worth much on the job market, is it? I don't really have anything, do I? No experience, no skills. It's my own fault, I know, but I just...never expected Arthur to *die*." She stopped and looked away, swallowing hard.

"What jobs for unskilled labor pay wouldn't cover your food and rent," the judge said thoughtfully. "What you need is to go back to school."

At that she brightened, straightening shoulders that had fallen into a dejected slump. "Oh, I'd love that. Do you think I could? I lived on very little when I was in college, I don't see why I couldn't do it again! All I need is a place to live—just a room, really—someplace near a college campus so I wouldn't need a car. And a part-time job, just enough to pay expenses, so I would have time to study."

Expanding on the new idea animated her features and infused them with warmth and color. It struck the judge that she was really a very lovely woman, in an unorthodox sort of way. She even reminded him a little of his wife, who had the same kind of off-beat, almost whimsical beauty.

"I know!" she cried, interrupting those pleasant thoughts, "What about some kind of domestic job? I could live in!"

The judge winced. "You mean, a *maid*?"

"A maid, housekeeper, I don't care. I don't mind that kind of work, and—" she shrugged and smiled lopsidedly "—if there's one thing I do know how to do, it's run a house."

Arthur Thomas's widow, a maid? The judge tried to imagine the slender, elegant figure in the leather chair doing domestic labor. How straight she sat, like a schoolgirl, her small, manicured fingers gripping the edge of his desk in her eagerness. The lambswool suit she was wearing was without a doubt a Chanel—a little formal for a Southern California spring, perhaps, but then, she *was* bereaved—and its deep lavender color was perfect for her coloring, pale ivory skin and that cloud of black hair, fine as . . .

No! The very idea was offensive to him. There had to be something else she could do. A lovely young—yes, young!—woman, intelligent and charming, eager and motivated, any employer should be tickled to death to get her! To think of her scrubbing floors . . . What a waste, he thought. What a damned shame.

And then he had a flash of déjà vu, suddenly remembering the first time he'd ever laid eyes on Toby Delancy Thomas. It had been right here in this office, come to think of it, almost twenty years ago, the day Arthur had come to change his will, bringing with him his new bride. She'd been just a kid, then, not even out of her teens, ill at ease and shy. And the judge remembered thinking then, what a waste. What a damned shame.

"I'll see what I can do," he heard himself saying. "My wife has a friend who teaches at the university. He may be able to pull some strings and get you into a graduate program. It'll take some doing—I'd imagine most enrollments are filled, this late in the spring. As far as a job and a place to live—well, let me work on that, okay? Maybe I can come up with something. In the meantime, it will take a few months to liquidate the estate, so you should be all right where you are for now. As executor, I will be able to handle most of the red tape, but I probably should have you sign a power of attorney, unless you'd like to—''

"No." Her mouth was set, her voice firm. "I'd like you to take care of everything, as my attorney. I'll pay you, of course."

The judge just sighed and handed her a pen.

After she had gone, he sat for a few minutes, drumming his fingers on his desktop and gazing at the framed picture of his wife that occupied a prominent place upon it. Presently, feeling calmer and much uplifted in spirits, he spun his Rolodex, pulled out a card and reached for the phone.

"Economics Department, please," he said to the university operator. "Professor Wu."

It took several tries and a considerable wait before he was connected with the professor, but when he finally got through, his patience and inspiration were rewarded. The professor, it seemed, regularly played bridge with the head of the psych department. He promised to see what could be done to facilitate Toby Thomas's enrollment in the graduate program.

"She's going to need a job and a place to live, too," the judge said when the primary question had been resolved. "You don't happen to know of anybody who's looking for a—" he almost choked on the word "—a maid, do you? Or a housekeeper?"

"I don't," the professor replied, "but I will be happy to ask Mrs. Wu. Her field of acquaintance is somewhat broader than mine."

The judge couldn't help but smile at the understatement. The professor's gregarious Italian wife knew everyone.

"Great, thanks a lot!" he said and rang off with a sigh of relief, knowing that Toby's problem was in capable hands.

Still, even he was a little surprised when he answered the phone only a few minutes later and heard rich, mellow laughter followed by a familiar voice.

"Michael, you must be psychic! How could you possibly have known?"

"Hello, Nancy." The judge chuckled. "Known what?"

"That the Gamma Pi's housekeeper is resigning, as of the end of the quarter."

"Gamma *what's*?"

"My sorority, Michael. Wu just called and told me about your friend and her problem, and I think I have the perfect solution. My sorority needs a housemother. What do you think? Doesn't that sound perfect?"

"A *housemother*? Good Lord." It wasn't any easier to visualize Toby Thomas playing surrogate mom to a bunch of sorority girls than it was mopping floors.

"They call them house directors now, of course, which is why I thought of your friend. Wu mentioned she's experienced at running a large house—it's the same thing, really. And the degree in psychology is nice. *And* her experience with young people—"

"What experience? She doesn't have any children."

"Two stepdaughters and a younger sister. That qualifies, I should think."

"I don't think she saw much of the stepdaughters," the judge said doubtfully, "and the younger sister was a long time ago. Times have changed. Kids have changed. Nancy, I don't know—"

"I think the job and your friend are perfectly suited, Michael. Of course, age will be a problem—the average age of housemothers, excuse me, directors, is *deceased*, you know." Mrs. Wu chuckled, then continued a trifle smugly, "Oh, well, I'm sure that can be gotten around. As president of the alumni board, I do have some say in the matter. Listen, I have a wonderful idea. Why don't you come to dinner tonight and bring Toby? That way, I can meet her and we can talk about the job while you and Wu discuss politics in the library. And, of course, you are not to come without that adorable wife of yours. I hardly ever get to see Brady anymore."

"I don't know," the judge demurred halfheartedly, knowing what was coming next, "I'll have to check with—"

"I have lasagna in the oven." The contralto voice was seductive.

The judge whispered, "Lasagna?" in reverent tones.

"And a great big pot of linguine is simmering on the stove, even as we speak."

"We'll be there," the judge breathed, mopping his brow.

He was grinning when he hung up the phone, thinking of his wife's face when he told her where they were going to be dining that evening. As much as she loved the Wus, Brady *hated* Italian food.

# Chapter 1

With an air of triumph, Toby Delancy Thomas punched the Escape key and sat back, rubbing eyes unaccustomed to the glare of green characters on a muddy black screen. She supposed she ought to be grateful to her predecessor for committing to computer all the information needed for the smooth operation of a large sorority house. She *was* grateful, especially now that, thanks to a two-hour crash course at Computerland, she was beginning to understand how to retrieve that information when she needed it. Unlike a lot of people she knew who belonged to those generations that hadn't grown up with computers, she wasn't intimidated by them. In fact, after an initial wariness, she had begun to feel quite warmly toward the tidy little PC purring away on her desktop.

However, like most people she knew who had not grown up with computers, she didn't entirely trust them. So after she had given hers an affectionate good-night pat and turned it off, she picked up the familiar leather-bound daily ap-

pointment book in which she had always kept her house-
hold schedule and flipped it open to the list she'd made of
things still to be done before Monday's opening. She drew
a line through Fire Safety Inspection, which had gone off
that morning without any major hitches, and after a moment's thought, added Change Smoke Alarm Batteries to
the bottom of the list. One item made her frown in mild an-
noyance. The installation of the new salad bar had been de-
layed, and it would not be available for Rush Week as had
been promised. She made a note to discuss alternatives with
Malcolm, the cook, first thing Monday morning, then
closed the notebook with a soft, satisfied sigh.

It was going so well, so much easier than she'd expected,
not much different, really, from opening up one of Arthur's
houses after a prolonged absence. Notify the utility com-
panies, hire a housekeeping service and handyman, discuss
menus with the cook and flowers with the gardener, ar-
range for deliveries of milk and produce and for pickup of
laundry and garbage. Nothing she hadn't done a hundred
times before. As Arthur would say, "Piece o'cake."

But here it was—she glanced at her watch—one o'clock
on Sunday morning, and she was still at her desk, with a
stomach too full of butterflies to let her sleep.

Tossing down her pen, Toby stood and walked slowly to
the doorway of her office. Beyond it was the front parlor, a
large and gracious room with the Georgian elegance of high
ceilings, polished hardwood floors and painted moldings,
tastefully decorated in muted tones of slate blue, dusty rose
and ivory. It was empty and silent now, except for the loud
ticking of the mantel clock. But on Monday morning it
would begin to fill up with young women—bright, beautiful, self-assured young women—holding *her* future in their
hands.

Would they like her? Would they think she was too
young? She'd thought about aging herself—streaking her

fine black hair with gray, wearing dowdy clothes to camouflage her slender body—but Mrs. Wu had firmly rejected that idea.

"Sororities are very image conscious," Mrs. Wu had cautioned her, "and don't forget that you will be, in effect, the front person for the sorority. The girls will expect maturity, yes, but also a certain amount of style. It's a fine balance, my dear, I grant you, but I think you will do nicely. Don't worry—trust me—just be yourself."

Toby wasn't really worried, not about the image part. Twenty years of marriage to Arthur Thomas had definitely matured her, and if there was one thing he'd always insisted on in his companions, it was style. But still the question haunted her: *would they like her?*

It was ridiculous of her to worry, of course. She'd hosted dinners for congressmen and bank presidents, and, what was even more difficult, luncheons for their wives! Why should she be intimidated by a bunch of college girls? Even if they did have the final word as to whether or not she would be their new housemoth—*director*—on a permanent basis.

What if I can't talk to them? she thought in sudden unreasoning panic. I don't know how they think. I don't remember what it was like to be young!

For some reason her eyes went to her old guitar, which lay propped against the wall near the door. She'd brought it with her from the Bel-Air house, one of the few things she hadn't sold—goodness knows why, she hadn't played it in years. She supposed it was silly, but she hadn't been able to bring herself to get rid of it. How she'd loved that old guitar, found in a secondhand store, so old there had been depressions worn in the neck from fingers pressing down on the strings. Her father had bought it for her when she was twelve, during one of his down times, to replace the piano they hadn't been able to take with them to the tiny upstairs apartment. She'd kept it with her ever since, refusing to replace it when good times came again and she could have had any musical instrument of her choosing. Refusing to part with it even though, as the wife of a big-time entrepreneur, she'd had no time for music.

She touched it, trailing her fingers across the pebbled case, her mind suddenly filled with images of a young girl sitting cross-legged in the grass, flowers woven through her hair, cradling the guitar and singing softly while sparks rose from a campfire and vanished into a summer nighttime sky. With unexpected clarity she remembered the words of the song and the poignant ache in her heart as she sang....

*Where have all the flowers gone?*

She drew a quick, catching breath and gathered her hair into one hand to lift it off the back of her neck as she slowly crossed the parlor to the front windows. She could see herself reflected in them, but not distinctly, so that she could almost, *almost* believe it was still that same young girl with flowers in her hair, looking back at her.

Where had she gone? The haunting words of the old protest song echoed softly in her memory.

Impulsively, she unlatched one of the old-fashioned casement windows, cranked it open and drew in a full breath of cool, jasmine-scented air.

*Gone,* she thought, staring up into the starless city night. Like the sparks from that dying fire, like the flowers in the song. *A long time ago.*

But that's life, she told herself, resolutely shaking off a sense of wistful longing with the bittersweet memories. Life and the inevitability of change. Seasons come and go, flowers bloom and fade, people grow older. Change was natural and right. It needn't be sad. She wasn't old, not yet forty, and she was starting a whole new life full of all sorts of possibilities. Change was exciting—and terrifying! Why shouldn't she have butterflies? She was scared to death, nervous, uncertain. And that in itself made her feel... young!

Laughing softly at that discovery, as well as at her maudlin thoughts and fears, Toby began to crank the window shut. But in the next moment she felt herself go cold with fear of another sort. A more concrete and immediate kind of fear.

She'd distinctly heard a rustling sound. Something was moving in the bushes beneath the window.

She called out sharply, "Who's there?" and then wished she hadn't. She was suddenly much too aware of the huge house behind her and of being alone in it. She'd never thought about it before—goodness knows, she'd been alone often enough while Arthur was away on business trips. But there had always been someone nearby, one of the servants and, of course, the dogs, Bruno and Kate. But this was Sorority Row; on the other side of the street was the university campus, dark and deserted now, while all up and down this side there were only other big, empty houses like this one, most of them occupied by a single elderly housemoth—director, most of whom, unlike her, were undoubtedly sound asleep at this hour.

"Hello," she said again, with more authority. "Is someone there?"

The rustling grew louder; the bushes quivered violently. Toby heard a muffled sniff, and then in the tense, careful manner of one attempting to hide the effects of tears a voice said, "Um, I'm sorry to bother you. Is Mrs. Bower here?"

Toby's heart began to beat again. Relief weakened her knees. The voice was young and female. "I'm sorry," she said kindly, "Mrs. Bower retired last spring."

A face appeared below the window, a pale oval with dark smudges for eyes. Toby just caught the shine of tears before a hand flashed briefly, obliterating the telltale traces, if only temporarily. There was another sniff. "Are you the new housemom?"

Housemom? Smiling to herself, Toby said, "Yes, I'm Mrs. Thomas. Are you a...umm..." She hesitated, searching her memory for the proper combination of Greek letters.

"A Gee Pi," the girl supplied. "Yeah. My name's Christine Brand. I'm living here this year. And, um, I was wondering—"

"I'm sorry," Toby said firmly, "the house doesn't open until Monday morning." The rules had been very specific about early arrivals.

"Oh, yeah, I know. I don't—it wasn't...um." There was a pause, and then, in the same low, deliberate voice with which she'd begun Christine said, "I'm sort of...stranded, and I was wondering if I could maybe just come in and use the phone?"

Toby hesitated, chewing her lip. The girl seemed genuine, and was apparently in some kind of trouble, but one heard such awful stories.

There was another sniff, and the face disappeared. A hurried voice drifted through the window, almost lost in the renewed rustling of the bushes. "I'm sorry, I shouldn't have bothered you. It's very late. I'm sorry."

Toby muttered, "Damn!" under her breath, then cried, "Wait!" and sprinted for the front door. Throwing it open, she called softly into the night, "Christine—wait. Please come in. Of course you can use the phone." Just because she was alone now, she thought grimly, she was damned if she'd let herself succumb to raving paranoia.

Halfway down the walk, the girl hesitated and then turned, hugging her arms across her middle. "Are you sure? I mean, I'd never have bothered you, but I saw a light and I thought Mrs. Bower..."

"It's all right," Toby said with a reassuring chuckle. "I'm obviously up. Come in and use the phone. You say you're stranded?"

As the girl moved forward, up the steps and into the light, Toby's hand went to her lips, too late to stop a soft gasp of shock. The girl's arms were folded across her body for a reason. They held together the torn remnants of her shirt.

Pressing her lips together to hold back the questions, Toby stood aside and held the door open while the girl walked past her, into the house. A tall girl, she noted, with long, sleek legs that justified the blue denim miniskirt. There were smudges on those legs, more smudges on her arms and neck and chest and another high on one cheek. Smudges that were either dirt or bruises.

"Come in here," Toby said, leading the way into her office. "Use the phone on my desk." Her voice was calm, but her mind was casting wildly about for explanations. An automobile accident? A bad fall? A fight with her boyfriend? For some reason, she couldn't bring herself to ask. The girl was a stranger, but it was more than that. She seemed to have a kind of wall around her—of pride, maybe, or self-control—that Toby didn't know how to breach.

With a mumbled, "Thank you," the girl picked up the receiver and tucked it between her ear and shoulder, holding her shirt together with one hand while she dialed. She waited patiently while it rang, shoulders hunched, staring straight ahead into nothing, ignoring Toby's suggestion that she sit down. Her blond hair was wild and tumbled; its disarray had probably begun the evening as artful, but now it was simply a mess. Mascara made inky runnels down her cheeks, and her lower lip was cut and swollen. She seemed not to be aware of any of it.

After what seemed like a long time she said in her low, careful voice, "Hi, Jake, it's Chris. I'm sorry to disturb you, but would you please beep my dad?" On the last word her eyes closed and a little spasm jerked at her lips, but the tenor of her voice didn't change. "Yes, I'll wait. Would you please tell him it's urgent?"

Suddenly unable to bear watching her any longer, Toby turned and left the room. She went into the kitchen, turned on the lights and filled a cup with water and put it in the microwave. After some indecision she selected an envelope of hot cocoa mix and stirred it into the hot water. When she went back into her office, Chris was just putting the receiver onto its cradle.

"Were you able to reach your dad?" Toby inquired, keeping it casual. For some reason, the butterflies were back. She felt as if she were tiptoeing across a river on slippery stones.

Chris shook her head. Her eyes slid away from Toby's. "No, he's out on a job and he's not answering his page. But that just means he's probably where he can't get to a phone right now. He'll call back, though, it just might take a little while. I gave Jake—that's Dad's assistant—this number. I hope that's all right. I didn't know what else to do...."

"Of course it's all right," Toby said, holding out the cup. "Here, I made you some hot cocoa."

"Cocoa?" As the girl stared down at the cup in her hands, her face began to lose its aloofness. It seemed to soften and blur, shedding years along with a thin shell of sophistication the way a snake sheds its skin, leaving her with a shiny, fragile look, like that of a small child one hiccup away from tears.

Toby's throat began to hurt. With her heart pounding and those persistent butterflies rampaging through her insides, she said, "Chris, if something's wrong, I'd like to help. Is there anything I can do?"

Chris gave a short, brittle laugh and shook her head. "No, I don't think so."

I was right, I don't know how to talk to her, Toby thought, frightened by her own helplessness. I don't belong in this job.

But she persisted anyway, shyly touching the girl's arm. "Chris, what happened to you? These are bruises, aren't they? I don't mean to pry, but...were you in an accident or something?"

"No." There was a muffled sound that might have been a laugh or a sob. "It wasn't an accident." She was silent, then, for a long time, but Toby waited, not making a sound. There were no sounds at all, not even from outside. It was as if the whole city waited.

"I think—" Chris said, and paused again to clear her throat. She shook her head, and the words came finally, reluctantly, "I think, umm... I've just been raped."

*Raped.* The shock of that single ugly word tore through Toby like a bullet. Her first response was a reflex, like arms thrown up to ward off such a missile—a sharp, incredulous question. "You *think*?" The girl's head came up and around. The look she gave Toby was like a blow, forcing air from her lungs in a single breath, a silent, empathetic, "Oh...God."

She'd seen that look before, on her little sister's face—oh, how well she'd remembered that hot summer day. It had been Margie's birthday, her fifth. They'd been playing near the pool, laughing, having so much fun—and then Margie had been stung by a bee. Shocked and in pain, she had turned upon her older sister a look of reproach and betrayal, a look that said, Why has this happened to me? I thought the world was wonderful and I trusted you to keep me safe. How could you let this happen to me?

Just like that, Toby's butterflies were gone and without even thinking about it she knew what to say, what to do. Gently removing the cup of cocoa from Chris's cold hands, she took them in hers and held on tightly. In a calm, firm voice she said, "Chris, I want you to tell me what happened to you. Why do you only think you were raped?"

The effort to think and speak rationally etched furrows in the girl's smooth forehead. "He was sort of a friend . . . of a friend, but I mean, I *knew* him, you know? And we were sort of . . . pretty much *together*, at this party. So, I don't know, he might have—maybe he thought—maybe it was my—"

"Chris." Toby gripped her hands more tightly and gave them a little shake. "Whoever he is—did you want to make love with him?"

Chris's throat convulsed. She shook her head violently and gulped. "No. It wasn't—no."

"Did you try to tell him so, either with or without words? And did he force you to have sex with him anyway?" Toby's words were hard, her jaws tight. The answer was graphically written in bruises all over the girl's slender body.

Chris's head jerked up and down. She shut her eyes, and her face contorted like a child's as words tumbled from her on the crest of a great sob. "I tried to make him stop—I tried—I didn't want . . . I hadn't ever . . . before, and I didn't want it to be like this. I didn't want it to be like this!"

Again Toby whispered, "Oh, God." And then her arms were around the sobbing girl and she was holding her and comforting her as easily and naturally as she'd once comforted her little sister through a hundred childhood heartbreaks.

What a baptism for the new housemom, she thought as she swallowed the lump in her throat and murmured the meaningless calming phrases. At least after this I should be able to handle *anything*.

The storm was brief. Chris stirred and Toby let her go, watching as she swiped at leftover tears, smearing the last vestiges of her mascara across her cheeks. Then Toby handed her a box of tissues and said with quiet sympathy,

"If you can, I think you should tell me just exactly what happened." Above a wad of Kleenex, Chris's eyes looked stricken. Toby took her hand and gently squeezed it. "I know it's hard, but you're going to have to tell the police eventually, and if you've already talked about it, it will make it easier."

"The police?" Chris said faintly, looking appalled. "I don't think—I can't go to the police!"

"Why not?"

The question seemed to confuse her. Her eyes darted around the room, as if looking for a way out of it. "But . . . he's a friend! Or anyway, my friend's friend. I can't—I don't want him to go to jail."

Toby felt anger rising inside her, like a cold gray ocean wave, but she kept her voice calm and reasonable. "Chris, he's not your friend. Friends don't do this. Do you want him to get away with what he did to you?"

"It wouldn't do any good anyway," Chris said on a little choking sob as she jerked her hand out of Toby's and turned away. "He'll just deny it. He'll make it sound like it was me, you know? Like I led him on and then chickened out at the last minute."

"Even if you did that, it's still rape," Toby said quietly. "Isn't it?"

Chris looked at her with swimming eyes, then shut them tightly, put a hand over her mouth and nodded. After a few moments she wiped her eyes and said almost matter-of-factly, "Last year, one of my friends was raped at a frat party. The guy told this big lie about how she was all over him, and they told my friend if she pressed charges, she'd be in trouble for drinking underage. So she just dropped it. Nobody did anything to the guy—nothing! My friend would even see him around sometimes, and he'd just act like she wasn't there. She kept having nightmares, and so finally she just...dropped out." Her voice broke on the last word. The tears, always close to the edge, threatened to spill again.

Very gently, Toby asked, "Were you drinking? Is that why you're afraid?"

Chris nodded, sniffed and dropped into Toby's swivel chair, where she sat hunched over with her hands pressed between her knees, looking frightened and very, very young. "If I hadn't been drinking, it wouldn't have happened. I'd had too much to drink and I wanted to go back to the apartment. See, I was staying with these friends of mine, because my dad had to go out of town and the house doesn't open till Monday. Some guys in the building were having a party. My friends knew them better than I did, but anyway, we went, and this guy—Steve—was there. I'd seen him around and thought he was pretty attractive." She paused, shuddering. "At the party he was really paying attention to me, and I was...well, flirting with him, I guess, and, of course, I was drinking. After a while I started feeling bad— you know, like I'd had too much to drink—and I wanted to go back to my friends' apartment and lie down. Steve said he'd walk me. I thought, why not? He seemed really nice, fun, and it was...well, *you* know."

Toby did know. The first steps in the dance, fraught with so many possibilities, both scary and exhilarating. A sudden and unexpected wave of empathy shook her; so vividly did she feel the girl's fear and pain and confusion that she wanted to put her hands over her ears and close her eyes and cry, No! That's enough! But she only nodded and murmured, "Yes."

Chris swallowed, waited a moment and then went on. "We were laughing, just being weird. And then I guess I sort of tripped, and he—Steve—decided he'd carry me. I didn't mind, it was just silliness, but when we got to the apartment and I wanted him to put me down, he wouldn't. He said he'd carry me over the threshold, or something like that. So I got my key and opened the door—we were fumbling around, because I'd had too much to drink and I think maybe he had, too—and he carried me in. And he still wouldn't put me down. I started to struggle a little, just playing, you know? Laughing. And then . . . he kissed me.''

Her words began to come more rapidly, as if they were something repulsive that she wanted to rid herself of as quickly as possible. "I didn't really mind that, in fact I even liked it—I mean, I'd thought he was attractive, and I had been flirting with him all night—so I kissed him back. And then the next thing I knew we were in the bedroom and he was putting me down on the bed and lying down with me, and his hand was on my leg . . . and I started getting scared. I pushed him away and he . . . grabbed my arms and h-held them—''

"It's okay," Toby said, taking her hands. "It's okay." But she wondered bleakly how long it would be before anything was okay again for this girl.

Chris gulped in air like an oxygen-starved runner. "I struggled and fought. And then I guess I screamed, because I think that's when he hit me." She touched her swollen lip with her tongue. After one brief look, her pain-filled eyes slid away from Toby's; again they flitted desperately around the room, searching for an escape from the pictures in her mind.

"The police will want you to tell exactly what happened," Toby said through tensed jaws, masking her own emotions. "They'll ask very specific questions."

She was prepared for another protest, but Chris was apparently reconciled to the idea of going to the police. She took a deep breath, nodded and began to talk in a flat, toneless voice that somehow made the descriptions all the more vivid. Toby held her hands and fortified her own heart and mind as best she could, but it didn't help much. She kept wondering if it was Chris's calling her "housemom," or that single look of stark reproach, reminding her so much of her sister, that made her feel like a grief-stricken parent.

"So," Chris said after a forlorn little silence, "I guess I have to call the police now, huh?"

"You don't have to," Toby said, carefully clearing her throat. "It's up to you, but I think you should."

Chris sniffed. "Oh, yeah? Why?" She sounded belligerent, which Toby took as a good sign.

"For one thing, something has happened to you that I'm not sure you're going to be able to handle by yourself. You might need some help, and I don't—"

"You mean, like a shrink?"

"Maybe." Toby leaned forward and touched her arm and felt her flinch. "Chris," she said gravely, "this isn't exactly a skinned knee, and a kiss and a Band-Aid aren't going to fix it. The person who attacked you took some precious things away from you, not the least of which is your self-esteem. I'm not sure what it's going to take for you to get that back, but I think it might help you if you fight back—let him know that he's not going to get away with what he did and that you aren't going to be defeated, as your friend was. Do you understand what I'm saying? It isn't revenge I'm concerned with, it's your own emotional well-being."

Chris nodded, wiped her cheeks in a determined manner and stood up. She reached for the telephone and then paused, looking uncertain. "Okay, so what do I do? Call 911?"

Toby released some of her tension in a little gust of laughter. "You know, I'm not really sure. I've never been in this situation before. I'm sort of new at being a house-mom."

Chris tried a shaky laugh of her own. "What a great way to start, huh?" But she went on looking at the telephone as if she'd never seen one before, then relinquished it gratefully when Toby offered to make the call for her.

"They want you to go to the hospital," she said a few minutes later as she was hanging up. "The officer will meet you there, to take your statement." At the look on Chris's face, Toby caught her hand and gave it a reassuring squeeze. "Honey, it's standard procedure. You can have someone with you all the time, if you want. Is there someone I can call for you? Your mom?"

Chris shook her head. "My mom died when I was little. There's just—" She clapped a hand over her mouth; above it, her violet eyes widened in dismay. "Oh, my God. My dad's going to have to know about this, isn't he? I shouldn't have called him. I wasn't thinking clearly. Oh, God, I can't let him find out about this. Maybe if I call Jake back—"

She put a shaking hand on the telephone. Toby covered it with hers. She said gently, "Chris, I don't see how you're going to be able to keep this from your father. And even if you could, I certainly don't think you should. Do you?"

Chris shook her head, but it was only a reflex. She still looked as if she'd rather face a firing squad than her father. With a quaver in her voice she said, "I guess not. I just don't know how I'm going to tell him. This is going to *kill* him. He's going to want to kill someone, and he just might!"

She seemed in danger of crying again, so Toby said soothingly, "Don't worry about your father, okay? I'm sure he'll be more concerned about you."

But mentally she was trying—not very successfully—to keep from forming unfavorable impressions of what Chris's father must be like. Of course he was going to be upset. Toby knew that the shock and anger she was experiencing now were only a tiny fraction of the pain a parent would feel under the circumstances. And it was natural that Chris should want to protect the father she loved from that pain. But it bothered her that the girl's fear and concern for her father should keep her from turning to him when she needed him most.

"And I'm sure he'd want to be here for you," she said mildly.

Some of Toby's private censure must have crept into her tone, because Chris said hurriedly, "No, no, you don't understand. My dad's great, but, see…after my mother died, my dad raised me all by himself. He just worries about me so much…"

"All the more reason he'd want to be here with you," Toby said firmly as she opened her desk drawer to look for her car keys. "Meanwhile, I think you'd better get over to the hospital to meet that officer. I'll drive you. They said to go to the university's emergency center—do you know where that is?"

Chris nodded and mumbled, "Yeah, I know where it is." But she went on standing there, shoulders hunched, arms once again protectively crisscrossing her body. A tangle of blond curls falling into her face made her look like a lost, frightened child. She blurted, "Umm, do you think you could, you know, stay with me? I know it's a lot to ask…"

"Of course I'll stay with you," Toby said crisply, marveling at the small but wrenching pain in the vicinity of her heart. She put her arm around the girl's slender shoulders. "As long as you need me."

As she was steering Chris through the door, a thought occurred to her. "Didn't you say you had left word for your father to get in touch with you here? Would you like to leave him a message on the answering machine? I don't think anyone else is likely to call tonight."

"Oh," Chris said. "Yeah, I guess so." But she looked as if the task were beyond her capabilities. She was, Toby realized, nearing physical and emotional exhaustion. So she went back into her office and programmed the answering machine with a brief message, saying that Chris was all right and that she could be reached at the university emergency center.

"He's going to flip out when he hears that," Chris said from the doorway as Toby was resetting the machine. "He worries about me so much, you wouldn't believe." She gave a liquid laugh. "One time I remember, in third grade, I broke my arm. I thought he was going to take the emergency room apart." The tears were flowing again. "I just don't know if he can handle this."

"People handle what they have to," Toby said flatly as she turned out the lights. "You'd be surprised."

She put her arm around Chris's shoulders and guided her through the door, down the front walk and into her car, thinking as she did so that "great guy" or not, she really wasn't looking forward to meeting Mr. Brand.

That night reminded Toby in some ways of the day Arthur died. There was the sameness of feeling emotionally drained and physically exhausted, of being forced to stay in unfamiliar places and in the company of kind but emotionally distanced strangers. Of wishing that it would all be over, that someone strong and kind and capable would come and relieve her of the responsibility, that she could just go home and crawl into her own bed and the blessed oblivion of sleep.

She'd sat with Chris—her hand still ached from the force of the girl's grip on it—while she told her story all over again to a female uniformed officer. She'd encouraged her through the indignity of having her bruises and torn clothing photographed in minute and graphic detail. Now Chris was being examined by a doctor, an ordeal she'd decided at the last minute to face alone.

Meanwhile, tired beyond the ability to sleep, Toby had curled up on a vinyl sofa in the emergency center's waiting room. Her head was pillowed in the crook of her arm, and she was staring at an abstract wall mural consisting of wavy horizontal lines in shades of aqua and sand that she took to represent the ocean. She wondered if it was meant to be a calming influence.

The man who burst through the center's double doors was about as calm as a nor'easter. And like a nor'easter he brought with him a blast of cold wind, the smell of the sea and something else—a kind of raw energy, electricity, an aura of excitement.

Toby sat up as he passed her with only the briefest of glances, and something in her quickened, as if stirred by a freshening breeze.

She knew at once that he was Chris's father. Who else could he be? As the man strode to the reception counter, she carefully unfolded herself and stood up, her movements slowed by a stiffness that was only partly physical, consciously fortifying herself, bracing for what was to come.

The man placed both hands flat on the countertop, leaned his weight on them and said, "I'm Stony Brand. Is my daughter here?" His voice wasn't loud but, made harsh and guttural by unbearable tension, it seemed to reverberate in the 3:00 a.m. quiet.

"Your daughter is with the doctor now," the nurse at the desk said with professional detachment. "Please have a seat, Mr. Brand. Someone will be with you in a moment."

"What do you mean, she's with the doctor?" The man's voice was escalating in volume; he seemed relieved to be finally shouting. "What's the matter with her? What's happened to my daughter?"

"I really can't tell you anything, Mr. Brand," the nurse said firmly. "If you will just have a seat, the doctor—"

"The hell I will!" Stony Brand roared. "I want to know what's happened to my daughter, and I want to know *now*. You find somebody who can tell me what's going on or I will, you got that?"

Toby touched the sleeve of his jacket. "Mr. Brand—"

Blue eyes, a lighter shade than his daughter's, lashed her like salt spray. "Who're you?"

"I'm Mrs. Thomas, the housem-mother. Mr. Brand—" She stopped because her tongue had stuck to the roof of her mouth. Somehow, she didn't know how...she was going to have to find a way to tell this tempest of a man that his beloved daughter had been raped.

## Chapter 2

You're the housemother. You left the message."

His face was as harsh as his voice—broad cheekbones, wind-scoured and sun-reddened, a pugnacious jaw and a nose that had met with unknown disaster. In spite of all that, it wasn't an insensitive face; the eyes had a probing, inquisitive sharpness, and the mouth, though set at the moment in stubborn, unyielding lines, looked as if it might smile easily. Lines were deeply etched in his forehead and around his mouth. A caring face, Toby thought. A loving face.

"Yes. Mr. Brand—"

He was holding her arm, unaware of the strength in his grip, never thinking that he might be hurting her, all his energy and concentration focused on just one thing. "You said she was all right. What the hell is she doing here if she's all right?"

"She *is* all right. Please, Mr. Brand—"

"Look, lady." His voice sounded as if he were tearing off words, one at a time. "Chris doesn't haul me in off a barge at 2:00 a.m. if she's all right!"

He was holding her by both arms now, looking into her face, searching it for the answers he needed so desperately. And staring back at him, Toby saw beyond the anger to a fear so black and terrible she could only begin to imagine it, a fear that perhaps only a parent could really understand: the fear that grave harm had befallen his child. She was so moved by it, her own fear suddenly seemed inconsequential. She felt calm and strong and in control.

She put her hands on his arms and felt the muscles in them, like chunks of granite. "Mr. Brand, I'll tell you what you want to know, if you'll just—"

Just then the door whooshed open and the two police officers came in, carrying disposable cups of coffee. Stony Brand's eyes flicked at them, narrowed and came back to Toby. He opened his mouth to say something, but at just that moment, from somewhere in the maze of curtained cubicles, a soprano voice quavered, "Daddy? Please don't shout, okay?"

*"Chris?"* With a hoarse cry, her father tore himself from Toby and lunged toward the sound. The two police officers and the desk nurse all leaped to stop him. There was a moment of bedlam.

"Here—sir, you can't go in there!"

"Whoa, where do you think you're going?"

"Hey, buddy, let's just take it easy now."

Above them all, Chris's voice came again, with greater urgency. "Daddy, *please* calm down."

"You can see her in a minute," the nurse said firmly. "As soon as the doctor is through examining her."

"Okay.... *Okay.*" Shaking himself free of the restraining hands, Stony Brand drew in a breath that pulled the fabric of his heavy jacket taut across his shoulders. He let it out carefully, looked at the two cops and in a calmer voice repeated, "Okay."

He turned then, scrubbed one hand across his ravaged, stubbled face and walked slowly back to Toby. "She's all right, I can hear that." His eyes caught and held hers in a purposeful grip, while his face and voice struggled with the relief and the fear. "So, Mrs. Thomas, are you going to tell me now what the hell's going on here?"

Toby glanced at the two police officers, but they had tactfully withdrawn to the other side of the room, thinking, perhaps, that it would be gentler coming from her. But she knew there was no gentle way to say it, so she took a deep breath and simply . . . said it.

"Mr. Brand, Chris was raped."

For a long time there was only silence. A terrible silence, Toby found it; a void in which the only sound and movement seemed to be her own pounding heart.

Stony's eyes narrowed suddenly. Toby could see only a cold glitter, like chips of glass. The word, when he finally uttered it, was hushed, the barest whisper, but louder than a shout and more heartrending than a cry of anguish. "Raped?"

Toby found that her throat had locked; she could only nod. She reached out her hand to him, but he backed away from it, shaking his head. Finding her voice at last, she tried to say something, something reassuring, something comforting, but he abruptly turned his back on her, leaving her floundering. She left him alone, then, knowing there was nothing she could say that he would hear, understanding that he would prefer privacy to comfort while he dealt with the shock in his own way.

For a moment, though, she couldn't resist watching him—a broad-shouldered man in navy blue coveralls and all-weather jacket. His wavy blond hair still bore the unmistakable imprint of a hardhat, hands, the scars and stains of heavy work. But his pain was so visible, so graphically stated in every muscle and bone and body line, that she finally had to look away. Why was it, she wondered with tight and aching throat, that emotions seemed so poignant in a person of great physical strength?

Presently he coughed and turned around. His eyes were intensely blue and rimmed in red. Lowering his head and scowling like a wounded bull about to charge, he asked brusquely, "Was she ... you know—" He made a gesture with his hand and then thrust it into his jacket pocket, as if he didn't trust himself not to strike something with it. "Was she ... hurt? Beaten, anything like that?"

Toby swallowed and shook her head. "No, just some bruises and a cut lip, from struggling with ... her attacker."

He made a hissing sound through his teeth and jerked his head toward the two police officers. In a rough, ragged voice he asked, "Have they caught the guy? Do they know who did this?"

"They haven't arrested him yet, I don't think, but they will. They do know who did it. Chris knew him."

His face contorted momentarily with anger and something else—a kind of helpless bewilderment that all at once made him human and vulnerable. "She *knew* him? What kind of a guy is he, anyway? Who would do something like this?" He had begun to pace, a few steps one way, then back, his voice beginning to escalate in volume again, a little more with each question. The cops were alert, Toby noticed, but still staying out of it. "How does something like this happen to a girl like Chris? She's a nice, sweet kid—a sensible kid. She knows how to keep herself out of trouble. How the hell could this happen, huh? Tell me that! I send her to the best college, in the best part of town, put her in a sorority, because that's supposed to be safer than living in an apartment—" All at once he rounded on Toby, hands balled into fists, eyes like steel splinters. "Where the hell were you? How could you let this happen?"

It was so unexpected, Toby took a reflexive step backward. Words of protest flashed through her mind like strobes, too quickly gone to provide any real illumination. She settled for a shake of the head and a confused, "What?"

"You're the one in charge, aren't you? Why weren't you looking out for her? Don't you have rules? Some kind of security? I want to know how this was allowed to happen!"

Thoughts formed themselves into sentences, but she never got to utter them. She was opening her mouth, prepared to gently—after all, he was a man in shock, angry, and understandably looking for a convenient target for his rage—point out a few things to Mr. Brand, when Chris's wail came floating down the corridor again.

"Daddy, *please* don't yell at Mrs. Thomas. It's not her fault!"

Her father was just drawing breath for a new onslaught. He froze for a second, then held one big finger a foot from Toby's nose and grated, "Don't you go anywhere. I want to talk to you."

"I wasn't planning to go anywhere," Toby replied with breathless dignity, wasted on Mr. Brand, who had already covered half the distance to Chris's cubicle. Toby saw the doctor intercept and skillfully maneuver the big, angry man a short way down the corridor while he spoke to him in calm, reassuring phrases. Across the room the cops stirred, tossed coffee cups into a wastebasket and went off to waylay the doctor. The waiting room was suddenly empty and unnaturally still, like the aftermath of a storm.

Poor man, Toby thought as she watched Mr. Brand pause at the entrance to his daughter's cubicle, take a deep breath then finally ease the curtain aside. Poor, poor man.

* * *

"Hi, kitten."

"Hi, Daddy."

Stony could tell she'd meant to be brave. He thought it was probably his calling her "kitten" that spoiled it for her. She was still smiling, but the tears were beginning to trickle down the sides of her face toward her ears. His own nose and eyes were prickling dangerously, so he rubbed at them and said gruffly, "Hey, how are you doin', huh?"

She gave a funny little laugh, more like a hiccup, and said, "Well, I guess I've been better."

Her voice seemed stuffy, as if she'd been doing a lot of crying. It was hard to imagine—Chris, his Chris, who hardly ever cried—a regular little toughy. The last time he'd really seen her cry, she must have been about seven or eight years old.

"Hey, Dad, remember when I broke my arm in the third grade?" She was giggling now, but crying, too, both at the same time. "And you carried me into the emergency room and you wouldn't let the nurse take me away from you? And you almost wrecked the place? Geez, Dad, I thought you were going to do the same thing out there just now."

"What?" Stony said. "Who, me?"

"I heard you yelling, Dad. The whole hospital heard you."

"Yeah, well..." Stony hauled in a breath and found no room for it in his chest. He coughed and said, "I guess I'm a little..."

In a broken voice Chris said, "I'm sorry, Daddy. You're really upset with me, aren't you?"

Oh, boy. Stony felt as if a whole herd of stampeding buffalo had been trampling on his insides. Damn it, he hurt—all over.

"Upset with *you*? God, kitten..." He wanted to pick her up, just gather her into his lap and rock her, the way he'd done when she was little. But this wasn't a skinned knee, and to his dismay he found that he didn't know how to touch her—that he was afraid to touch her. Helplessly, he lifted his hand and let it drop.

"Kitten, of course I'm upset, but not with you. This wasn't your fault."

"Yes, it was." She squeezed her eyes shut, dislodging more tears. It was almost more than Stony could stand. "I lied to you, Daddy."

With her eyes still closed up tight, she waited, like a small child having confessed to the ultimate sin, certain of swift and sure retribution. Stony looked down at her face, at the spiky clumped lashes, the dirt smudges and bruises, the sunshine sprinkling of freckles, the little scar on her chin from her first bicycle disaster, and he wondered how it was possible to love someone so much and hurt so bad.

He tweaked the end of her nose the way he used to do when she was little, forced a smile and said, "What are you talking about? Lied to me about what?"

"Dad, I haven't been staying at the Gee Pi house, I've been crashing with some friends, at their apartment. And...that's how it happened. There was this party in the building, and I, umm... Anyway, if I hadn't lied to you, it probably wouldn't have happened, and...I'm really sorry."

"Why?" Stony gently thumbed tears from the corners of Chris's eyes and then leaned on his hands. Very carefully, not wanting to upset her more, he asked, "Why aren't you living at the house, baby? I thought that was all set."

"It is all set. But...the house doesn't open till Monday."

He didn't want to come down on her, certainly not now, but there was one thing he had to ask. "Chris, if you knew the house wasn't open, why didn't you tell me?"

She hitched herself a little higher on the gurney's one hard pillow and wiped her face with her hands. "Because," she said with a sniff, "I didn't want you to worry."

"Ah, geez, Chris—"

"You hate it when you have to go out on a job and leave me alone, you know you do! So when that tanker thing came up, I told you I was moving into the house a week early, so you'd feel okay about leaving and you wouldn't have to think about it. It was okay, Dad, really. My friends were great, they let me have their couch for nothing, and I even had a parking space. I thought it was okay, it was just for a week...."

Stony pushed himself away from her, suddenly unable to take any more. Damn! he thought, addressing the curse to the ceiling. It was just like her, always worrying about *him*.

"Daddy?" Her voice was a teary squeak again; he'd never have believed she had so many tears in her. "So you see, it really wasn't Mrs. Thomas's fault. I mean, even if I had been living in the house, it still wouldn't be. The house-mom isn't responsible for me, Daddy. I'm nineteen years old, I'm not a child."

There was a kind of poignant irony in that, Stony thought, but he was suddenly too exhausted to figure it out. He turned back to the gurney, rubbing at the muscles in the back of his neck. "Okay, so if you're not living in the house, how does Mrs. Thomas come to be... How did you—" He waved a hand, frowning.

"It was the only place I could think of to go for help. She's been really great, Dad. I don't know what I'd have done if she hadn't been there. She even stayed with me when the cops were talking to me. I really think you should apologize to her, for yelling at her."

Stony thought so, too. "I will, kitten, I promise. Now, what about you? Are they about finished here? You ready to go home?"

She shook her head and grimaced. "Uh-uh. I think they want me to stay a while, for, quote, observation. They have to give me a whole bunch of antibiotics to prevent VD, I guess, and then they're going to give me something to make me sleep." Stony's stomach knotted. Chris saw the look on his face and said hurriedly, "It's okay, Daddy. I'm going to be okay, really. It's just, I can't seem to quit this damn—sorry—crying. I don't even know why I'm doing it. It's not like it's the end of the world or anything—certainly not 'a fate worse than death,' as they used to say—but every time I open my mouth, I start crying! I can't—"

"Shh, it's all right," Stony whispered, and discovered that he did know how to hold his little girl, after all.

Back outside the curtained cubicle once more, he paused, wishing he had something to blow his nose with. It was a helpless, desperate feeling that, come to think of it, pretty much summed up his mental state at the moment.

Jamming his hands deep into his coat pockets, he exhaled, rotated his neck a few times and wound up staring at the ceiling. What in the hell was he supposed to do now? It was going to be a while before they'd let him take Chris home. He knew he ought to try to get some sleep, something to eat, maybe a shower. A cup of coffee sounded great. Beyond that he couldn't think.

There was one thing, though, that had to be done before all the other things, and he'd best get it over with right now. He wasn't looking forward to it. He'd never been good at apologies, especially when he'd made an ass of himself.

He could see Mrs. Thomas, the housemother, still sitting there in the waiting room, one foot tucked under her, her head pillowed on her arm. He wondered if she'd fallen asleep. It occurred to him suddenly that she probably hadn't had any more sleep than he had, or for that matter, anything more to eat. It also occurred to him as he got closer to her that she looked awfully damn young to be a house-mother.

A jogger went by outside, the slapping of sneakers on pavement a rhythm bass accompaniment to the clinking of his dog's lead chain. Somewhere a scooter snarled its way through its whole sequence of gears before finally fading into the almost inaudible hum of a big-city Sunday morning. New sunlight pouring through the double glass doors found its way across the room to pool like melted butter around the sleeping woman's foot, sensibly clad, he noted, in a wedge-heeled sandal. A single feathery curl of hair wafted back and forth across her lips with each breath she took, like a wisp of black smoke.

"Mrs. Thomas." Stony touched her arm. Her eyes opened and flicked toward him—gray eyes, soft and hazy, like early-morning fog. He smiled crookedly and said, "Good morning."

She straightened instantly, placed both feet squarely on the floor and smoothed the fabric of her slacks—tan, possibly linen, Stony guessed—over her thighs. "I'm sorry, I must have dozed off." Her voice was morning husky, in spite of her best efforts to hide it.

"Don't apologize, it's been a long night." He took a deep breath and laughed a little. "Boy, I don't know—" Realizing his voice wasn't reliable, he tried a cough, then just shook his head and said anyway, "Every parent's worst nightmare."

"No," she replied pointedly, "not the worst."

"Well," Stony began, somewhat taken aback, then shook his head and sat down on the couch. "Yeah, I guess it does beat the hell out of what I was thinking on the way over here."

"She's not hurt, and the doctor says there's very little chance of pregnancy—"

Stony made a strangled sound and put a hand over his eyes. He felt a light touch on his arm.

A gentle voice said, "Mr. Brand, Chris is going to get over this. If she needs help, she couldn't be in a better place. This university has one of the best rape and abuse trauma programs in the country. But she's also going to need *your* understanding and support."

"Yeah, I know." Stony pressed his fingers into his burning eye sockets and took a deep breath, then hitched himself around and tried to smile. "I came over here to apologize. I acted like a jerk."

Her eyes were soft, compassionate. "It's all right, I understand."

"No, I had no right to come down on you like that. I'm sorry."

"No, please, Mr. Brand. You don't need to apologize."

"Yes, I do." The smile felt easier to him now. "And I'd like to do more. I'd like to buy you a cup of coffee—some breakfast, how's that? It looks like it's going to be a while before they let me take Chris home, and I don't know about you, but I'm running on empty. So how 'bout it? Will you let me buy you breakfast?"

She was studying him intently, her eyes creased just slightly with concern. Oddly, he found their touch gentle and easy, like that of a longtime friend rather than a stranger. A nice lady, he thought. A damn nice lady.

"Thank you," she said after a moment. "That would be nice. I hadn't realized it, but I am hungry. And coffee sounds wonderful."

"Great. I'll just go tell somebody where we're going, in case..."

When Stony came back from the reception counter, Mrs. Thomas was standing near the door with her back to him, making an effort to comb some kind of order into her hair with her fingers. When she heard him coming she abandoned the attempt and turned with a smile, as if her appearance didn't really concern her that much, after all. Stony thought that unusual, for an attractive woman.

"All set," he said, holding the door for her. "After you, Mrs. Thomas."

"Thank you, Mr. Brand."

Just outside the door, Stony halted. She did, too, and looked at him questioningly.

Stony smiled at her, squinting against the morning sun, and said, "Can we do something about that? I mean, I know there's a certain protocol involved here, but after what we've just been through together, does it really have to be Mrs. Thomas and Mr. Brand?"

She laughed, an unexpected and delightful sound. "Of course not. I'm Toby." She held out her hand.

He took it, nodding judiciously. "Hmm, unusual. Nickname?"

"No, my father wanted a boy. How about Stony?" He raised his eyebrows; she smiled. "I heard you tell the desk nurse."

"Ah. Definitely a nickname. Started in high school." He gestured toward his truck, which he'd left illegally parked in the emergency zone. "That's my real name."

"Houston Brand and Son, Salvage Operations," she read from the logo on the door, turning to give him a confused look. "Is that Houston or Son? Chris didn't mention a brother."

Stony chuckled. "Both. I'm Houston Jr. It's just me, now, though. My dad was lost in a hurricane off Bermuda."

"I'm sorry."

"It was twenty years ago," Stony said softly. "But, yeah, I'm sorry, too."

"Is that... marine salvage, then? I heard you mention a barge."

"Yep." He opened the door on the passenger side and held it for her while she climbed in, then slammed it hard after her. "You have to let it know who's boss," he explained as he slid behind the driver's seat, by way of apology. "Oops—here, let me clear that stuff off for you." She was delicately easing out from under her bottom various items from the assortment that regularly occupied the front seat: a small coil of rope, a flashlight, several large bolts, a pair of weather-stiffened leather gloves.

As he was waiting for the truck's engine to warm up, Stony noticed, though she was doing her best to hide it, that Toby was shivering. It was going to be a nice day later on, probably hit eighty, but right now the air had a damp chill to it, and he could definitely see goose bumps on the fair skin of her upper arms. A short-sleeved shirt, cream-colored, some silky kind of material—that's all she was wearing. She hadn't even thought or stopped to put on a sweater.

Something inside him tightened, twisted. "Here—" With movements suddenly become jerky and unreliable, he pulled off his jacket and pulled and tugged at it until he had it arranged where he wanted it, around Toby's shoulders. "You look like you could use this."

She turned her fog-gray eyes on him in confusion, and in so doing, unknowingly created in him a corresponding disorder. She opened her mouth to protest.

"I haven't thanked you," he blurted, not giving her the chance. "For what you did for Chris."

"But you don't—"

"*Yes.* I do." His voice sounded loud and rough to him, even above the noise of the truck's motor. "I don't think you realize what you—" With his hands gripping the steering wheel he paused, struggling for control. "You didn't have to let her in. It was 1:00 a.m., for God's sake! She was a stranger. And you . . . well, I just want you to know I'm glad—I'm grateful to you. That's all.''

He slapped the truck in gear, then, and drove out of the medical center parking lot, scowling through the windshield, driving with excessive care, like a man who knew he had one too many beers under his belt. He could feel the thing he'd been struggling to keep control of coming unraveled, and he knew he wasn't far from making a damn fool of himself.

Toby directed Stony to a place she'd discovered in the village that she knew had good strong coffee. Papa Jack's was popular with the university students, but with the fall quarter not yet underway, and especially at that hour on a Sunday morning, it wouldn't be crowded. Most of the students already in residence would be sleeping off their Saturday night— She pushed the thought away without completing it, but went on thinking anyway of Chris in sedated sleep in the emergency center and of the young man whose sleep was soon to be rudely interrupted.

"They have good omelets here," she said as they were seated in a window booth. "You can have almost anything you want in them."

"I'm a no-frills man myself. Bacon and eggs with the works, please, and a side of pancakes," Stony said to the hovering waitress. "And keep the coffee coming." He put his elbows on the tabletop and, with a sigh, let his head drop into the support of his hands.

Toby ordered a Spanish omelet and coffee, and when the waitress had gone away, sat gazing helplessly at the man opposite her, trying to find something to say. It was impossible; everything that came to mind seemed trite and inadequate. So she went on studying him—his hair, the color of antique brass, receding at the temples, long on the back of the neck, his weathered skin and big, big hands—as if he were a species of human being she'd never encountered before. And she almost felt that he might be, he was so very different from Arthur.

It came to her suddenly and with a small sense of shock that, for the first time in more than twenty years, she was sitting across a table all alone with a man not her husband.

"Well," Stony said, lifting bloodshot eyes to hers. He was smiling, but there was something not quite right about it, as if he'd sent the message but the muscles weren't cooperating. He shrugged and brushed a hand across his eyes. "Damned if I know what to say. I just . . . never expected to be in this position, I guess. I never thought something like this could happen. Not to me. Not to Chris."

"I know," Toby said softly. "Life throws curves sometimes."

He propped his chin in one hand. "You sound like the voice of experience."

The waitress came with coffee, so Toby thought she would be spared having to answer. She didn't intend to turn the conversation to herself when he was the one in need of solace. But when they were alone again Stony regarded her narrowly through the steam rising from his coffee mug and said, "What curves has life thrown you, Toby?"

She thought for a moment and then said, "Well, I never expected to be a housemother *and* part-time college student at my age!"

"How did you get to be a housemother and part-time college student, at your age?" Stony asked with a smile, putting a teasing emphasis on the last part. A charming set of lines appeared around his eyes.

She sipped scalding coffee and placed her mug carefully on the table. "My husband died. Four months ago—in May."

There was a little silence, and then, "I take it it was sudden?"

"Very," she said. "He was jogging."

"I'm sorry."

"What I mostly felt at the time," she went on thoughtfully, wondering even as she said the words what on earth was possessing her to say them to a stranger when she'd never acknowledged them even to herself, "was *betrayed*."

She didn't know what she expected—an awkward silence, perhaps, or an embarrassed little cough. She didn't expect the soft chuckle of sympathy. "I know what you mean," Stony said. "When my wife died, I was furious. I thought, how could she do this to me? How could she die and leave me with this tiny little person to care for? I didn't know anything about babies—and even less about little girls! Now all of it, the worry, the responsibility—it was all mine. God, I was overwhelmed. And it never got any better, either. The older Chris got, the worse it got. I mean, you name it, she did it—broke her arm playing soccer, chipped a tooth learning to ride a bike. Discovered boys and got her heart broken too many times to count. But I thought, since I'd got her through high school and learning to drive—*that* was a killer!—I thought— Ah, damn." His voice broke suddenly.

Toby tactfully shifted her gaze downward to the mug in her hands. "You know," she said after a moment, giving him time to regain control, "there was a television show I remember, oh, years and years ago. It was about this cantankerous old lady and a young, handsome guy who went bumming around the Old West together, having all sorts of adventures. At the end of every show, they'd be going along in this rickety old buckboard, talking philosophically together. Once, I remembered the old lady offered the opinion that all children should be placed in a barrel at birth and fed through the bunghole." Stony gave a snort of surprised laughter; Toby smiled. "And then she went on to say that when a kid turns eighteen—and she paused and you had to wait for the punch line, and then she said—'You plug up the bunghole!' Now, I know,'' Toby said, holding up her hand as Stony chuckled in rueful appreciation, ''what she was supposed to mean by that joke—she was kind of a female W. C. Fields, after all. But I've always thought that most parents at one time or another wish they could do just that, wish they could take each new little person and somehow insulate and protect it from all the bad things in the world. Only they can't do that, because then that child would never be able to come out of the barrel. He'd never be strong enough to survive in the world. Do you see?''

''Yeah,'' Stony said with a deep sigh, ''I do see. But it just hurts so damn much, you know? The worry, the fear. You do your best to prepare them, to protect them, and no matter what you do, it isn't enough. When I was teaching Chris to ride a bicycle, I'd run alongside, holding on to the bike, keeping it balanced. But all the time I was doing that, I knew she'd never learn to balance it herself unless I let go of it. So finally I did. I let go of her.'' He put a hand over his eyes and laughed painfully. ''God, it was hard to let go of that thing. And, of course, the first thing she did was get out of control and run full tilt into a curb. Flipped over the handlebars, chipped a permanent front tooth and cut a big gash in her chin. And I felt so damn bad, like it was my fault. Like, if I'd held on just a little longer...''

''No!'' Toby had never heard such anguish in a man's voice before, and it did things to her she didn't understand. Leaning toward him across the table, she impulsively touched his hand, laying her fingers across the back of it, the hard, solid strength of it at such poignant odds with the vulnerability in his eyes. ''No. You aren't to blame. You've done the best you could, and—'' she swallowed, hoping to tame the tremor that had crept unexpectedly into her voice ''—for what it's worth, I think you've done a—a damn fine job! Chris is a lovely girl.''

Stony's smile appeared again, slightly askew. "Yeah, she is, isn't she? But I tell you, there were times... Hey, I'm just glad she's my only one, you know? God, I'd hate to think of going through this all over again! What about you? You have any kids?"

Toby shook her head and withdrew her hand. "No. Arthur—my husband—had two by a former marriage, but I—we never had any." She coughed and changed the subject. "You never remarried?"

"Naw. I looked, at first. But then I realized I wasn't looking for a wife so much as I was looking for a nanny for Chris. So I hired one, and that solved that."

Toby was too polite, too reserved, to ask questions, but they lay there in the silence between them, anyway. After a moment Stony shifted and cleared his throat. "I hadn't made such a success of marriage the first time, and I couldn't see any way to change that. I still can't. My job and marriage—they just don't mix. There's an element of risk— calculated, to the finest detail, but it's there—and then, I have to be gone a lot, and always at the worst possible times. I missed so many important events in Chris's life. Do you know, I wasn't even there when she was born." He gave an ironic little snort and looked away, shaking his head. "No, I don't think I want to try that again. Not ever."

The waitress came just then with their plates, allowing those words to assume the finality of a punctuation mark.

While they ate, Toby kept Stony talking about the work he did, fascinating, dangerous work that might send him rushing off to some of the world's most inhospitable places to battle icebergs, jagged rocks and stormy seas. She listened—it was one of the things she did best—and learned that he'd never finished college because he'd had to quit to take over his family's salvage business when his father was killed. She learned that it had been Stony's company that had finally succeeded in capping a leaking oil well following the collapse of a drilling platform in the Santa Barbara Channel some years back—she'd read about the disaster in the newspapers. And she learned—mostly from things he didn't say—that if there were a marine disaster anywhere in the world, the cry for help would most likely not be SOS, but SSB—Send Stony Brand!

Talking came as easily to Stony as smiling, and by the time their plates were empty and their coffee cups had been refilled for the umpteenth time, Toby felt she knew quite a lot about Chris Brand's father, knew him as well as any man she'd ever met, other than Arthur, of course—who, she reminded herself, it turned out she hadn't known at all.

It gave her a strange feeling to realize that she would never see this man again, not like this. If she ever saw him again, it would be at some sorority social, casually, formally. Mrs. Thomas and Mr. Brand.

And that's as it should be, she told herself firmly as she sat beside Stony in his pickup truck on the way back to the emergency center. She was beginning to feel very odd—slightly light-headed and achy in her chest and behind her eyes. Fatigue, she told herself. Emotional exhaustion and lack of sleep.

She had Stony drop her off at her car in the emergency center parking lot. When he pulled up beside it, she got out of the pickup, then remembered that she was still wearing Stony's jacket over her shoulders. She cried, "Wait!" and he leaned across the seat to crank down the window.

"Your jacket," she said breathlessly, handing it through to him.

He caught her hand, just for a moment or two swallowing it up in a big, warm grasp that seemed somehow to encompass all of her. "Thank you," he said huskily, looking straight into her eyes. "For everything. From Chris and from me."

Toby nodded, but couldn't say anything. She got into her car and drove back to the Gamma Pi house with exaggerated care, like one under the influence of too many lunchtime margaritas.

It was a beautiful Sunday morning. The sun was warm, the eucalyptus trees were in bloom, and all over the city people were reading the Sunday papers, washing their cars, packing picnic lunches, putting on their Sunday best and driving to church. Inside the Gamma Pi sorority house all was cool, serene and quiet. The house still seemed to be awaiting the arrival of the girls with a kind of tense and hushed excitement, but Toby no longer shared it. At least her own fears and doubts on that score were gone. Monday, her new life would officially begin, that was all. The old one was over.

In her bedroom, she drew the shades, folded back the bedcovers and stepped out of her shoes. With her fingers on the buttons of her blouse she paused, then walked slowly to the dresser. The oval mirror there gave back the image of a tallish, slender woman with dark, flyaway hair, a pale face and gray eyes smudged and hollowed with fatigue.

*Where have all the young girls gone....*

She tilted her head, listening to the silence.

She was alone. All alone.

As she watched, the image in the mirror blurred, wavered and slowly dissolved. She turned, groped blindly for the bed and crawled between the sheets. And there, for the first time since her husband's death, she cried herself to sleep.

# Chapter 3

On her way into Toby's bedroom Chris stopped short, a look of horror on her face. "Oh, Mrs. Thomas, you can't wear that!"

Toby looked down at herself in dismay. It was one of her nicest casual outfits, chosen with great care for reasons she didn't wish to examine closely. "Why, what's wrong with it?"

"Nothing's wrong with it," Chris hastily assured her. "It's gorgeous. That's why you don't want to wear it. This is Dad's Day. It's a picnic—you know, with messy things to eat, dirt, grass, touch football . . ."

"I know, that's why I thought pants—"

"Yes, but not *silk*." Chris fingered the matching jacket that was lying across the foot of Toby's bed. "Don't you have any shorts or jeans?"

"Sorry," Toby said with a helpless shrug. She'd sold most of her clothes, keeping only the things she'd considered suitable for her new life as front person for a sorority, but in any case, her wardrobe had never included shorts and jeans. Arthur wouldn't have approved of her wearing anything so inelegant. "But don't worry, I'm certainly not going to be playing football! That's for you girls and your dads."

"Hmm," Chris said, chewing on her lip as she looked her up and down, "I'll bet you could wear some of mine. Hold on a minute—I'm going to go see what I can find. Stay there!"

She disappeared, leaving Toby to survey herself with some chagrin. Well, the pants *were* silk—raw silk, as a matter of fact—in a neutral tan that she'd considered just casual enough to wear to a picnic, yet classy enough to project the qualities of maturity and elegance the girls' parents might expect from their daughters' house director. Plus, the blouse was a shade of rose that she knew became her, bringing out more blue in her eyes and pink in her cheeks. Though why she should worry about looking nice for a bunch of doting Gee Pi daddies, she couldn't imagine.

"Here, try these." Chris was back, out of breath from dashing up and down two flights of stairs. She thrust an armload of rumpled clothing into Toby's arms. "I know there's something here that'll fit you. We're almost the same size."

"Well," Toby said as she untangled a pair of white shorts from the pile, letting the rest drop to the floor, "I certainly can't wear these. My legs are too pale."

There was a chorus of protest from the doorway, where, Toby observed, several of Chris's sorority sisters had gathered to kibitz with bright-eyed interest.

"Well, maybe for white," Chris conceded, diving into the pile on the floor. "How about these blue ones?"

"My legs," Toby said firmly, "are nearly forty years old. I am *not* wearing shorts."

The chorus came in on cue. "Aw, Mrs. Thomas—"
"Mrs. Thomas, you'd look so great—"

"Jeans!" Toby cried with relief, spying a familiar blue-denim leg and giving it a yank. She hadn't worn jeans in twenty years, but at least they'd cover up the parts of her she was least anxious to show. She held the garment up in front of her like a shield. "Okay, okay, I'll see if these fit."

There was applause from the doorway; the chorus had become a crowd. Chris beamed. Well, Toby thought, jeans wouldn't be too bad, especially with the rose-pink blouse, and she did have a rather nice pair of tortoiseshell sunglasses...

"And," Chris cried, diving once more into the pile and coming up with flushed cheeks, a grin of triumph, and, "a Gee Pi T-shirt!"

Toby gave up without a fight. It was the sparkle in Chris's eyes that did her in. She just couldn't bear to disappoint her. Since moving into the house two weeks late, following the stress and chaos of prerush and then Rush Week itself, Chris had seemed outwardly fine. She'd jumped right into the midst of sorority activities and her own busy class schedule with no apparent problems. Toby had noticed that she didn't go on dates, which, of course, wasn't surprising. But she never went to parties or football games with her friends, either. And what was of more concern was the fact that she seemed to spend a great deal of time in her room and that she never went on campus alone. Toby knew how much Chris had been looking forward to this Dad's Day picnic, though, and she wasn't about to do anything to lessen her enjoyment of it.

"All right." She sighed, taking the pink T-shirt with the Greek Letters Gamma Pi emblazoned in blue calico applique across the chest. "If you really think I should, but just don't expect me to play football."

This time the chorus in the doorway was mixed, about half of the girls assuring her that she didn't have to worry about a thing, the other half protesting, "Oh, come on, Mrs. Thomas, you'll have so much fun!"

Toby shooed them all out, including Chris, and changed quickly into the jeans and T-shirt. She was surveying herself doubtfully in the mirror when Chris knocked and then poked her head in the door.

"Mrs. Thomas? I brought you a pair of Nikes. I thought you might—oh, hey, you look *great*."

"Do I? Are you sure?" Toby put her hand flat on her stomach and turned sideways to the mirror, feeling nervous and awkward in a way she hadn't in many, many years. "Don't you think I look too . . . umm."

"Oh, no, you're perfect. Umm, well, maybe except for your hair."

"My hair?" Toby peered once more into the mirror, and reluctantly agreed with Chris. She usually wore her hair pulled back into a bun, which on her wasn't as severe as it sounded. Her curly, fine hair had a way of escaping all efforts to contain it; most attempts to do so were as futile as trying to tie smoke into neat bundles. But even so, she had to admit that a bun didn't look quite right with jeans and a T-shirt.

"How about a ponytail?" Chris suggested after thoughtful consideration.

"A ponytail! Good heavens." Toby thought that was pretty ridiculous, and was just about so say so when Mindy, the Gamma Pi president, stuck her head in the door to announce that the dads would be arriving any minute and Malcolm wanted to know where to set up the coffee and donuts.

"Oh . . ." Toby muttered, and daringly added "Damn!" under her breath. She couldn't believe it—here she was, dithering like a teenager over what to wear! Was she actually wringing her hands? This wasn't quite the image she'd hoped to present to the people whose support checks paid her salary.

"Here," Chris said decisively. She was already pulling pins out of Toby's hair. "Sit down and put on your shoes—oops, by the way, here's a pair of Gee Pi socks—and I'll fix your hair. Got a rubber band?"

Toby was beginning to feel a bit harassed. Making an effort to pull herself together, she closed her eyes and forced herself to concentrate. "Uh, in my desk. Top middle drawer." While one of the girls ran to fill the request, she said to Mindy, "Tell Malcolm to set up in the dining room. I think that's best, don't you? Tell him I'll be there in a minute—ouch!"

"Sorry," Chris said automatically. "Mrs. Thomas, you have the softest hair—hold still, I'm almost finished—it's naturally curly, isn't it?"

"Yes," Toby grunted, "unfortunately." She was bending over, trying to ignore Chris's pulling and tugging while she struggled with the unfamiliar complexities of cotton socks and shoe laces. "I still don't think this is really appropriate attire for...a housemother!" She straightened, pink faced and out of breath, to a round of applause.

"Mrs. Thomas, you look great!"

"Oh, wow!"

"You look fantastic, Mrs. Thomas."

"Yeah, a real Gee Pi mom!"

Chris's roommate, Kim, stepped forward. She had her hands behind her back and a big bright smile on her face. "Mrs. Thomas, I'd like to present you with your official Gamma Pi Dad's Day sun visor!"

Toby groaned and closed her eyes as the crowd of bouncing, clapping, laughing, chattering girls closed around her. The white sunshade with red letters proclaiming Gee Pi's Dad's Day was positioned on her head, and then the girls withdrew to survey their handiwork. There was another general babble of approval, and then Kim said, "Mrs. Thomas, you look just like one of us! No one would ever believe you're our housemom."

"Oh, dear," Toby murmured. That was the last thing she wanted to hear. "Listen, I don't really think—"

Mindy caught her hand and gave it an enthusiastic squeeze. "Mrs. Thomas, we think it's great that you're our housemom. We all want you to know we hope you'll be our housemom for a long, long time!"

There was another round of cheers, and several of the girls came up to hug her. Overwhelmed by a sudden and totally unexpected surge of emotion, Toby could only smile and whisper, "Thank you, I hope I will, too."

Incredible, she thought. She'd worried so about whether the girls would like her, whether she'd be accepted as their house director, whether they might think she was too young. And now...

"Hey," she said, laughing huskily as she straightened her sunshade and tugged it lower to hide the moisture in her eyes, "Get out of here now! I've got to go help Malcolm! And you'd better check to make sure everything's ready. Your dads will be here any minute."

That statement was prophetic. As Toby was passing through the door to the dining room she heard the front door buzzer, heralding the arrival of the first of the fathers. The sound went through Toby like a jolt of electricity. Which one? she wondered. Would it be Stony?

*Stony.* The name she'd been censoring from her thoughts for weeks. All right, damn it, she *was* looking forward to seeing Chris's father again, much more than she wanted to admit. And she knew very well that was what was making her feel this way—nervous and flustered and uncertain.

I'm being silly, she told herself, relaxing a little as she heard an unfamiliar masculine voice rise above the feminine babble in the front parlor. I'm too old to be acting like this.

Except that right now she didn't feel old at all. She felt nervous and flustered and uncertain—wasn't that just like any adolescent? She felt young, and suddenly life seemed both scary and exciting, full of wonder and limitless possibilities.

"Hut, forty-two! Hut, forty-two. Hike!"

The football shot between the slim golden legs of the center, straight and true into the quarterback's waiting hands. The quarterback dropped back into the pocket. The center easily deflected the middle guard, a paunchy man in madras shorts, then leaped into the air in triumph as the quarterback lofted the ball neatly into the arms of a girl wearing blue jeans, a pink T-shirt, a white sun visor and a dark ponytail.

The center's father, watching from the mottled shade of a yellowing sycamore, grinned with pride. Hot damn, he thought, just the way he'd taught her!

"Hi, are you Mr. Brand?" A pretty Oriental girl with long, dark glossy hair was standing at his elbow, smiling up at him. Stony smiled back. "Hi. I'm Kim Yee, Chris's roommate. I recognized you from the picture on Chris's desk. I'm glad you could come. Can I get you anything?"

Stony showed her the plastic glass in his hand. "Found the lemonade—thanks. Sorry I missed the kickoff. I told Chris I'd be a little late."

"Oh, that's all right," Kim assured him with another smile. "We haven't eaten yet. But I think the dads' team could have used a little help."

Stony chuckled. "So I see. Uh, by the way, where's your housemother?" He hoped the question was casual enough; he hadn't realized until he uttered the words how much he'd been looking forward to seeing her again.

"Mrs. Thomas? Oh, she's out there—in the game."

"You're kidding!"

"No, she's right there, see? The one with the ball."

Out on the grassy field, in the brilliant October sunshine, the girl with the dark ponytail was hugging the ball for dear life, apparently making her way, albeit in an erratic zigzag, toward the goal. She ran, Stony observed, like someone who wasn't used to doing much of it. As the opposition lumbered into position to cut her off, the quarterback, a tall girl with curly auburn hair, began jumping up and down, waving her arms and yelling, "Throw it, Mrs. Thomas, throw it!" Other members of her team, including his daughter, took up the cry, "Throw it, Mrs. Thomas, hurry! Throw it to Mindy!"

"Well, I'll be damned," Stony muttered.

The woman with the ponytail—could it possibly be the nice lady with the soothing voice and gentle eyes he remembered, so elegantly dressed in linen slacks and wedge-heeled sandals?—had finally spotted the frantically waving quarterback and unloaded the football just seconds before a fit-looking silver-haired man tagged her on her neat blue-jeaned rump.

The pass wasn't pretty, but the quarterback managed to scoop the football into her arms and scramble the last few yards to the goal line unopposed. The housemother and the quarterback both disappeared in a sea of leaping, cheering bodies.

At his elbow, Kim said, "Isn't she great? We think we're so lucky to have her for our housemom. She's so much fun. She plays the guitar, too—sixties stuff, folk songs and things like that. We just think she's super."

Stony muttered some sort of response, he wasn't sure what. He was busy watching Toby. In fact, he couldn't take his eyes off her.

For weeks, now, she'd been making unexpected visits to his thoughts, dropping in on them like a butterfly alighting on a leaf, elusive, ephemeral, leaving him with a sense of surprise and wonder. Out on a job, with his hands full of steel cable and salt spray stinging his eyes, he'd suddenly recall the way her fingers had felt on the back of his hand, soft and cool as silk. Or he'd see her eyes, gray as the fog that rolled in from the Pacific, gazing at him with such gentleness and compassion. In the middle of conversations he'd hear her voice, just a word or a phrase she'd spoken, and then for the rest of the day that phrase would play in his mind like a line from some half-remembered song.

He'd wondered about it, wondered why he should be thinking of a woman he'd only met once, and then under such traumatic circumstances that he hadn't really been aware of her as a woman. Not that he hadn't noticed that she was attractive. He had. But not with that gut-level, man-woman awareness that sets the hormones flowing, the heart pumping and all senses into overdrive. Come to think of it, he hadn't felt those particular symptoms in a long, long time.

The football game was breaking up, apparently called by mutual consent, or for mercy's sake. Chris came running up to him, looking hot and sweaty, but wearing a grin that did his heart good.

"Hi, Dad," she panted. "Glad you made it."

"Hi, kitten," Stony said as he hauled her into a hug. "Sorry I'm late."

"Oh, that's okay, we haven't eaten yet. Did you have any trouble finding the park? Did you see the game?"

"Just the last part. You looked good, kid."

"Wasn't it great? We won by three touchdowns. Mrs. Thomas almost made a touchdown, did you see? And then at the last minute she threw it to Mindy and *she* made the touchdown. But I think Mrs. Thomas should get some of the credit."

"Yeah, I'd give her an assist," Stony murmured thoughtfully, watching the subject of the conversation walk toward them, flanked by her celebrating teammates. Her walk was neither athletic nor artful, nor even especially graceful, but there was something about it that stoked his fires and warmed his blood. Mrs. Thomas, he was beginning to realize, was one very sexy lady, and all the more so because she seemed to have no idea how sexy she was.

Chris grabbed his hand. "Come on, Dad, you have to say hello to Mrs. Thomas. Mrs. Thomas!" she yelled, waving her over. "My dad's here. He finally made it. He even got to see the last part of the game. Dad, you remember Mrs. Thomas."

"Oh, dear," the house director murmured, looking acutely embarrassed. Then she laughed—that low chuckle he'd liked so much the first time he'd heard it—and held out her hand. "Hello, Mr. Brand."

"Mrs. Thomas," Stony murmured, pleased to note that her hand and her voice were both as soft as he remembered. "Nice play."

"How embarrassing," she muttered under her breath. "I can't believe I let myself be talked into playing football! At my age . . ."

Stony barely heard what she said or what Chris replied. He was suddenly immersed in the way Mrs. Thomas's chest moved, the way her T-shirt clung, the way the sweat shimmered on her skin, like dew on rose petals; in what it would feel like to taste that salt-sweet moisture with his mouth, what it would taste like on his tongue, the way her pulse would throb against his lips. It was as graphic and unsettling a fantasy as he'd had since adolescence.

"Oops," Chris cried, jarring him out of his erotic reverie, "there's the catering truck! I'm on food detail. Gotta go—see you guys later, okay?" She stood on tiptoe to plant a noisy kiss on Stony's cheek and then was gone.

In the ensuing silence Toby cleared her throat, a tiny sound, but it served to remind Stony that he was still holding her hand. He let go of it, but the urge to touch her was still strong, and he didn't know what to do with his hand to keep it from seeking new contact. Eventually he jammed it into his pocket and said, "Well, I, uh . . ."

Fortunately, Toby broke in on that pretty attempt at speech. "Really, I must apologize."

Stony blinked and said, "For what?"

She swept a hand vaguely across her front. "Well, for my appearance and behavior. The girls insisted, but I should have—"

"You look cute," Stony said bluntly. And then, because he didn't know whether that was still considered a compliment or not, amended it to, "I like the way you look. You look just right for the, uh, occasion." But damn it, she did look cute, in that ridiculous visor and ponytail, with little curly wisps of hair clinging to the dampness on her neck and around her face. Inside his pocket, his fingers curled with the desire to touch her.

She stared at him for a moment, then coughed, mumbled "Thank you," and looked away. Stony realized with both surprise and regret that he'd embarrassed her. He always had been too quick to speak his mind. It had gotten him into trouble more than once.

Making a conscious effort to downshift, to put her at ease, he said casually, "Chris looks happy. How's she doing?"

Toby glanced at him, then back toward the noisy group setting up lunch under the trees. "Yes, she does look happy today, doesn't she?"

But there had been a hint of a shadow in those gray eyes, and something in her voice. Stony frowned and put a hand on her arm, turning her back to face him. "Toby, tell me the truth—how is she? She won't talk to me about it—about what happened to her. She hasn't said a word since I brought her home from the hospital. Is this . . . normal, you know, in cases like this? Do you think she's okay?"

Her slender shoulders rose and fell again with her exhaled breath. "Actually, Mr. Brand—"

"Stony, remember?"

"Stony, I've been wanting to talk to you about that."

He was conscious, suddenly, of a quickening within him, a sort of cautious excitement. Concern for his daughter kept him from taking advantage of the opening Toby'd just provided him, but the awareness was there, in the back of his mind. "Shoot," he said gravely.

"Well, frankly," Toby said, "I don't think she is okay. Outwardly she seems fine—well, you can see for yourself. But there are things . . . symptoms, that make me think—"

"What kind of things?"

Toby shrugged. "Oh, a lot of little things." She hesitated, then took a quick breath and said, "Kim says she has nightmares."

"Ah, geez." Stony put his head back and looked up at the sky. He had that squeezing sensation in his chest again, the feeling he'd gotten when he'd first heard what had happened to Chris. When he'd first heard the word. *Rape.* He turned and started walking slowly toward a stand of pines and eucalyptus trees away from the rest of the group. After a moment's hesitation Toby followed him. He felt her touch on his arm.

She said gently, "Stony, it's unrealistic to suppose Chris would come through something like this completely unscathed."

He nodded and said, "Yeah, I suppose so."

"There's so much that happens to a woman with an assault like this—fear, of course, anger, loss of trust and self-esteem. But it's a lot more than that. I don't know if I can explain it to you, but rape is such a personal assault. It's a violation of the innermost core of a person's being. What has been violently taken away from Chris is her control over her own body, and until she gets back that feeling of being in control, she's not going to be able to get over the rest—the fear, anger and so on.''

''You sound like you know something about this.'' He was sorry for the harshness in his voice. He couldn't help it, his throat hurt.

''I've been reading a lot about it lately,'' she said dryly, looking up at him. ''I wish I'd known more . . . before.''

Stony hooked his thumbs in his hip pockets and walked on, studying his feet as they crunched through eucalyptus debris. Presently, he said, ''So, you're telling me Chris needs some kind of professional help?''

''I would certainly recommend it, yes. But whether that means private counseling, group therapy or even some kind of self-defense training, I think you and Chris should decide.''

''All right,'' Stony said, taking a deep breath, ''I'll talk to her.'' He walked awhile in silence, listening to the distant voices of the girls and their fathers and the papery rustling of leaves, the slow footsteps of the woman beside him, keeping pace with his own. ''Toby?'' He stopped walking.

She stopped, too, and looked at him expectantly.

In response, his heart began a slow, heavy thumping. Over it, he heard himself say, ''Would you like to have dinner with me?''

''Dinner?'' She said it as if it were a word she didn't know the meaning of. Then the confusion in her eyes cleared away, like clouds, Stony thought, before the sun. She smiled. ''Oh, yes, I think that's a good idea. We can talk about this more fully, and I can give you the names of some excellent—''

"You can give me the names, but that's not why I want to have dinner with you," Stony said frankly. "I don't want to have dinner with you so we can talk about Chris. I want to talk about others things—you, for instance."

"M-me?" The clouds were back, darker now. Storm clouds.

"Yeah," Stony said, smiling at her confusion. "Like, what kind of music you like and what makes you laugh and whether you prefer movies to dancing, just in case we wanted to do either after dinner. That kind of thing."

"You mean, like a . . . *date*?"

He threw back his head and laughed out loud. He couldn't help it; she looked so shocked, anyone would think he'd suggested doing something illegal. "Well, let's see," he said, clearing his throat and composing his features. "A date. Let's see, is that where I get my car washed, including the inside, and you worry about what to wear, and I shave twice in one day and you wash your hair with something that smells nice, and we both put on clean underwear, and then I pick you up and take you someplace I hope will impress the hell out of you, while you try to remember everything your mother told you about how to keep a conversation going, and we both watch our table manners and try not to do anything embarrassing, and all the time you're worrying about what you should do if I try to kiss you good-night, and I'm worrying about whether or not there's a condom in the glove compartment—excuse me, did you say something?"

"No! I...no." She sounded winded. "Nothing." But her lips were slightly parted and her straight black brows had drawn together in a puzzled frown.

Stony touched her cheek with one finger and found it soft as velvet and very warm. Once again he felt ashamed of himself for his glibness; this, obviously, was a woman who didn't know how to flirt. "Toby," he said gently, "I've made you blush, and I'm sorry. But I do want very much to have dinner with you. What do you say?''

''I—uh . . .'' Her swallow was almost audible. At last she closed her eyes and whispered, ''I really don't think I should.''

''You don't think you should? Why not?''

''Because I'm—it's only been six months since—''

''Since your husband died. I see.'' Stony let his breath out on a long, slow exhalation. What a heel he was. He was causing her pain. He knew he should back off, stop pressing her, give her more time, but he couldn't. There was a strange urgency in him, something that wouldn't let him leave it alone. He could feel it, hear it in the air around them, a kind of humming that was more than just the natural background murmur of a warm autumn afternoon. He almost wanted to point it out to her and say, There—do you hear that? That's electricity, baby. It's real, and it's here, between us. Don't you feel it? We have to do something about this.

But he didn't.

Unable to resist, he did touch her again, though, lightly along her hairline, just above her ear, gently fingering back some loose wisps of fine black hair as he'd been wanting to do all day. And he said very softly, ''Toby, it's only dinner. Nothing more.''

She whispered, ''I know. It just seems . . . wrong.''

He tipped her chin upward, but her eyes refused to meet his. With that peculiar urgency rasping in his voice he asked, ''Toby, do you *want* to have dinner with me?''

She hesitated for what seemed like forever. The humming all around them grew louder in Stony's ears; couldn't she hear it? Finally, as if admitting to something shameful, she nodded and said, ''Yes.''

''Then it's not wrong,'' he said, injecting into it all he could of his own conviction. ''It isn't wrong to need the company of other adult human beings. Toby, if you want to, it means you're ready." He gazed down into her eyes, feeling as if he were floating in a soft gray fog.

"Dad, Mrs. Thomas, come on! Lunch is ready!"

To Stony the voice seemed to come from far away, somewhere in that fog. But Toby started and turned toward the sound, like a wild animal poised for flight. Stony caught her arms. "Toby," he said urgently, "have dinner with me. Please."

"I—all right, I will!" She sounded fierce, almost angry, and as breathless as if she'd just gone ninety-three yards for a touchdown. "I'll have dinner with you."

She'd have pulled away from him then, but he held on to her, determined to pin her down. "Tomorrow night?"

"Yes. I don't know. All right."

"Dad! Come and eat, you guys!"

Finally, but very reluctantly, he let go of Toby's arms and moved away from her. Chris was coming to get them, and he didn't want her to sense the electricity, not yet. He wasn't sure Chris was ready for that just yet. It occurred to him that he wasn't entirely sure he was ready for it, either, but there wasn't much he could do about it now.

"Coming, Chris," he called, "we'll be right there." To Toby he said in a hoarse whisper, "I'll pick you up, say, seven o'clock?"

"Fine," she whispered back, flustered. "No, wait! Don't pick me up. I'll meet you."

"Meet me?" There wasn't time to argue. "Okay. Where? Uh, let's see, how about the Rendezvous, on Sunset. Do you know it?"

"I'll find it. I'll be there—seven o'clock. I promise."

"Okay," Stony said, walking backward, away from her. "I'll see you then." He grinned crookedly. "I'll be the one in the polka-dot tie."

A little bubble of nervous laughter escaped her, sounding almost like a cry of pain.

Halfway to Chris, Stony turned once more. Toby was standing where he'd left her, arms folded protectively across her chest, looking younger than he'd have thought possible, and scared. Damn—he probably had frightened her with his bulldozer tactics. He knew he ought to feel guilty about pressing her so hard—what if she wasn't ready?—but he didn't. What he felt instead was almost ridiculously happy. His knees felt weak, his heart was pumping like a steam locomotive, and he was grinning from ear to ear; he wanted to leap in the air and crow, find a fence to walk, a rock to throw. He felt young, like a schoolboy, a love-smitten Tom Sawyer.

## Chapter 4

Toby knew when she saw the look on Stony's face that he hadn't been certain she was going to come. Which wasn't surprising. Until only moments ago, she hadn't been certain of it herself.

After struggling with it for a night and a day, she still wasn't sure she was doing the right thing. She felt disloyal. She felt sneaky. She also felt excited, exhilarated, nervous and incredibly, thrillingly alive. She kept thinking about what Stony had said about it not being wrong if it was what she wanted. Well, she knew that she wanted to have dinner with Stony more than anything in the world. So why did she still have this queasy feeling in the pit of her stomach?

The trouble was, she didn't know her own mind anymore. It was a stranger to her lately, producing thoughts and emotions she didn't even recognize. While half was dealing efficiently with business as usual, the other half seemed to be wandering around in a state of dazed unrest, yearning vaguely for something—but she didn't know what it was.

"You were serious about the tie," she said to Stony, breathless although it had been only a short walk from the parking lot to the restaurant. He looked different tonight, all dressed up in a camel-colored suede sport jacket and a tie that did, indeed, have polka-dots on it—tasteful little blue dots ringed in navy on a maroon background.

"What? Oh yeah." He looked down at the tie as if surprised to see it there. "It was either this or blue paisley. I think Chris bought 'em for me one Christmas—I can't remember."

"I take it you don't often wear one?" she said with a smile. Some men looked comfortable in ties. Stony didn't.

"Not any oftener than I have to," he admitted with rueful candor.

"Do they require you to wear a tie here?"

"I don't know. I don't think so." He craned his neck to survey what he could see of the dining room. "Doesn't look like it."

"In that case," Toby said, "why don't you take it off? You don't have to wear a tie for me."

"Really?" He looked like a boy who'd just been told school was canceled.

Toby laughed. "Really."

"You know, damned if I don't believe I will." He gave the tie a tug and then paused. "You're sure you don't mind? Here, let me take that for you...."

She was already shrugging out of the coat she'd worn against the evening chill—the only dressy coat she'd kept, a nice lightweight, cream-colored cashmere. He took it from her and turned it over to the attendant, then finished removing his tie and handed that over to her, as well. When he turned back to Toby, her breath caught. Somewhere inside she felt a peculiar sensation, as if something vital had shifted.

With the top button of his shirt undone he looked more like the man that had swept into that hospital waiting room frowning like a thundercloud and smelling of the sea—a little rough, a little wild, a little dangerous. Only tonight it wasn't storm winds and cold seas he brought to mind. Some trick of the lighting had turned his weathered skin the color of honey and his hair to molten gold. He seemed all light and warmth to her, a haven in the storm. Looking at him, she felt herself drawn like a homeless child to a lighted window.

"You look very nice," she said inadequately. "Even without the tie, I mean."

"So do you," Stony said. The look in his eyes was not a trick of light. No trick of light could have done to her what that look did, sensitize every nerve ending in her skin so that she felt . . . everything. She felt the panty hose that hugged her thighs, the whisper of silk on silk where her skirt brushed her legs; she felt the chafe of lace over her nipples, the cool kiss of the drop pearl pendant between her breasts, the stirring of air across her skin. The air itself had become a caress.

Stony coughed and said gruffly, "Nice dress. Did you spend the day worrying about what to wear?"

"What? Oh!" She smiled, remembering his unsettling soliloquy of the day before. "Well, a little." As a matter of fact, everything she owned was, at the moment, spread out on her bed. Not until five minutes before time to walk out the door had she decided once and for all on this one, a classic peach silk shirtwaist with long sleeves, a gracefully flared skirt and a deep V neckline—just a hint of décolletage.

Resisting a nervous impulse to cover that décolletage with her hand, she rejoined brightly, "And did you wash your car?"

"No, I didn't bother, since you weren't going to let me pick you up. By the way, why didn't you?"

She blinked and felt herself coloring. "Well, I—I just didn't think it was a good idea. I don't know how the girls would feel about my... umm." She couldn't quite bring herself to say the word *dating*.

"Fraternizing?" Stony supplied, looking amused.

"Well, yes. It just didn't seem quite... I don't think there's anything in my contract that specifically forbids it— given the average age of most housemothers, I doubt that it's ever come up before—but I just don't know how they'd react."

Actually, the girls had ragged her unmercifully about her mysterious "date," and had made nuisances of themselves with totally inappropriate suggestions as to what she should wear and what to do with her hair and makeup.

"And then," she said, "there was Chris."

"Yeah," Stony said, "I thought of that myself." After a brief, somber moment, he grinned at her and lowered his voice to a seductive murmur. "So, this is beginning to sound like a secret rendezvous, an assignation. A tryst. I think I like the sound of that—makes it all the more interesting."

Toby tried to laugh, but it had a forced, hollow sound. Stony's smile faded instantly. "But you're nervous about it, I can tell," he said softly, touching her arm. "Are you feeling unfaithful to your husband, is that it?"

"No." She shook her head emphatically, although she knew there may have been something of that in the confusion of feelings within her. "No, that isn't it. I think it's just that—" She took a deep breath and released it in a little gust of rueful laughter. "Stony, I haven't been on a date in... a *very* long time. It feels very strange. I'm not sure I even know what to do anymore."

"Monsieur Brand, your table is ready," the maitre d' intoned. "Right zis way, please."

"Don't worry about a thing," Stony whispered out of the side of his mouth as he tucked her hand firmly into the crook of his arm. "I told you, remember? All you have to do is remember everything your mother ever told you—"

"About keeping a conversation going," Toby chimed in, laughing. "Right—so why is my mind a blank?"

It was a blank because, by taking her hand and placing it in that warm envelope of his arm and body, Stony had brought her to a place where thought was impossible, where past thoughts were wiped away and future thoughts were just pinpoints of light beginning a journey from some distant star, much too far away to be of any consequence. A warm little cocoon, inside which she could neither see nor hear, just feel. With those hypersensitive nerve endings of hers she seemed to be able to feel, like Superman, through the layers of jacket and shirt to the firm and vital flesh beneath. And where his hand touched hers, to feel the slow, erratic pulsing of her own heart.

The restaurant was elegant but dark, with an ambience appropriate for its name. Though the room was crowded, each table seemed isolated in its own intimate aureole of rosy golden light. Toby stumbled through the seating ritual, nervous and clumsy as a teenager at her first cotillion, though she'd dined in formal elegance with Arthur so many times it should have been second nature to her.

She wondered how she could so quickly have lost all the poise and assurance Arthur had taught her. Was that what happened when you began a new life? Was everything useful and good forgotten right along with the bitter regrets and painful memories? Or had she ever really had that assurance at all? Perhaps it had been only a facade, a lie, like so many other things about her life with Arthur.

She wasn't feeling hungry, so she let Stony order. He did so with a minimum of fuss. No frills. He'd said that about himself, she remembered, on another occasion when they'd shared a meal together. She hadn't felt nervous and awkward then. She'd felt calm and in control, her mind full of nothing but compassion and concern for Stony. She had even, she remembered, put her hand on his....

His hands. How fascinating, the incongruence of those big, hard-worn hands—hands more suited to grappling with hawsers or holding the helm of a sailing ship steady in a gale—instead caressing white linen, manipulating the delicate crystal stem of a wineglass. How gentle, she wondered, would their touch be on a woman's skin? The unheralded thought made her skin shiver with the same awareness she'd felt when his eyes touched her.

"Well," Stony said when the wine steward had gone. He lifted his glass to Toby with a smile. "Assuming you've been properly impressed by my choice of restaurants, I think this is the part where we both try not to do anything embarrassing. Shall we drink to that?"

"Hear, hear," Toby said faintly. There was a gleam in his eyes as he watched her across the silver rim of his glass, as if he knew very well she'd be thinking about what came next on that date agenda he'd recited so glibly. About—what was it?—good-night kisses and—good heavens—condoms in the glove compartment!

She took a quick sip of wine and found it blessedly dry and cool and, for some reason, intensely evocative of long summer afternoons in southern France. "Umm, that's good," she said, closing her eyes and breathing in the familiar aroma. "It's been a long time."

Opening her eyes, she found that the wine and that brief intrusion of her past life had helped to restore both her composure and a sense of perspective.

"I must apologize for my nervousness," she said formally. "I didn't expect to react this way."

"Oh, well, hell," Stony drawled, gently teasing, "I guess you gotta expect it, your first date in—how long?"

"Twenty-one years. But that's no excuse. I expected to handle it better."

"Holy sh..." Stony set his wineglass down on the tines of his fork, slopping a little of its contents onto the tablecloth. "Did you say, twenty-one years?" Toby nodded. He shook his head and looked away, muttering, "I had no idea." It was a moment or two before he brought his gaze back to her, and when he did, his eyes were once more very blue and very intent, but this time without that particular chemistry that produced such unsettling physical reactions in her. In a gentler voice he asked, "Toby, how long were you married?"

"Twenty years," she said, somewhat in awe of it herself.

"Damn," Stony said, and muttered something under his breath again. "Toby, listen—I'm sorry. No wonder you're having trouble with this. I've been a jerk for even suggesting—"

"No!" The protest came from Toby involuntarily, in sudden panicky fear that she might be about to lose a chance for something precious and wonderful. And then, having said that, she wasn't sure what to say next. How could she explain? It wasn't that she hadn't grieved for Arthur or that she didn't miss him sometimes. "My marriage was... a little unusual," she said finally.

Stony's frown was wary. "Unusual how?"

"Well, I guess you could say I didn't marry for the usual reasons."

"You mean, it was a marriage of convenience?"

"Well, yes and no," Toby hedged, reluctant to explain the details of her marriage to a comparative stranger.

"What do you mean, 'yes and no'?" Stony, apparently, had no such reservations.

"Yes, it was a marriage of convenience, but..."

"You slept together?"

Though brusque to the point of rudeness, the question made Toby smile a little. Stony, she was discovering, was a man who said what was on his mind. For some reason, that fact made it easier for her to do the same.

"Yes," she said quietly, "we slept together."

"Did you love him?" Stony's eyes were like searchlights, probing her soul.

She took a sip of wine; swallowing it felt like swallowing shards of glass. It was a long time before she finally said, "I was fond of him."

Stony let out his breath in a soft hiss and reached for the wine bottle. "Tell me about it," he said curiously as he filled her glass and then his. "Why was it convenient for you to marry a man you didn't love? And then, for God's sake, why did you stay married to him for twenty years?"

"I'm not sure I can explain." Any more than she could explain why she wanted to or why she should suddenly feel like crying. She only knew that all at once she was overwhelmed by self-doubts and regrets and the realization that twenty years of her life were gone, and she could never get them back.

She drank some more wine and it seemed to help. That Stony could be a patient and attentive listener when he chose to be no doubt helped, too. In any case, as soon as the lump in her throat allowed her to, she began to talk, staring into her wineglass as if the right words might be found written there.

"You see, my parents were killed in a plane crash when I was in my second year of college and my sister, Margie, was still in high school." Abandoning the glass, she lifted her eyes to Stony, appealing to him to understand how it had felt to have the world kicked out from under you. "We were... devastated, in more ways than one. My dad was a great guy in many ways, but he wasn't very good at planning for the future." She laughed painfully, remembering.

"He had this incredible talent for making money, and an equal facility for losing it. I'm sure he must have made and lost several fortunes while I was growing up, and never saved a dime. So, sometimes we lived in big houses with swimming pools, and sometimes we lived in little apartments that smelled of the neighbors' cooking. Since we moved around a lot, we never had any really close friends. My mom and dad didn't have any other family—just each other...and us, I suppose. They were devoted to each other—inseparable." She paused, frowned and rubbed mechanically at the tightness in her throat. "Mom always went with Dad on business trips, which was why they both died in that crash. I always thought it was what they'd have wanted."

Stony refilled their glasses, though they didn't need it, giving her time.

"So anyway, because their preoccupation with each other didn't leave much time for us, I always felt sort of responsible for my little sister. Margie was a very bright girl, very focused. I was what I guess you'd call an indifferent student. I just went through school the easiest way I could, without any idea what I wanted to do with my life. Margie was different. She had her heart set on being a doctor, and she knew exactly how she was going to do it. She was going to go to Stanford, then on to medical school there, and so on. And then our parents died. It happened to be one of Dad's down times, financially, so...there we were. No money, no family, no close friends."

Stony shifted and nodded grimly, as if he knew what was coming. Toby gathered her courage and went on. "But Arthur was...there. He was Dad's new business partner and pretty close to his age. As I understand it, they were going in together on some fantastic new venture that was going to make them both rich." As if the idea had just come to her, she said thoughtfully, "Arthur was a lot like Dad, in many ways—you know, a wheeler dealer, an entrepreneur. Only better at it. At least I thought so at the time. Anyway, when my parents were killed, Arthur came to me with a proposition. He said he'd see that both my sister and I got our college educations, including Margie's medical degree, if I'd marry him.''

Unable to restrain himself, Stony shifted again, muttering under his breath. Sensing his disapproval, Toby flashed him a beseeching look. "I was nineteen and scared," she said with quiet dignity, remembering so clearly the fear and the emptiness. "And don't forget, this was before Women's Lib. Plus, there was Margie to think about. I was at a very idealistic age, I suppose, but I didn't think of what I was doing as noble or self-sacrificing." Pride gave a lift to her chin and her voice a defiant edge. "Arthur was not only wealthy, you know. He was quite an attractive man, too— very suave, polished, worldly, sophisticated, everything I was not. I was a shy, self-conscious college student, and very flattered that someone like Arthur Thomas wanted to marry me."

"Why—" Stony croaked, cleared his throat and tried again, frowning. "Why did he?"

Trust Stony to cut to the bottom line, Toby thought wryly. Relaxing a little, she said, "I take it you don't consider that he might have been madly in love with me? Which was what I convinced myself at the time—I told you I was idealistic." She smiled. "It was just like one of those romance novels, you know? Where this poor, innocent little nobody gets swept away by some rich, handsome older man." She laughed and then grew thoughtful again. "Looking back at it now, I think he may have seen himself as some sort of Pygmalion. I certainly made a classic Eliza Dolittle. And then, I suppose he might have just been lonely."

Stony snorted.

"He'd been divorced from his first wife for a long time," Toby explained defensively, stung by his skepticism.

"If the guy was so damn lonely, why didn't he marry somebody his own age?" Stony's voice was escalating in volume. Heads were beginning to turn their way. Remembering the scene in the hospital emergency room, Toby reached across the table and put a hand on his arm. He made an exasperated noise, but lowered his voice to a more discreet level. "You were young enough to be his daughter, for God's sake!"

Toby removed her hand and sat back. "I didn't think you'd understand," she said, letting her disappointment show in her voice.

Stony scowled. "I'm trying to understand." He took a deep breath and held it as an exercise in self-control. "All right, so lots of men marry younger women. He had kids of his own, didn't you say? What did they think about all this, about having a stepmother close to their own age?"

"His daughters were both in their early teens, then, but he almost never saw them. They were in boarding schools in the East and in Europe, and I guess because Arthur's relationship with their mother was so awful—they really couldn't stand each other—they grew up and just never bothered to keep in touch with their father. I always thought it was sad, especially because..."

She didn't finish it, but Stony did, with typical forthrightness and unexpected perception. "Because you two never had kids?"

Toby nodded.

There was a stiff little silence, interrupted by the timely arrival of the waiter with their salads. When he had gone, Stony surveyed his with a frown and said, "This thing about children—is it painful for you? I mean, I'd like to know if it is. I don't like making you uncomfortable."

"Oh, you're not," Toby hastily assured him. "Really. Oh, it bothered me at first. I'd always just taken it for granted that I'd have children—I guess almost everyone does, don't they? But my life was so full, I was so busy traveling, entertaining Arthur's business contacts and so forth, that after a while I realized that my life-style really didn't have room in it for children. So it was probably just as well." The words came easily to her now. She'd said them so many times, both out loud and to herself. "You said yourself that being a parent was frightening, demanding— a full-time job. I don't know how anyone manages to do anything else and raise a child at the same time."

"You manage," Stony said dryly. "You just do, that's all."

It was a perfect opening for one of Toby's best gambits. She'd always been adept at steering troubled conversations into calmer waters. She smiled into Stony's glittering blue eyes and said warmly, "Well, you certainly 'managed' beautifully with Chris. I think she's a very special person."

Stony grunted, "So do I," and stabbed into his salad. But it became obvious he wasn't going to be easily distracted when, after disposing of a cherry tomato, he leveled another hard blue stare at Toby and said, "So. You married a man old enough to be your father, a man you didn't love, but were in awe of. Then what? Did it work out? Were you happy?"

Toby toyed with a piece of endive, unable to meet his eyes. At last she decided on, "I wasn't unhappy."

"Uh-huh."

Her chin came up. "Listen, Arthur was very good to me. He gave me everything I could possibly want. After I graduated from college—"

"Oh, yeah, what about that? What about your sister? Did she ever get to be a doctor?"

"No," Toby said. "She met an electronics engineer from Japan during her second year of med school. They have four children and live on the outskirts of Tokyo."

"So your noble sacrifice was all for nothing."

Anger rose like carbonation to sting her nose and throat. "I told you, it wasn't a 'noble sacrifice.' I wanted to marry Arthur, do you understand? It was my choice—mine!" Now it was she who was causing heads to turn. With a quick, horrified glance around, she dropped her voice to a whisper that couldn't quite hide the tremor in it. "Arthur was good to me. I had everything—beautiful clothes, cars, a gorgeous home, vacation places. I've traveled all over the world. I speak French and a spattering of German. I can converse on any subject you choose—just try me! I've entertained U.S. senators in my home, Mr. Brand. Don't sneer at—at my choices!"

When she finished, Stony just looked at her with a quizzical light in his eyes and for a few moments didn't say anything at all. Well, she'd surprised him, she supposed. She waited, poking angrily at her salad, for him to ask the obvious question, but when he spoke, it was she who was surprised.

"So," he said in that soft and gentle tone that was such a devastating contrast to his usual brusqueness, "there were no second thoughts? No...doubts? No regrets?"

*Regrets.* Toby's throat closed up. She placed her fork carefully beside her plate and murmured, "No, none." She couldn't look at him; she dared not look at him. She felt fragile as blown glass and just as transparent.

"Toby," he persisted, quiet and relentless as dripping water, "in twenty years of marriage, everybody has second thoughts at one time or another. Even the best marriages. It's natural."

"Perhaps," she said stiffly, and pushed back her chair. "Will you excuse me for a moment please?"

Stony opened his mouth, then closed it again. Toby choked out something about going to the ladies' room. He murmured, "Of course," and rose politely when she did, then watched her as she wove her way through the maze of tables, walking carefully on her fragile, blown-glass legs.

At the maitre d's station she paused. I could leave, she thought in a moment of childish panic. Just slip out and go home. I have my own car.

Looking back, she could see Stony sitting where she'd left him, with his chin propped on one hand, eyes on the tablecloth in front of him. Rosy-gold light gleamed in his hair and sparkled on the wineglass he lifted slowly to his lips. The scent of flowers drifted to her from an arrangement nearby. She heard music; a band she hadn't even been aware of before was weaving delicate strands of melody through the clutter of dining room noise. She even recognized the tune, a Peter, Paul and Mary song from the sixties.

How ridiculous. Of course she didn't want to go. She asked the maitre d' for directions to the ladies' room, scolding herself for her foolishness. Why was it that lately she seemed to keep reverting to adolescence? If she couldn't conduct herself with more poise than she had so far, then she obviously wasn't ready for dating in the nineties, that's all. Stony's questions were a little blunt, perhaps, but not entirely out of line. It was she, after all, who had tried to explain her marriage. She could hardly blame him for wanting to understand.

But would he understand? she wondered, pausing before the softly lighted vanity in the ladies' lounge. Would anyone, if he knew the truth? The eyes that gazed back at her were dark and doubtful.

Everyone has second thoughts, Stony had said. Everyone has regrets. It's normal. But had anyone ever felt as she so often had, contemplating her life and her future with Arthur? As if it were a vast, treeless, trackless plain, devoid of all life, utterly and completely empty.

* * *

Stony was mentally kicking himself, calling himself every kind of tactless bastard and making impossible promises to God if He'd let her come back. When he saw her weaving through the tables toward him, he broke into a cold sweat of relief and began composing eloquent apologies in his mind, but she looked so serene and composed he decided it might be better to leave it alone. Instead he vowed to behave himself and never let his big mouth get away from him like that again. Toby's marriage was none of his business.

But damn it, there were still questions he wanted to ask her, questions that were boiling and seething inside him, threatening to blow the lid right off his resolve. Valiantly clamping down that lid, he rose to pull back Toby's chair.

"Perfect timing," he said smoothly. "The food just arrived."

"So I see. It looks wonderful." Her voice seemed breathless. As he seated her she turned slightly to smile at him, and he caught a whiff of fragrance—from her hair, he thought—delicate and elusive as the wind-carried scent of wildflowers.

He didn't respond to her comment for the simple reason that all of a sudden he couldn't think of a thing to say. He was too busy fighting urges he hadn't experienced in a long, long time. The urge to put his hands on her, to touch her. Everywhere. But beginning, he thought, with her shoulders and then her neck, her throat, the sweet, soft undercurve of her chin. He'd tilt her chin upward with the lightest touch of his fingers, her lips would part and her eyelashes settle like black feathers onto her cheeks, and her hair would pour like warm rain over his hands as he cradled her head and kissed her....

"*Madame, monsieur*—eez everysing all right here?"

Stony frowned at his plate with a strange sense of having suffered some kind of memory loss. He seemed to have disposed of his blackened Cajun swordfish, although he couldn't remember what it had tasted like, or what they'd talked about while he'd eaten it. Small talk, he supposed—no, Chris. He remembered now. They'd talked about Chris again. He'd been regaling Toby with hair-raising tales of his life as a single father.

"Fine," he assured the hovering waiter. "Great." He looked at Toby. "How about you?"

She informed him that her veal had been absolutely wonderful.

"Perhaps you would like to select somesing from our dessert cart?" the waiter suggested. "No? Zen may I bring you some coffee? Perhaps a cognac?"

Stony said that coffee would be fine. The waiter removed their plates and went away.

"By the way," Toby murmured, leaning toward Stony across the table, "did I tell you that you have succeeded in impressing the hell out of me?"

The language startled him, until he remembered that it was his own. He laughed. "No, you didn't."

"Well, I am."

He doubted it, based on what little she'd told him of her wealthy and sophisticated ex-husband, but he let it go. Instead he grinned and drawled, "Well, I just thought it would be appropriate. You know—for a tryst."

Gray eyes, sparkling with amusement, met his. "I see."

Unlike him, she was too reserved to pry, but he could see the question forming itself in her mind. "I haven't eaten here in years," he said, answering it. "Or trysted, either. As a matter of fact," he went on when she didn't respond, "I rarely tryst at all."

She still didn't say anything, but the silence and her quickly downcast eyes were eloquent.

"Believe it or not, it's true," Stony protested glibly, watching a faint tinge of pink wash beneath the surface of her skin. "Short-term liaisons are emotionally wrenching, and nowadays, downright dangerous. And like I said, my life-style isn't exactly conducive to long-term relationships. So..."

"So," she said quietly, meeting his eyes with a solemn and searching gaze, "what are we doing here?"

Well, he had no answer to that, either for her or for himself. What was he doing here? When he tried to answer the question in his own mind he felt disoriented and uncertain, unable to see where his footsteps were leading him. It was her eyes, he thought; they seemed to shroud him in soft gray fog.

The silence lasted until he broke it with a bark of ironic laughter. "Making a liar out of me, I guess. Come on," he said roughly, reaching for her hand, "let's find out."

She rose with him, but slowly. "Where—"

"Let's dance." Her reluctance dragged at him like an anchor. Looking back, he saw her eyes darken and her mouth open in protest. "What's the matter?"

"I don't think—I haven't danced in years."

"Come on, don't tell me you and your husband never—"

'She shook her head. "No. Arthur didn't like to dance."

Alien feelings writhed in his stomach, the same ones that earlier had made him keep asking her questions even though he knew they would cause her pain, something akin to anger, only gentler and much more complex. Whatever it was, he responded to it as he usually did to anger, with brusque voice and quiet, watchful eyes.

"It's like riding a bike," he said, pulling her to him. "Some things you don't forget how to do."

He put his hand on her back, just above her waist. Guiding her through the room seemed part of the dance to him, as the music swelled and blossomed and the dining-room chatter faded away. When they reached the dance floor and he turned her to face him, she just naturally lifted her hand to his shoulder. He murmured, "See, what did I tell you?" She didn't reply.

He held her lightly, not bringing her closer to him because it was what he wanted to do so badly. His response to her surprised him, and he wasn't sure how he was going to handle it. Strangers touching for the first time in artificial intimacy—there should have been an awkwardness, a resistance to that breaching of comfort-zone barriers. But instead, he felt tuned to her. Touching only in the conventional places—hands and small of the back, with her hand a tentative weight on his shoulder—somehow he felt her, every inch of her. For the effect she was having on him he might as well have been holding her naked body in the most intimate of embraces, and it shocked him to realize how much he wanted to do just exactly that.

The song ended and another one began, an old pop standard he recognized and liked. Apparently Toby liked it, too, because she made a small sound of pleasure and looked up at him, smiling. He smiled back at her, and then it seemed the most natural thing in the world to draw her closer. He could feel a trembling in her, a tight, deep trembling, almost like a strong current of electricity running through her core.

"You see?" he whispered, not entirely steady himself. "Piece of cake, right?"

Her hair brushed his cheek as she nodded. He closed his eyes and inhaled the fragrance of it. "Piece of cake," she whispered back. Then, a moment later, "What dance are we doing?"

He laughed and murmured, "Damned if I know." He was too preoccupied to try anything complicated. "But it feels good, doesn't it?"

He couldn't believe how good she felt to him. The only trouble was, he didn't know what he wanted from her. He'd spoken so blithely of avoiding relationships, both short-term and long, and then she'd stopped him in his tracks with that damned question: *Then what are we doing here?*

He hadn't had an answer for it, and he still didn't. Because the truth was, he wanted to take this woman to bed—of that much he was certain—and yet he knew it wasn't something he was going to be able to manage on a short-term basis. It may have sounded like a cliché, but Toby just wasn't that kind of woman. He had a feeling she was going to complicate his life in ways he wasn't ready for.

"Oh, dear," said Toby as her toe made unexpected contact with his. "I'm sorry."

"My fault," Stony muttered, steering her to a less-crowded part of the floor.

"I'm very rusty. It's been so long—"

"You keep saying that." He pulled away from her a little so he could look at her. "Seems to me it's been a long time since you've done a lot of things—dating, drinking wine, dancing." Letting go of her hand, he brought his fingers instead to her face, watching as they brushed the matte velvet softness of her cheek, traced the outer curve of her jaw, smoothed back errant wisps of smoke-fine hair. "I wonder..."

She made a small, breathy sound. "What?"

"I just wonder what else you haven't done...in a long, long time."

Silence swept them into its vortex. The music, the dancers whirled away, receding farther and farther until the two of them were alone at the center of a very small universe. He heard only the soft hiss of her indrawn breath, felt nothing but her hand—the one he'd abandoned—on his chest, the moist warmth of it spreading like a stain across his shirtfront. And his own hand, cradling her face, his thumb stroking the kitten-soft place just under her chin. He saw her mouth, lush, inviting...and vulnerable. He saw her eyes darken and grow apprehensive. Tenderness filled him, and a strange kind of ruthlessness.

"Mrs. Thomas," he whispered, "don't look so distressed." His lips curved gently. "I'm only going to kiss you."

"Yes," Toby whispered, "I know."

## Chapter 5

Having declared his intentions to kiss her, for some reason Stony hesitated, the way a novice diver hesitates at the end of the high board as his stomach turns over and fear washes coldly through him, taking the strength from his limbs and the wind from his lungs, and then with fatalistic acceptance of the consequences, closes his eyes and leaps into the unknown. He could see the same fearful acknowledgment in her eyes, feel the same cessation of breath and heartbeat, the tenseness in her muscles, as if her body were bracing for imminent calamity.

Calamity? Geez, he thought, it was only a kiss!

"Aw, hell," he muttered, and stepped off the high board.

Impact was soft and warm and sweet . . . and devastating. He brushed her lips and they clung to his as if infused with their own static electricity, soft as a whisper, and yet he couldn't seem to pull away. All through his insides he felt things swelling, heating. He expanded his chest and held himself very still, for fear he might explode.

It was she who broke the contact, with a long sigh that told him she'd been holding her breath, too.

"The music's stopped," she said, her words slurred and drunken.

Stony gave their surroundings a brief, dismissive glance and growled, "So what?" All around them on the dark floor other couples were nuzzling and whispering, aware of nothing but each other. He chuckled. "It's easy to see why ballroom dancing is making a comeback, isn't it?"

"Yeah." She was leaning against him, but with both hands flat against his chest, forming a barrier between her body and his. Even so, he could feel her tremble.

"They'll start another in a minute," he said. "Shall we just stay here?"

She nodded, but when the music began again it was too uptempo for Stony's mood, and after a minute or two he muttered, "Let's get out of here, okay?" He kept her close to him as he steered her through the throng of dancers, and as they left the dance floor he put his hands on her shoulders and leaned over to whisper in her ear, "I want to kiss you again, somewhere a little more private this time."

Toby gave him a quick, startled look, but didn't reply.

Back at the table their coffee was waiting for them, and so was their check. Stony frowned at it, then at the steaming coffee cups. With one hand on the back of Toby's chair he asked gruffly, "Do you want to stay?"

She shook her head. Stony nodded. He got out his wallet and counted bills into the tray, then turned to take her elbow. Beneath the silky fabric of her dress he could feel the slenderness of her bones, the tensile strength of ligaments and tendons, the warm resilience of muscle, the satin texture of skin. In all of that, and in the way she held her shoulders and refused to meet his eyes, he read confusion. He moved his fingers on the inner bend of her elbow, just lightly stroking, up and down, and instantly felt the trembling.

From out of nowhere came a line from an old song—had he just been dancing to it? It was possible, he hadn't been paying much attention. *Bewitched, bothered and bewildered.* It was the *bewildered* that got to him the most.

Why in hell was she making this so complicated? For that matter, why was he? She was a woman, he was a man, they were obviously both attracted to each other, they'd had dinner together, danced a little and then he'd kissed her. If it was all right with her, he meant to kiss her again and see what that led to; and if nothing, well, *c'est la vie*. Standard procedure. What was there in any of that to make chaos out of his insides? Why this feeling like he might have just lifted the lid off Pandora's box?

Toby stood in the foyer feeling miserable and awkward while Stony got her coat and his tie from the attendant. Emotions rolled through her like waves, one after the other, standard dating-anxiety emotions. Elation—he'd kissed her. Excitement, or was it apprehension—he might do so again. Confusion—what should she do if he did? Depression— what if he didn't? Insecurity—he was frowning at her; what on earth did that mean?

She watched him loop the tie haphazardly around his neck and remembered the moment he'd taken it off, his grin and the warmth she'd been so drawn to. It seemed ages ago to her now. Still frowning—with preoccupation, she concluded—he held her coat for her, settling it over her shoulders while she lifted her hair out of its collar, leaving one big hand on her back, high up near her collar, so that when she let go of her hair it tumbled down and covered his hand. With his other hand he reached around her to open the door, and the desire to feel his arms around her was so overpowering that she shivered.

"Getting chilly," he remarked.

"Yes, but I like it," she said, speaking rapidly through the tremors. "It's a beautiful night, really. I love a clear night like this. Look at the stars."

Stony looked up at the dirty gray city sky and snorted. "You ought to see 'em on a clear dark night at sea. People who grow up in the city don't even know what stars are." He sniffed the air like a wild animal. "It's clear because there's a Santa Ana on its way. Smell it? Going to be windy tomorrow."

"Oh, God, I hope not," Toby moaned. "I hate wind. It does terrible things to my hair."

"Oh, yeah? What kind of things?" His hand turned; his fingers caught and tangled themselves in her hair.

She gave a breathy, shaken laugh. "Oh, you know, static electricity. It just goes everywhere."

He stopped walking and faced her, crushing her hair in his hand like flower petals and raising it to his face to inhale the fragrance. "Your hair fascinates me," he said, his voice rough and wondering. "There seems to be so much of it, but when I gather it up like this, there's nothing. It's like spiderwebs. Smoke."

She smiled and murmured, "Well, I think I prefer smoke to spiderwebs." But he wasn't smiling. His rugged face was grave. In the antiseptic blue light of the parking lot it seemed almost austere. His eyes held hers just long enough for her to read his intent before he lowered his mouth to hers, pinning the weightless mass of her hair between his hand and the curve of her skull.

Had she ever been kissed before tonight? If so, she didn't remember it. Nothing in her experience had felt like this—nothing. Stony's mouth, the moist-heat, firm-texture reality of it, the taste of him, uniquely him, colored slightly with wine and spices. Neither gentle nor demanding, not an invasion or a conquest, but a seduction. He courted and wooed her mouth, coaxing and cajoling her lips until they opened for him naturally, eagerly, penetrating so delicately at first, then with abandon, making love to her mouth with subtle rhythms, with caresses so erotic they left her shocked and gasping.

Sensation exploded inside her, white-hot at her core, expanding outward in a billion points of multicolored light that tingled in her hands and left her legs weak. She clutched at his arms and with one anguished sob, tried to tear her mouth away, and found that she could not. His hands held her face in a firm but gentle embrace, while his fingertips pushed starry shivers into her hair. Her breathing grew labored; tears rushed stinging to her eyelids and throat.

She heard him murmur something, felt the shape of words against her lips, but had no idea what they were. Holding her face between his hands, he slid his open mouth over hers, gently back and forth, glazing her lips and his own. He tormented her with the cooling moisture, hardening his tongue, teasing her sensitized lips with a delicate, fluttering penetration until she whimpered and reached hungrily for him, seeking relief in his mouth.

As he gave her what she demanded, she heard a deep-throated chuckle of masculine satisfaction. His hands left her face and skimmed downward over her body, reaching inside her coat to knead the taut flesh at the sides of her waist, to splay upward from there across her ribs and lightly explore the firm, full weight of her breasts. When he touched her nipples, a bolt of heat shot through her, straight to her core.

Panic took her. Stunned, she thought, It's too much! Too soon! I'm not ready!

Her cry of desperation was muffled in his mouth, but he heard it. She felt him tense, and this time when she struggled he let her go. She gulped in air and said, "You must do this a lot."

He jerked as if she'd slapped him. "What the hell is that supposed to mean?"

Strung tightly as a guitar string, still she managed to keep her tone light. "You're so good at it. I'm sorry—I'm not."

"Aw—" Stony lifted his head and swore at the stars.

Feeling thin-shelled and hollow, Toby rushed on. "After all, you've been single almost as long as I was married. I've only made love with one man in my life."

"Look—" The word burst from him in an exasperated gust. "I'm not going to tell you I've been a monk since my divorce. I haven't. But, damn it, I'm not some kind of playboy, either. I'm pretty damn particular about who I kiss, as a matter of fact. I wanted to kiss you. Can you blame me?" He felt himself gentling as he looked at her, felt his anger dissolving like sea foam on the sand. Touching her cheek with the backs of his fingers, he said softly, "I like you, Mrs. Thomas. You're warm and intelligent and very attractive. You have fantastic eyes and a sexy voice. Your hair is soft and your skin is soft and you smell nice. I like kissing you. But, Toby, if you don't want me to, then you just have to tell me, that's all. Is that the big problem? You don't want me to kiss you?"

Her eyes were luminous, reflecting the sky. "No," she whispered. "The trouble is, I want you to...too much." Dark lashes drifted down over shimmering tears. "Stony, it's been so long since anyone's held me. Since anyone's touched me, or..."

"Longer than six months?" Stony asked softly, cradling her cheek in his hand.

She nodded, and he felt the warm flood of her tears on his fingers. "Yes. I'm hungry, Stony, I admit that. And I'm vulnerable, and I'm scared."

"Say that to the wrong man, lady, and you could find yourself in big trouble." His voice was rough, as it always was when he was feeling especially tender.

Toby gave a little hiccup and tried to smile. "You mean I'm not?"

Stony didn't smile. "No," he said somberly, "absolutely not. I mean that. We'll take this thing anywhere you want to, as fast as you want to. I'll warn you right now, I want to make love with you, and I'm going to proceed on that basis just as far as you'll let me go. But—" he stopped her soft gasp with his thumb "—anytime you say the word, I'll stop, do you understand? *Any*time."

She nodded, sniffling a little. Before she could bring her hand to her face, he leaned down and kissed her, savoring the salty sweetness of her tear-drenched mouth. Dear God, he thought, as once again something swelled and tightened inside him, what am I getting into?

Pulling himself away, he asked gruffly, "Where's your car?"

"There." She pointed, then dove into her handbag, looking, he presumed, for her keys. But after finding them and handing them over to him without a glance, she went on rummaging. "Damn," she said in a muffled voice, "how come there's never a Kleenex when you need one?"

"Feel free to use my sleeve," Stony said blandly. "Or my shirtfront or any other part of me you'd care to." He was ridiculously pleased when she laughed.

"Is this it?" he asked a minute later, gazing doubtfully at a sedan of indeterminate color and advanced age. Japanese, he thought, from a bygone era when Japanese cars were still cheap and fondly known as "tin cans."

Toby nodded. Without comment he opened the door for her, handed her the keys, waited while she got in and fired up the engine, then slammed the door shut. Instantly overwhelmed by the need to touch her one more time, he rapped on the window with his knuckle. The window rode slowly down.

"I'll call you," he said, resting both hands on the top edge of the glass. Her face swiveled toward him, pale as milk in the man-made twilight. "I have to go back to work tomorrow. I just flew in for this Dad's Day thing. But we're just about to get this one wrapped up—should be finished by Thanksgiving. I'll call you when I get back, okay?"

Her lips moved, forming the word, *okay*. He leaned down and touched them with his, then straightened and gave the car door a little slap. "Good night, Mrs. Thomas."

He watched her drive out of the parking lot, wondering why he'd let her go without asking her the question that was nagging at him: If her late husband had been so all-fired prosperous, what in the hell was his widow doing, driving a beat-up old Datsun and working as housemother for a sorority?

"Hi, Mrs. Thomas, how was your date?"

"Oh, fine," Toby said, her voice cracking. She'd been hoping to slink into the sanctuary of her own quarters unobserved. Fat chance. Living in a sorority house, she was discovering, was like having fifty doting parents monitoring her every move. Parents, moreover, who never, ever seemed to sleep.

This time it was Mindy, who was sitting on the couch in the living room with one foot tucked under her, books and papers fanned out across the cushions and coffee table. Toby paused in the doorway and said, "You're up pretty late, aren't you?"

"It's only ten-thirty."

"Oh," Toby said, frowning at the clock on the mantel. "So it is." It didn't seem possible that just four hours had passed since she'd left the house to meet Stony for dinner.

"Yeah," Mindy drawled in midyawn, "I've got this paper due tomorrow. What a bummer. So—" yawn completed, she bounced up, bright-eyed and curious "—how'd it go? Did you have a good time?"

A good time? How would she classify this evening? Toby really wasn't sure.

"It went fine," she said. "I had a very nice time."

"Did you? That's great," Mindy said warmly. "Just great."

Toby muttered, "Well, good night," and went on down the hallway, through the dining room and into the huge, dark kitchen. She turned on a small light above the sink, then opened the stainless-steel-and-glass refrigerator and took out an individual-size carton of orange juice. She was back at the sink, pouring the juice into a glass, when the kitchen door cracked open.

"Mrs. Thomas?" Mindy stuck her head in, then slipped through the door and closed it behind her. "Are you okay? You seem, I don't know, kind of upset." Toby turned around and leaned against the sink, the glass of orange juice in her hand. Mindy said, "I don't mean to intrude, it's just—did something, you know, happen?"

"No," said Toby. "Yes. Sort of." She gave a short, surprised little laugh, because she wasn't given to such confidences.

"Do you want to talk about it?"

Toby shook her head and gulped orange juice.

Mindy said, "Okay, well, if you change your mind..."

She had the kitchen door open and was about to go through it when Toby blurted, "I don't think I'm ready for this!"

Mindy halted and the door clicked softly shut again. "Ready for what, Mrs. Thomas?"

"This—" she waved her glass vaguely "—this dating thing. I haven't in so long. Actually, I don't think I ever did do much of it. I had a social life, but I don't remember it being this..." She searched for a word and settled at last on "complicated."

"Complicated?" Mindy repeated, cautious but concerned. "I guess I don't know what you mean."

Toby laughed. "I don't, either. Would you like some orange juice?"

"Sure, that'd be great."

Toby got another carton out of the refrigerator, poured it into a glass and handed it to Mindy, who by this time had found a convenient seat on top of the worktable. "Malcolm would have a fit if he caught you doing that," Toby remarked.

"Malcolm's a pussycat," said Mindy with a complacent chuckle.

At that, Toby couldn't help but smile. It was true, although at first meeting it was hard to imagine a man less likely to fit that description than the Gee Pi sorority's cook. A Mr. T look-alike, he was built like an offensive lineman, wore three earrings—in the same ear—and played saxophone in a band that had a regular four night a week gig at a club in Santa Monica. That last wasn't common knowledge. Toby happened to know about it because, after her first encounter with him, she'd called up his employment records from the computer files. As it turned out, Malcolm himself did more to reassure her than anything in those files. He was gentle, funny, wise and a superb cook. Not surprisingly, the girls adored him.

"Mrs. Thomas?" Mindy said after they'd sipped in silence for a while. "What did you mean about dating being complicated?"

Toby sighed. "I don't know, it just seems like things were simpler when I was growing up. Or at least, more clearly defined."

Mindy considered that, her head tilted to one side. "Well, I don't know what it was like back *then* but I guess it is harder now. Nobody really tells you what's right or wrong. It's like—you sort of have to decide that for yourself."

Laughter bounced painfully through Toby's chest. "That's the part I'm having trouble with, I guess. Deciding for myself."

"Really? About what?"

"Oh, you know. About..." Toby paused, amazed at how hard it was to say the word. Was it her generation, she wondered? Just one more thing that separated her from the realities of this alien world she now found herself in. Struggling to make her voice matter-of-fact, she plowed on, grateful for the dim light. "About sex. How do you decide about going to bed with someone?" Her breath exploded from her in a nervous rush. "Oh, boy, I can't believe I'm saying this. I'm the housemother, and I'm asking you for advice!"

"Oh, it's okay," Mindy said easily. "My mom just got divorced last year. She talks to me a lot, too. So what happened? Did this guy put pressure on you to go to bed with him?"

"No," said Toby, "not really." He hadn't; the pressure had all come from within. From her own body. "It's just that—well, it would have been so easy to let myself go, just be swept away. But I just *can't*. It's so irresponsible. It might be excusable in a...a teenager who doesn't know any better—"

"It's pretty irresponsible at any age," Mindy said flatly. "I know lots of people who do, but it's stupid. I mean, the consequences are so serious. You have to think about birth control and, of course, now it's a good idea to know somebody pretty well, first, because of AIDS."

There was a little silence. Then Toby coughed and said, "I think I'm pretty safe on both those counts. So I guess it just boils down to..."

"What's right for you," Mindy chimed in, sounding more like her usual, perky sorority self. "And nobody should decide that but you, Mrs. Thomas. So don't let yourself be pressured into doing something you don't want to do, okay?"

"Easier said than done," Toby muttered, searching for the words to explain that it was what she did want to do that was the problem. She didn't know whether Mindy's generation ever suffered these awful internal tug-of-wars.

"You know what I do?" Mindy said, hopping down off of the table. "When I'm getting ready to go out, I decide right up front whether I'm going to go to bed with the guy or not. That way I don't get all confused if the issue suddenly comes up, you know what I mean?" She caught Toby in a quick, unexpected hug. "Gotta get back to my paper. It's tough, Mrs. Thomas, I know. But you're going to do just fine. And if you ever need to talk, just ask, okay?" She sounded remarkably like a mother soothing a distraught child.

And Toby felt like that child, as panic rose to clog her throat and sting her eyes. "I'm not so sure," she said in a low voice, hanging back as Mindy paused in the doorway. "What if you really want to, but..." If she didn't say the words to somebody, she was going to explode! She gulped in air like a pearl diver, shut her eyes and blurted, "The thing is, I'm scared. I've never slept with anyone except my husband. I've never even—" She bit off those words, because even in panic it was too painful to admit that at nearly forty, she'd never been in love.

"Oh, Mrs. Thomas," Mindy said, giving her another hug. "It'll be all right, you'll see." But a moment later as they walked together down the quiet hallway she said thoughtfully, "You know, maybe if you aren't ready and you think you won't be able to handle the pressure, maybe you shouldn't go out with him. At least until you're sure. That's what I'd do.''

The telephone shrilled in its alcove, making them both jump.

''Oops, I'll get that,'' Mindy said, reaching for it as several heads popped expectantly over the stair railings. ''Hello, Gee Pi House, may I help you? Sure, hold on just a minute, I'll get her.'' Covering the mouthpiece with her hand, she bellowed up the stairwell, ''Chris! Would one of you guys please go tell Chris her dad's on the phone? Thanks.'' In a soft, mellow tone she said into the phone, ''She's coming, Mr. Brand. It'll be just a minute, okay?'' She punched the Hold button and cradled the receiver.

''Well,'' she said, turning back to Toby with a smile, ''gotta get back to work. 'Night, Mrs. Thomas. If you ever need to talk, just let me know, okay?''

Toby muttered something and gave Mindy a distracted wave. She was gazing, bemused, at the telephone, wondering when it had turned into a monster—a monster that had the power to turn her stomach upside down and her legs to jelly.

It was only Stony's voice, she told herself, reproduced through one of those incomprehensible electronic mysteries she couldn't even begin to understand. He was miles away.

But somehow he was there, an arm's length away. She could feel his heat and energy, smell his warm, masculine scent, see the light shining soft in his hair and hard as diamonds in his eyes.

Oh, God, she thought as she made her way on wobbly legs to the privacy of her own quarters. He said he'd call. What will I do if he does?

''Daddy?''

''Hi, kitten, I got your message. Everything okay?''

"Oh, yeah, everything's fine. So where were you?" Chris's voice was teasing. "Did you have a date? Hmm?"

"He-e-ey." Stony laughed. "That's none of your business, kid."

"Oh, yeah? What if one of these dates turns out to be my stepmother? That's kind of my business, Dad."

"Chris, you know I wouldn't do that."

"Oh, come on, Dad. Why not?"

"You know how I feel about that. I was a lousy husband. Who's going to put up with a husband that's gone all the time?"

"Yeah, and you probably think you were a lousy father, too, only I don't think you're a lousy father, and I bet you wouldn't be a lousy husband, either."

"What are you talking about? I missed every major event in your childhood. I missed your first steps, your school plays, your eighth-grade graduation—I missed your birth, for Pete's sake!"

"So what? I don't remember that anyway. And I was a stupid tomato in my school play, I didn't even have any lines. I always knew you'd be there if you could. And you were there when I really needed you, like when I...got hurt. When I broke my arm, who took me to the hospital?"

Stony was silent, listening to what she hadn't said. She hadn't mentioned her most recent trip to the hospital, and it bothered him that she hadn't. It also reminded him of what Toby had said and the fact that he needed to talk to Chris about some kind of counseling. He wasn't looking forward to that. Dammit, what he wanted to do was put it all behind him and try to forget it had ever happened. Trouble was, he was pretty sure Chris hadn't forgotten—not yet.

"Hey, what's gotten into you tonight?" he said through gruff laughter. "Why this sudden interest in my love life?"

"I just don't think you should be alone, that's all," Chris said in a stubborn tone he recognized, refusing to join his laughter. "You should have someone, Dad. Someone really terrific."

"I have someone really terrific," Stony joked, hoping to head her off before she really got rolling. "You."

"You know what I mean. I don't want you to be lonely."

"I'm not lonely."

"Dad . . ."

"What is this 'lonely' stuff all of a sudden? Geez, I just got home from a date, how could I be lonely?"

"You're shouting, Dad."

"Aah," Stony said, "I don't want to talk about this. It's late, and I have to get back to the job tomorrow. I want to know how you're doin', kiddo."

"I told you, Dad. I'm fine."

"You sure about that?"

"Yeah, everything's fine."

"Yeah, well I've been thinking maybe you should talk to someone about . . . what happened to you. Maybe a group or something. What do you think?"

"Dad, I'm okay about it. Really. I wish you'd stop worrying about me."

Stony exhaled slowly and audibly. "Heard anything new about the case?"

"Oh, yeah, I guess I forgot to tell you. Someone from the D.A.'s office came by last week—my victim's advocate. I have to go and testify in a couple of weeks, but she told me Steve is going to plead no contest, and they'll probably give him probation." Her voice was flat, disinterested.

"How do you feel about that?" Stony said cautiously, not wanting to upset her by voicing his own opinions.

He could almost hear her shrug. "It's okay, I guess. It's about what I expected."

Stony waited for a moment, then coughed and said, "Well, if you change your mind about talking to somebody, just let me know, okay? Jake will always know where to reach me. I'm hoping to have this job wrapped up by Thanksgiving, anyway, so I'll see you then."

"Oh! Oh my gosh, I almost forgot. That's why I called you. It's about Thanksgiving. Uh, Dad, I was wondering if you'd mind if I went skiing over Thanksgiving weekend. Kim—you know, my roommate, you met her yesterday?— Kim and her family are going up to Mammoth and they asked if I'd like to go along. They have a condo, so it wouldn't cost for a room, and I have enough left from my allowance to pay for lift tickets. Dad, I know we've always spent Thanksgiving together whenever we could, but—"

"Yeah, yeah," Stony broke in, "now I get it. Now I know why you're so concerned about my love life. It's guilt, right? You're standing me up, and you want a clear conscience, I know. Hey, listen, I can take it. You just go on, leave your old man out in the cold."

"Dad—"

Stony chuckled. He was teasing her, so relieved to hear some enthusiasm in her voice again that he could ignore his own disappointment. The way she'd sounded when they'd been talking about the rape scared him. "Kitten, I think it's great. You go on—go skiing. I'll send you some money. Don't worry about a thing, you got that?" His voice was so full of emotion it was choking him. "Say hello to Kim for me, okay? Have a good time, and . . . I'll see you when you get back."

"But what are you—"

"I said, don't worry. Geez, you're such a nag!"

Chris's giggle had a liquid sound. "Thanks, Dad. I love you."

"I love you, too, kitten. Hey, no broken bones, now!"

"Now who's a nag? G'night, Daddy."

"'Night."

After he cradled the receiver, Stony sat for a while, listening to the silence. He noticed that it had a different texture now, a hollow emptiness that seemed to whisper and echo the word, *lonely*.

Well, hell, he thought, shaking it off, laughing at himself, of course he got lonely sometimes. Didn't everybody? Being alone didn't scare him, he was used to it. In fact, he was so used to going his own way, even if Chris was right and he could find somebody willing to put up with him, he didn't think he could ever get used to having to account to somebody again.

Besides, Chris was wrong about what kind of husband he'd been. She didn't know the whole story. He was a coward. He'd never been able to tell her that if it hadn't been for him, her mother might still be alive.

Nah, he thought, shaking his head and pressing his fingers against his burning eyelids, marriage wasn't for him. He'd never get married again. Crazy to even think about it.

And suddenly he was thinking of Toby and knew that she'd been there all along in his mind, coming quietly as she often did, like ground fog, so that he wasn't even aware of her until she'd enveloped him completely, filling his mind and all his senses. The unimaginable softness of her hair and the wildflower scent of it; the matte velvet warmth of her cheek, the husky-sweet timbre of her voice. The way she'd felt in his arms tonight, slender but supple and strong; the trembling deep, deep inside her. The taste of her mouth.

Thinking about her didn't make the silence less lonely. It only made it less bearable.

He wondered what Toby was doing for Thanksgiving. She'd probably already made plans. He was thinking about calling her to find out when somewhere in the dark house a clock emitted a tiny electronic beep, signaling the hour. The diver's watch on his wrist verified the fact that it was midnight. Well, he thought, too late to call her now. And he'd be leaving at the crack of dawn. It would have to wait until he got back.

"Mrs. Thomas?" A sun-streaked blond head poked cautiously into the doorway of Toby's office. "Telephone—it's that same guy, the one that called a little while ago. What shall I tell him?"

"The same thing I told you to tell him a little while ago," Toby said with a calm she didn't feel. "That I've left for the holidays. And you don't know where I can be reached."

The girl shrugged and said, "Okay." Toby breathed a shaky "Thank you, Paige," to the empty doorway.

Abandoning all pretense of working, she stood and wandered into the hallway, which had become an obstacle course of assorted luggage, backpacks and totebags.

"Who's left?" she asked Paige, who was just turning away from the telephone alcove.

"Just Katie and Terry and me—we're sharing a cab to the airport. I called, so they should be here any minute."

"Well. Okay, then, that's..." Toby murmured as Paige dashed off up the stairs for another load. She shrugged and called after her, "Have a happy Thanksgiving!"

She was gazing in bemusement at the pile in the hallway, trying to calculate the odds that it was all going to fit into one cab, when a soft voice behind her said, "You, too, Mrs. Thomas."

It no longer startled her that a man the cook's size and build could move with such quietness. She turned with a smile and said, "Thank you, Malcolm, same to you. Are you leaving?"

"Just about to. I left you a little somethin' in the icebox for your Thanksgiving dinner."

"Malcolm, I told you you didn't..."

He just looked at her, dark eyes holding steady as he shrugged into his fringed leather jacket, then said in his whiskey-soft voice, "Mrs. Thomas, you take care now. You need anything, you give me a call."

"I will. Thank you."

"I'll be leavin', then. See you Monday."

"Yes," Toby said. "Bye."

A car's horn blared from the driveway, signaling the arrival of the cab. Malcolm paused long enough to bestow bear hugs and farewells upon the last three departing girls as they came hurtling down the stairs, and then was gone, vanishing through the kitchen doorway as swiftly and silently as an Indian scout on a moonless night. There was a small whirlwind of activity while the girls gathered their belongings and dished out their own hugs and noisy goodbyes, finally bumping and thumping their way through the front door and all piling miraculously into the waiting cab. The door closed after them with a sigh and a click, and Toby was left alone with the silence.

It didn't last long. Behind her in the alcove the telephone began to ring. She stood still and counted while every muscle in her body tensed and tightened and her heartbeat echoed hollowly in her stomach. Two rings...three. On the fourth ring there was a click and a whirring, and then, "Hi, you've reached the Gamma Pi Sorority house. Nobody's here right now, because we've all gone home for Thanksgiving...."

Toby didn't wait to hear the rest. She went on down the hall and into the kitchen at a pace that felt very much like flight.

In the refrigerator she found a small turkey, not more than eight or ten pounds, stuffed and neatly trussed. A piece of sticky backed notepaper was affixed to the aluminum foil covering the turkey. "Three hundred and twenty-five degrees for four hours," she read in bold, black printing, followed by heavily underlined, "Do Not Overcook!" That made her smile. Malcolm may have been a pussycat, but he took his cooking seriously.

The note went on in the cook's distinctive handwriting. *Call me if you need anything. If you get tired of your own company, come on down to The Duke's. The boys and I'll buy you a drink, play you a song. Nobody should be alone on a holiday. Have a good one.* It ended with the indecipherable squiggle with which Malcolm signed all communications.

With tears forming unexpectedly in her throat, Toby dropped the note onto the worktable and went upstairs to inspect the dorm rooms and bathrooms.

Satisfied that the house was secure and safe from fire and plumbing disasters, she went back to her office and turned on the computer. Ah, she thought, four whole days of peace and quiet. Four whole days in which to work on the research paper for her psych class that was due the end of the quarter. Four days to catch up on her reading, to organize her notes and start studying for the finals that were coming up in a couple of weeks. It was important to her that she do well, this first quarter back in school after so many years. She had things to prove, to herself, if to no one else. This time alone was just what she needed, and she meant to put it to good use. Four days...

The computer whirred patiently; its screen remained blank. Outside, the city bus roared by and voices called farewells from one of the other sorority houses on the street. A car door slammed. The silence came again, only to be invaded by the loud ticking of the mantel clock in the parlor across the hall.

It occurred to Toby that the telephone hadn't rung in quite a while. It had rung twice while she was upstairs, but not since, and in the disconcerting way that feelings have of sometimes turning around on you, she found that she was sorry. She kept listening for it, telling herself that if it rang again, she would answer it. It might not even be Stony, and if it was, what would it hurt her just to talk to him? She was being childish. If she couldn't trust herself to go out with him again, the least she could do was tell him so in person.

But the phone didn't ring.

After a while, she turned off the computer, got her guitar out of its case and took it with her into the front yard. There was a porch swing there, popular with the girls as a photo spot because of its pretty setting beneath the big old silk tree. She made herself comfortable in the swing, cradled her guitar and sent a few tentative chords quivering into the November dusk. The next chords she took inside herself, letting them seep into her fingers, her chest, her stomach, spreading a fine and gentle warmth through her body and soothing the turmoil in her soul.

When she felt better, she joined her own voice to the guitar's, singing Dylan songs, and Simon and Garfunkel, while the twilight settled in around her and pink blossoms drifted down from the tree like snowflakes. *Parsley, sage, rosemary and thyme....*

She didn't notice the black sports car with the dark tinted windows until it pulled into the narrow driveway beside her, its big engine adding a throbbing bass to her own music. Her fingers stilled, then flattened on the strings, stifling the last chords. She sat up slowly, a pulse in the pit of her stomach picking up the beat of the car's engine. The window on the driver's side rode smoothly down.

"Hello, Mrs. Thomas," Stony said pleasantly. "Have a nice trip?"

## Chapter 6

He'd been angry, at first. Angry that she wouldn't talk to him, angry that she'd lied. The most recent explosion had hit him just a moment ago, when he'd pulled up and there she was, sitting in that swing, just happily singing away, oblivious to the upheaval she'd brought into his life. But Stony's explosions were like fireworks—loud, colorful and harmless. The last spark had died before he was even out of the car.

Not that the death of the spark left him feeling easy. Far from it! He hadn't felt easy in weeks. Anger was easy, clean and uncomplicated. He wished to God he could just get good and angry and stay that way. But what Toby had done to him was tie all his emotions in knots, until he didn't know anymore what he felt or what he wanted. He couldn't even trust his own actions. When she'd refused his calls, he'd told himself to leave it alone. She obviously felt she wasn't ready to handle a relationship, and since he'd left it up to her, he pretty much had to accept her decision. When she'd instructed the girls to say she was out of town—when he knew damn well she wasn't—he'd thought, Fine. If she wanted to be alone, he'd leave her alone.

But then he'd grabbed up his coat and keys hopped into his car and the next thing he knew, he was pulling into her driveway. And now, seeing her sitting there in that swing, with pink flowers in her fine black hair, he knew that leaving her alone was the one thing he wasn't going to be able to do.

"Chris isn't here," she said, rising to face him as he came up the steps. She wore the slightly hunched look of a child caught in a fib. "She went skiing with—"

"I know," Stony said flatly. "I came to see you."

He heard a faint sound, a slight catch in the rhythm of her breathing. "Why? I mean, how did you know I'd be here? I told—I left word that I was going away for Thanksgiving."

"I talked to Chris just before she left. She told me you were here. I took a chance you hadn't gone yet."

"Oh." She caught her lower lip in her teeth. Looking around for a way out of the trap, her eyes lit with obvious relief upon the guitar. Snatching it up, she cried, "Oh, good heavens, I didn't realize it was so late. I just came out here to relax for a minute, and I completely lost track of time. I haven't even packed yet."

She didn't like lying, he could tell; she did it so badly. She couldn't keep her hands still, her eyes were too bright, her cheeks too pink and she was sweating. As a matter of fact, he would have thought she looked cute if he hadn't been so exasperated with her. He didn't know whether to kiss her or shake her until her teeth rattled.

"What time are you leaving?" he asked, keeping his tone neutral.

"Oh, whenever I get ready to go." She tried to sound offhand and only succeeded in sounding distracted. "That's the nice thing about being single, I guess. I don't have to think about anyone else. But I guess I had better get going. I don't like to drive too late at night."

"Where are you going?" Stony asked interestedly, keeping pace with her as she edged toward the front door.

"Uh, San Diego. I, umm, have some friends there. I'm spending Thanksgiving with them."

"I see," Stony murmured. "Won't your friends be expecting you? If you're going to be late, maybe you'd better give them a call." She threw him a harassed look, which he met with a bland smile. "Traffic's bad, too—getaway day, you know. Radio says all freeways heading out of town are pretty much at a standstill."

At the front door she hesitated, no doubt trying to think what she could say that would make him go away and leave her alone. But he had no intention of leaving, not until he'd found out what he wanted to know, so he reached around to open the door for her, putting a hand on her shoulder and leaning into her as he did. A shudder rippled through her, answering one of his questions.

"Would you, umm, like some coffee?" she asked helplessly, the tremor finding its way into her voice. It was dark in the hallway and he was closer to her than she wanted him to be, or maybe not close enough. It sure as hell wasn't close enough for him.

Calling on all his self-control, Stony murmured, "That would be nice. Thank you."

"Please, sit down. Make yourself comfortable." She caught at the conventional hostess's phrases with relief, like a lost traveler spotting familiar landmarks. "It will only take a minute..."

But instead of going into the living room, as she indicated he should, Stony followed her down the hall and into the kitchen.

"I hope Chris and Kim didn't run into traffic," Toby said in a bright, conversational voice as she scooted past him to turn on a light. "They did get a little bit of a late start. I think it was nearly four o'clock when Kim's father picked them up." She kept herself busy while she chattered, taking things out of cupboards, running water, flitting between sink and microwave. "It's such a long drive to Mammoth, a tedious drive, once you get out on the desert..."

"I believe they were going to fly," Stony said absently. His attention had been captured by a small piece of yellow paper that was lying on the table—cooking instructions of some kind. He picked it up.

"I hope you don't mind instant. Everything's been put away. Do you take cream and—" she turned and the bright little hostess's smile froze on her face "—sugar."

"Those friends of yours," Stony said quietly, waving the piece of paper between his first two fingers. "Their name wouldn't happen to be The Dukes, would it?" She closed her eyes. He heard the soft sigh of an exhalation. "Toby, why'd you do this? Why would you lie?" Anger rose in him again at this final proof of the lie, even though he'd known from the beginning. "I told you I was going to call you when I got back. If you didn't want to see me, all you had to do was tell me. What were you, afraid to face me? I never thought you'd pull this—this chicken kind of stunt."

He caught her by the shoulders and just as quickly let her go. Skimming his fingers lightly up and down her arms as an exercise in self-control, he said tightly, "Damn it, Toby. I told you how I felt about you weeks ago, and nothing happened out there on that boat to make me change my mind. I'd like to see you. I'd like to get to know you better—a whole lot better. But I told you I'd take it just as slow and easy as you want me to, and I meant that. If you don't believe me, if you're still scared about this, if you just don't want to have anything to do with me, then dammit, tell me to my face!''

When he stopped talking the silence was so profound he knew that he must have been shouting. Chris would have told him to keep his voice down. Toby just stood and took it, eyes closed and body braced against the onslaught. He took a deep breath and began again, softly. "What is it, Toby? Is it that you don't want to see me?"

She shook her head and whispered, "No."

Stony's heart stopped. "No, that's not it, or no, you don't want to see me?"

"No, that's not it."

His heart resumed its painful thumping. "Do you still not trust me?"

"No."

"No, that's not it, or no, you don't trust me?"

An anguished bubble of laughter escaped her. "No, that's not it."

"Then what—"

She held her hands up, palms out. He immediately held his up, too, breaking his only tenuous physical contact with her.

"I haven't—" Her voice cracked, and she went on in a whisper, "I haven't changed the way I feel, either. It's still myself I don't trust. I didn't dare talk to you because I knew I wouldn't be able to say no to you."

"Then why say it?" She just looked at him, her distress starkly written on her face and in her eyes, and he let his hands drop helplessly to his sides.

He wasn't communicating with her. He thought he knew what was going on inside her. He could feel both the yearning and the fear in her, and understood that what she yearned for and what she feared were one and the same thing. He understood that it was painful and confusing for her, but what he couldn't accept was that she'd actually let it keep them from seeing each other. He wanted to tell her it was going to be all right, that it would work itself out, if she'd let it, but she didn't seem to be listening.

He put his head back and looked at the ceiling, hoping to find the solution to his problem written there in nice, easy phrases. When he didn't, he swore softly and struck out on his own. "Listen, my feelings for you aren't very complicated. I'm not a complicated man. I'm pretty up-front, I say what I feel, and I won't ever lie to you. You'll always know where you stand with me."

He'd doubled his hands into fists to keep from touching her, but then he suddenly thought, What the hell am I doing this for? I'm a toucher, that's all there is to it! So he put his hands on her shoulders and let them wander inward, slipping his fingers under her hair to gently massage the taut muscles in her neck.

"Toby," he said, his voice thickening as he watched her eyes grow dark and her lips soften, "I know that your feelings are more complicated than mine. I don't want to make things difficult for you, I'm trying to make them simpler. I just don't want you to be afraid—of yourself or me or whoever. If we got to know each other a little better, don't you think it would help?"

"Makes sense." Her words were slurred and indistinct.

Stony smiled, letting his fingers slow upon her neck, easing the pressure, lengthening the stroke, making it less a massage and more a caress. "Yeah," he said softly, "of course, it does. The better we know each other, the simpler it gets."

He had no idea, then, how naive he was being. And apparently, neither did she. Her eyes were closed and her laughter had a husky sound that warmed his blood and sent it rushing through his body in predictable paths. Hell, he thought, with the kind of chemistry they had going here, all they'd have to do was spend a little time together and let things follow their natural course. Convergence was inevitable.

Convergence was definitely on his mind as he leaned toward her. Her mouth looked soft and blurred, as if she'd already been thoroughly kissed, evoking powerful sensual memories of the way she'd felt and tasted the last time he'd kissed her. Those same memories and his body's natural responses to them had been giving him fits during the past few weeks, too. All it took to build a bonfire in his loins was a momentary flashback—the imprint of her mouth wet-burned onto his, his tongue warmly enveloped, her wild-flower scent drowning him. And he knew that kissing her now wasn't going to make him feel better. It was only going to make it a whole lot harder to leave.

In a voice that felt and sounded like ninety miles of bad road he said, "Know what I think we should do?"

She murmured, "Hmm?" without opening her eyes.

"I think you should spend Thanksgiving with me."

Her eyes opened but remained unfocused. "Spend... Thanksgiving with you?"

"Sure." He moved his hands back to her shoulders and gave them a friendly squeeze. "You're alone, I'm alone. And like the note says, nobody should be alone on Thanksgiving. So you come over to my house—in your car, so you can leave anytime you want to. I'll pick up a turkey—"

"I already have a turkey," she said, sounding slightly dazed.

"Even better. Bring it, and we'll see what else we can find to go with it. What do you say?"

"All right," she murmured, and carefully cleared her throat before she added, "What time?"

"What time? Uh, how long does it take to cook a turkey?" he asked, stalling while he tried to calculate how long it would take him to get his house looking reasonably presentable. "What is it, a little one? Four, maybe five hours, right? So why don't you come around noon? We can put the turkey in and then nibble all afternoon—did you used to do that when you were a kid?''

She was gazing at him with great, luminous eyes. It had the darnedest effect on him when she looked at him like that. It made him feel happy. Just plain happy. He wanted to laugh out loud. He had to go on talking just to keep himself from picking her up in his arms and swinging her around until she was too dizzy to stand up.

''By the time dinner was finally on the table, I was never hungry because I'd been stealing olives and carrot sticks and bites of stuffing all day. And the best part was when my dad went to carve the turkey. He'd pull off these big pieces of nice crisp, greasy skin and give them to us kids to eat—the part that's supposed to be bad for you, now, right? Can't eat it now without feeling guilty as hell. Scientists sure know how to take the joy out of things, don't they?''

She laughed softly. He grinned at her. ''Then we have a date? Oops—I'd better give you my address.'' He took a pen out of his shirt pocket and scrawled the information on the back of the little yellow note.

''See you tomorrow,'' he said, feeling winded as a sprinter. He tipped her chin with his thumb and first finger and touched a kiss to her lips. Then quickly, before the effects of it could short-circuit his good intentions, went out and left her standing there.

By ten o'clock Thanksgiving morning, Toby had come to the conclusion that when it came to sex, it was easier to be swept away than it was to make an intelligent decision. She almost wished Stony would be a little less patient and understanding. If he'd pushed her harder, if he'd gone on stroking her neck like that just a little longer, if he'd kissed her, she'd probably have hopped right into bed with him last night and it would all be over and done with now. But—the louse!—he'd left it up to her.

It had sounded so easy when Mindy said it—just decide right up front whether you're going to go to bed or not, so you don't get caught off guard when the subject comes up unexpectedly. Simple? For someone of Mindy's generation, maybe, but not for someone like Toby, who had missed the entire sexual revolution. There were times when she felt like Rip Van Winkle, waking up after a twenty-year nap to a new and puzzling world.

In her youth, the answer to the question, Should she or shouldn't she, was unequivocal: Nice girls didn't. But she wasn't a girl anymore, she was almost a forty-year-old woman, and these days, nice women did, all the time. Two decades ago she might have reasoned that she didn't know Stony well enough; that after all, they'd only had one date and the subject of sex shouldn't be coming up this soon, anyway. But this was the era of the one-night stand, and as far as she could tell, not even the threat of dire consequences had done much to curtail it. And she wasn't kidding herself—with chemistry as powerful as that which seemed to be working between her and Stony, the subject was definitely already up and was going to continue to be.

She could rationalize away everything but the fear, which was real and was rooted in the very core of her femininity, her confidence and self-esteem. Intimacy was frightening, that's all there was to it. This man, this stranger she barely knew—what would he think of her body? It had never been spectacular, and now there were bulges and sags and veins that hadn't been there twenty years ago. And how would her body react to his? It had been so long! Dear God, would she even know how to touch him? What if she was a disappointment to him? What if the whole thing was a disaster? It probably *would* be a disaster, at least the first time, or at the very least, awkward and embarrassing.

But in spite of everything, she wanted to make love with Stony. It had been so long since she'd been touched in that special way. She longed to be held, stroked, caressed. And she liked Stony, she found him exceedingly attractive, and all her instincts and good sense told her that she could trust him. He was a good man, a decent man, and in spite of his bluntness, a gentle, even a sensitive man. If she had to go through this awkward business of losing her virginity all over again—which was what it was beginning to feel like to her—then she probably couldn't wish for a better person to do it with than Stony.

That was the logical part of her wanting. But it wasn't what made her cast aside all her reservations, pick out her prettiest underwear, shave her legs with minute care and select a purse big enough to discreetly harbor a few essential toilet articles and a change of underwear. She did those things because in all of her life she had never felt the way she did when Stony touched her. She hadn't known it was possible to feel like that, so wonderful it terrified her. She wanted to feel that way again.

For so many years her life had been a bleak and lonely desert. Now she felt like a hungry prospector who's just been given one golden nugget and a map to the mother lode.

"Hi, come on in!" Stony said with a smile, apparently delighted, though not too surprised, to find Toby on his doorstep.

"Hi," she breathlessly rejoined, but didn't accept his invitation to enter for the simple reason that her knees had locked and the entire field of the last Kentucky Derby was at that moment thundering through her midsection.

Stony took the foil-covered roasting pan out of her hands and surveyed her with a thoughtful frown. Accurately diagnosing her predicament, he gently touched her elbow and murmured, "Come in, Little Red Riding Hood."

She let go of a husky giggle. "Does it show?"

His eyes were shining with tender amusement. "Oh, yes."

"Well," she said, thrusting her hands deep in her coat pockets and casting a look of longing back over her shoulder to where her car sat parked under a golden canopy of sycamores. "Nice place you have here. Nice neighborhood. Quiet." She didn't know what she'd expected. Certainly not a neat little Cape Cod with white siding and gray shingles in a neighborhood of sloping, tree-lined streets on the edge of Griffith Park.

"My mom and dad built this place," Stony explained. "They were originally from New England." His grin became lopsided. "Except for learning to ride a bike, it was a good place to raise a kid." He cleared his throat. "Uh, Toby?"

"Yes?"

In a voice that quivered with gentle laughter he said, "I'm really not a wolf in disguise, and I'm not planning to make you my Thanksgiving dinner. It's okay to come in."

"I know," Toby said. "I'm not nervous." It was just that he looked so good to her standing there, his hair showing signs of having just been washed, his crisp blue cotton shirt open at the throat, sleeves rolled to the elbows, revealing smooth brown skin and curly golden hair. She realized that it was true, she wasn't nervous. It was something else that was making her legs feel weak and her stomach queasy. Something else entirely.

"I'm glad you're not nervous," Stony said, taking her arm and dragging her over the threshold. "Because I sure am. I've been cleaning house all morning."

"You didn't have to do that."

"Yeah, I did." He grinned wryly. "A housecleaning service comes once a week, usually on Thursdays. So this week they skip. And I am not a neat person. Here, the kitchen's this way."

The inside of the house was like the outside, smaller than expected, very traditional and very homey. There were hardwood floors and braided rugs, fruitwood furniture polished to a high gloss, brass lamps, tall bookcases filled with well-thumbed books, pictures of sailing ships on the walls. Chris's high school graduation portrait and a smaller photo of her as a toddler occupied places of honor on the piano. Toby's heart gave a leap when she saw the piano, a beautiful baby grand, but she only had time to draw her fingertips reverently across its polished top before Stony whisked her on, through the formal dining room and into the kitchen.

The only sign Toby could see of Stony's supposed untidiness was a sweatshirt draped over a kitchen stool. He spotted it, too, and quickly scooped it up, bundled it into a ball and lobbed it through a door at the far end of the kitchen where it missed an overflowing laundry hamper by a foot.

A little ripple passed through Toby's chest. A strange exhilaration pulled at the corners of her mouth so that she had to turn quickly to hide the smile from Stony. A smile that, along with the look in her eyes, would surely have given her away.

To give herself breathing space, she walked over to the window above the kitchen sink. It looked out on a swing set, a sandbox and a playhouse complete with front porch and window boxes. Chris had been a lucky little girl, she thought. For all his protestations, Stony must have been a wonderful father. She knew it as well as she knew he was there in the room with her, bending over an oven while the November sunshine turned his wheat-brown hair to gold.

Something twisted painfully inside her, something she hadn't felt in years, something she thought she'd gotten over, that yearning for something she knew she would never have. It caught her off guard, like a cloud of pollen on a summer day.

"What's the matter?" Stony asked softly from behind her.

She turned, blinking rapidly, to smile at him. "Nothing. Just . . . emotions, I guess."

"Good emotions?" His expression was somber, concerned.

She nodded. "Yes."

He knuckled away the one tear she hadn't been able to contain. "Glad you came?"

"Oh, yes." The last word was barely a sigh. His fingers were motionless, just touching her cheek. She felt the hesitation in him, and it shook her profoundly to think that such a man as he—so brash and brawny, so straightforward and strong—should feel uncertain because of her.

With tenderness blossoming inside her, she took his hand in both of hers, marveling at the strength and the gentleness in it, tracing the hard ridges of his fingers and the valleys between them, measuring the breadth of his palm against hers. Touching. Feeling. The sensation in her fingertips and in her palms was so exquisite it frightened her. I can't feel this wonderful, she thought. It isn't possible.

"Oh, Grandma," she said with a shaken laugh, "what big hands you have."

"Toby." His eyes were watchful and quiet. "What are you doing?"

She closed her eyes and brought his hand to her cheek. "That's not your line," she murmured, smiling slightly.

"Right now I'm speechless. Does this mean you've had a change of heart?"

"Not of heart," Toby whispered, no longer smiling. "A change of mind. In my heart I'm still scared."

His fingers curled against her cheek. "So'm I," he mumbled as he leaned over to kiss her. "Tell me if I go too fast for you. Remember, you're in control."

Which was ridiculous, of course. Things were already going too fast for her. But like a child running too quickly down a steep hill, she couldn't stop. All she could do now was keep going and hope for the best.

His lips were smooth and firm, his breath warm and pleasantly toothpasty. His mouth moved lightly over hers, softening, waiting until she parted willingly for him before altering the shape and rhythm of the kiss, and then so slowly that her flesh tingled in anticipation of his touch, craving it, hungering for it, reaching for it. She made a small, hungry sound and clutched at his wrist as if it were her only anchor.

There was no uncertainty in him now. Deliberately, almost lazily, he caressed her mouth, invading with long, slow strokes, giving her time, making her feel with each and every nerve ending, with every part of her, never realizing that, in trying not to rush her, he was tantalizing her beyond bearing, driving her to the brink of panic. Dear God, she thought, she couldn't stand this—her heart would burst, it was beating so.

Frightened and reeling, a helpless rider on a runaway merry-go-round, she felt him pull away from her, felt his hands on her shoulders and the coldness of space between their bodies. The world stopped spinning but remained blurred and out of focus.

"It's all right," he said, soothing her. "I'll stop, if you want me to."

She shook her head, frowning. "I fall apart when you touch me, but I don't want you to stop. Am I an idiot?"

"You're not an idiot," he said with tender laughter. "I want you to fall apart when I touch you. It does great things for my male ego."

"We aim to please," Toby mumbled, swaying drunkenly toward him.

His hands held her lightly, skimming her sides, pulling shivers to the surface of her skin in a thousand hot-cold points of light.

"Hold me," he said against her mouth. "Touch me just like this."

She did and was awed by the surging forces she felt beneath her hands. So much heat and strength—how could she ever control this? She would be overwhelmed, consumed.

"If I touch you," she panted, "will you fall apart, too?"

"I can almost guarantee it."

She doubted it. She wasn't experienced enough or skilled enough. There was no way she could possibly do to him what he was doing to her, reducing her to a molten, mindless state, a quivering mass of wanton desires and primal urges. Stony was steady as a rock. He must be, to be supporting her weight as well as his own; her bones were no help at all.

"Pull my shirt loose," he whispered, touching words to the tingling flesh of her lower lip. "Let me feel your hands on my skin."

Though shaking, she did as he asked, pushed her hands up under his shirt, spread her fingers wide over his rib cage and around to knead the rounded ridges of muscle along his spine. She felt ridiculously pleased when he groaned. It gave her confidence. Enough so that when he finally tore his mouth from hers and pressed it, hot and open, against her temple, she muttered testily, "Hey, aren't you falling behind, here?"

His hands tightened on her waist. "Ah, Toby." He lifted his head and chuckled dryly and painfully. "Are you sure you want me to?"

"Yes," she said. "Definitely." She held her breath while he tugged her blouse from the waistband of her slacks, and released it in a shaken sigh when she felt his hands on her skin. Tears and laughter bubbled through her, an effervescent stew of purest joy.

His hands were so big they seemed to encompass her, sliding upward over ribs and other ticklish places that should have recoiled from such intense stimulation but somehow didn't. Her flesh seemed to soften and grow malleable in the warmth of his hands. When his thumbs explored, her breasts swelled and tingled, rebelling against the confines of her bra; panting, she tried to tell him where it fastened, but he didn't need her help. One deft movement of his fingers released her of that torment. With a little whimper of need, she arched her back, pushing into his hands. His mouth trailed hot and open along the cords of her neck, closed with gentle, drawing pressure on its sensitive inward curve. Her breathing grew quick and shallow.

"That feels . . . good," she gasped, a statement of monumental inadequacy.

She felt his body shake with silent, rueful laughter. "I don't know about you," he said, muffling his words in her hair, "but I think we need to find a more comfortable place for this."

Toby's eyelids weighed several tons, but she managed to open one of them. "Oh, my goodness," she murmured, "we're in the kitchen."

Moving her hands experimentally lower on Stony's back, she encountered a cold, hard ridge of tile. Something—an oven mitt—was caught between his hip and the edge of the sink. "The turkey . . ." she muttered, trying to bring her mind back from the edge.

"In the oven. Cooking. It'll be done in four hours or so."

"Oh, yeah. I thought we were supposed to be nibbling."

"I am nibbling," Stony said, proceeding to do so beginning with her collarbone and ending with her earlobes. "Feel free to join me anytime."

It was a delicious idea, Toby thought, and discovered that by turning her head she could just reach his ear.

"Oh boy," Stony said, air exploding from his chest as he caught her to him in a quick, hard hug, "that's enough of that. At least until—do you suppose we could move this into the living room?"

"We could..." Toby murmured absently, nuzzling with her open mouth in the V of his shirt. Nibbling on Stony was proving to be habit-forming. "Or, we could go upstairs."

# SILHOUETTE GIVES YOU SIX REASONS TO CELEBRATE!

# Yes, become a Silhouette subscriber and the celebration goes on forever.

## To begin with we'll send you:

**4 new Silhouette Intimate Moments® novels — FREE**

**a lovely 20k gold electroplated chain—FREE**

**an exciting mystery bonus—FREE**

## And that's not all! Special extras— Three more reasons to celebrate.

**4. FREE Home Delivery!** That's right! We'll send you 4 FREE books, and you'll be under no obligation to purchase any in the future. You may keep the books and return the accompanying statement marked cancel.

If we don't hear from you, about a month later we'll send you four additional novels to read and enjoy. If you decide to keep them, you'll pay the low members only discount price of just $2.74* each — that's 21 cents less than the cover price — AND there's no extra charge for delivery! There are no hidden extras! **You may cancel at any time!** But as long as you wish to continue, every month we'll send you four more books, which you can purchase or return at our cost, cancelling your subscription.

**5. Free Monthly Newsletter!** It's the indispensable insiders' look at our most popular writers and their upcoming novels. Now you can have a behind-the-scenes look at the fascinating world of Silhouette! It's an added bonus you'll look forward to every month!

**6. More Surprise Gifts!** Because our home subscribers are our most valued readers, we'll be sending you additional free gifts from time to time — as a token of our appreciation.

## FREE! 20k GOLD ELECTROPLATED CHAIN!

You'll love this 20k gold electroplated chain! The necklace is finely crafted with 160 double-soldered links, and is electroplate finished in genuine 20k gold. It's nearly 1/8" wide, fully 20" long — and has the look and feel of the real thing. "Glamorous" is the perfect word for it, and it can be yours FREE in this amazing Silhouette celebration!

# SILHOUETTE INTIMATE MOMENTS®

# FREE OFFER CARD

**4 FREE BOOKS**

**20k GOLD ELECTROPLATED CHAIN—FREE**

**FREE MYSTERY BONUS**

*PLACE YOUR BALLOON STICKER HERE!*

**FREE HOME DELIVERY**

**FREE FACT-FILLED NEWSLETTER**

**MORE SURPRISE GIFTS THROUGHOUT THE YEAR—FREE**

**YES!** Please send me my four Silhouette Intimate Moments® novels **FREE**, along with my 20k Electroplated Gold Chain and my free mystery gift, as explained on the opposite page. I understand that accepting these books and gifts places me under no obligation ever to buy any books. I may cancel at any time for any reason, and the free books and gifts will be mine to keep!          240 CIS YAET (U-S-IM-02/90)

NAME

(PLEASE PRINT)

ADDRESS                                    APT

CITY                                        STATE

ZIP

FILL OUT THIS POSTPAID CARD AND MAIL TODAY!

Postage will be paid by addressee

**BUSINESS REPLY CARD**
FIRST CLASS    PERMIT NO. 717    BUFFALO, N.Y.

**SILHOUETTE BOOKS**®
901 Fuhrmann Blvd.,
P.O. Box 1867
Buffalo, N.Y. 14240-9952

NO POSTAGE
NECESSARY
IF MAILED
IN THE
UNITED STATES

## Chapter 7

"What?" Stony said, holding himself very still. He couldn't believe he'd heard her right. Or if he had, that she had any idea what she'd said.

She drew back a little to look up at him. Behind the passion glaze in her eyes he could see uncertainty forming. "I said," she mumbled, licking her lips, "that we could go upstairs."

"You mean—"

Color stained her cheeks, poignant and subtle as a wild rose. "I think it would be simpler...in the long run. Unless you'd rather not. If you don't want to—"

"Of course I want to," he said, gentling his tone, unable to resist brushing that delicate bloom in her skin with his fingertips. "That should be obvious. I'm just...a little surprised."

"Are you?" She pulled away from him to look into his eyes. The accusation in her gaze took him back a bit, but then her mouth quivered and he knew she was only a breath away from a smile. "Do you mean to tell me you didn't know this would happen when you invited me to come here today?"

He wasn't going to lie to her. "Oh yeah," he growled, "I knew. I changed my sheets. I just didn't know that you did."

A little bubble of laughter burst from her. Stifling it as if she'd committed an indiscretion, she murmured, "I brought a toothbrush."

Warmth and wonder slowly filled him. "You did?"

She nodded, and with a quiet dignity that humbled him, said, "Stony, I'm out of practice and scared out of my wits, but I'm not a child. Why do you think I was afraid to talk to you? After the way I felt when we danced together, when you kissed me, I knew this would happen if I saw you again. I just had to make sure I was ready for it."

"And now," he said gently, brushing his thumb across her lower lip, "you are?"

"Yes."

He didn't ask her what had made her change her mind. He knew her reasons would be too complex to put into words. He had an idea, though, that it could all be distilled down to an elemental truth: that when it came to a battle of primal urges, sex and hunger would always win out over fear.

Nevertheless he cautioned himself to go slowly. The fear was still a part of her. "Are you sure?" he asked, smiling a little and keeping his tone light to let her know it was all right if she wasn't. "Even now that you've cooled down a little?"

She gave another of those ripples of self-conscious laughter. "It's better this way, actually. You won't have to carry me. I think I can walk now."

Stony put back his head and laughed with pure, unadulterated pleasure. Pleasure in her. He'd never met anyone like her before. Everything she said and did surprised and delighted him. "This way, my lady," he said huskily, carrying her hand to his lips and pressing a lingering kiss into it before tucking it securely into the crook of his arm. If he used every ounce of self-control he possessed, he thought he just might be able to make it as far as his bedroom before he kissed her again.

For all of her avowed certainty, though, he knew she was still apprehensive. He could feel the nerve tremors cascading through her body as they walked close together up the stairs. He wondered if she had any idea how nervous he was. He'd been single a long time, but he was no Lothario. He had no practiced line or standard method for dealing with situations like this. He'd always just pretty much played it by ear, and sometimes it worked out well and sometimes it didn't. It had never seemed to matter much to him, one way or the other. Before today.

But Toby was different. He knew that she was special to him, though in what way she was special he couldn't have said. He just knew that he wanted this to be good. He wanted it to be . . . right.

"Here we are," he murmured, pausing in his bedroom doorway. The room was suffused with hazy golden light. Late November sunshine slanting through the dormers had painted windowpane-checked rectangles on the hardwood floor. It was warm and inviting, and thanks to his foresight, reasonably tidy, but he found himself suddenly wishing, with a fierce and protective tenderness, that it was night. He had an idea the light was going to make it harder for her.

"Maybe it would have been easier if you'd carried me." Hushed and breathless, Toby confirmed his thoughts.

Stony looked down at her. "I still can," he said, and scooped her up before she knew he was going to. She gave a startled gulp and wrapped her arms around his neck. "Yes," ne murmured approvingly, "that's the idea. Now...kiss me."

She tilted her head, smiling a little, as if it were a new idea. When her lips touched his, their sweetness nearly took his breath away. He let his lips part just slightly, but left the rest up to her; and when he felt the shy and tentative explorations of her tongue, he knew that to her, it was a new idea.

The awareness that she'd never done such a thing before, never taken the lead in kissing a man, absolutely shattered him. Questions exploded through his consciousness, but before they could take on coherent form, Toby's tongue found his and drove them all out of his mind. She was a fast learner. Stony groaned. She chuckled, gaining confidence and expertise by leaps and bounds. The desire he'd so carefully banked flared to life and in seconds became a roaring blaze.

"Hey," he said thickly as he set her feet on the rug by his bed, "what the hell was that?" Though he felt ready to explode, she was looking more flustered than aroused.

Licking lips already glistening with moisture from the kiss, she muttered, "I want to..." then stopped, frowning. "I don't know...what you like. I'm afraid I won't—" She caught a quick, exasperated breath. "You're not going to help me with this, are you?"

"Nope," Stony said, gulping back laughter, "you're doin' just fine."

She closed her eyes and leaned her forehead against his chin. "Why is this so hard to talk about?"

"It just is," he said tenderly. "It's a rule. It's supposed to be easier to do than talk about."

Gazing hungrily at his mouth, she whispered, "Is that a hint?"

"It is."

"Oh..."

He didn't undress her, guessing that she would be shy about her body, though he was certain she'd have no reason to be. And he knew that when the time came, the clothes would come off, almost of their own accord and without her even being aware of it. Instead, he took her mouth in a slow and sensuous kiss, and while she was thus distracted, placed her hands with firm intent on the front of his shirt. That mind-blowing kiss of hers had shown him the way to ease her past the awkwardness. He would simply let her undress *him*.

The buttons were easy. With flattened palms she rode the separated halves of his shirt upward across the planes of his chest and over his shoulders, letting it drop unheeded to the floor. She began, then, to explore his body, not just with hands and eyes, but with all her senses, leaning forward to rub her face against his chest, nuzzling with her nose like a kitten, inhaling deeply of his scent, tasting him with her tongue, burying her fingers in his hair and discovering smooth flat nipples and hard-pebbled tips and then, as if unable to resist, tasting him there, too.

Stony stood motionless, dumbfounded, wondering when she would ever stop surprising him. He'd never known anyone like her before, never known a woman could be so completely enthralled by him, so totally immersed in the sensual enjoyment of his body.

"Toby," he said raggedly, struggling for sanity as her hands sought his belt buckle. "I want you to know something." She paused, lifting her enraptured gaze to his face. "There is no imaginary line, no point of no return. If you want to slow down or stop, I will. Just tell me." He wondered if she believed him. He wasn't all that sure about it himself. Not anymore.

She smiled at him, her face soft and radiant as a sunrise, and with tears shimmering in her eyes said simply, "Thank you."

She had no thought in the world of stopping him, but his sensitivity and concern banished all remaining doubt and a good deal of the fear. She wanted him with a fierce and single-minded passion that defied rational thought. Later, perhaps, she would wonder about the stranger who had taken over her mind and body, and search for reasons and justifications. For now, there was only Stony.

His body fascinated her, so big and broad and strong. He was a feast for the senses, and she was hungry. She loved the way he smelled and the way his chest hair felt on her face. She loved the way his arms wrapped so firmly around her and the steady thumping of his heart against her cheek. Her breasts ached and swelled, wanting that vibrant warmth and textured caress, wanting the contact her blouse denied them.

She moved restlessly against him, unable to voice her need except with a fretful little growl.

"What is it?" he whispered. "Tell me."

"I want..." Her lips felt stiff. Why, oh why was it so hard? "I want to feel you."

Somehow he understood. "Here..." His fingers slipped between them. A moment later she felt the cool rush of air on her heated skin and then his hands on her sides, lightly skimming the outer curve of her breasts as he drew her to him and nested her taut and aching nipples in the furry warmth of his chest.

She made a uniquely feminine sound of pleasure. He answered it with a chuckle of masculine satisfaction and catching her hair out of the way with one hand, lowered his mouth to her bared nape. Sensation washed through her body in hot-cold rivers, weakening her knees. Her pleasure sound became a long, openmouthed gasp.

With hands splayed wide across her shoulder blades to support her, he laid her gently down, staying with her, his mouth drawing heat from the core of her body to the surface of her skin, blazing a trail of love bites from her throat to the rising swell of her breast. She moaned softly and arched her back, and when his mouth moved lower, moaned again. His lips caught the tender bead of a nipple; his tongue flicked it to hardness, then gently laved it. Shudders wracked her. Her fingers curled and uncurled, making useless, frustrated forays across his chest and belly, always coming back to the insurmountable obstacle of his belt buckle.

Frustrated, she drew one leg up slightly and turned toward him, pushing with her hand against the hot, throbbing pressure in her lower body. His hand followed hers and displaced it—oh, the difference, so sweet and wonderful she wanted to cry. Bringing his mouth back to hers, he bathed her lips with slow, drugging strokes, slipping his tongue almost lazily in and out of her mouth while his hand explored the intricacies of her waistband fastenings.

After a few tense and frustrating moments, Stony pulled his mouth from hers and said, "Toby, how in the hell—" just as she gasped, "I . . . can't . . . get it!" They both began to shake with rueful laughter.

"Well," Stony said in a hoarse whisper, "I guess we'll have to call the whole thing off."

Toby whispered, "I'm sorry I'm so clumsy."

His fingers traced the line of her eyebrow, the top of her cheekbone, the shell of her ear. "Toby, look at me," he ordered, his rough voice at odds with the delicacy of his touch. She did and felt herself fill up with light and warmth, like a fountain full of rainbow bubbles. With indescribable tenderness in his eyes, Stony said, "Lady, you are many things—beautiful, sexy, funny, shy, passionate, delightful, to name a few—but clumsy isn't one of 'em."

She drew a shaky breath. "It's just . . . so awkward."

"Of course it is," he said, drawing her irresistibly into his smile. "There is just no way to get out of a pair of pants that isn't awkward. The Scots have the right idea—they wear kilts." His hand, resting lightly on her stomach, rode the ripples of her laughter. "So," he whispered, bending to blow lascivious puffs into her ear, "what do you say you do yours and I do mine—"

"And I'll be in Scotland before you," Toby said on a gulp.

Stony's laughter exploded in the hollow of her neck.

For a few moments they held each other, rocking with mirth that released the tension but in no way diminished the depths of their arousal. The shared laughter was another new experience for Toby, and a revelation. Sex could be awkward—and disconcerting, exciting, exhilarating, surprising and fun. She was embarrassed—a little—but it was all right. Her body wasn't perfect, but it didn't matter. She was risking the most fragile, vulnerable parts of herself, body and soul, opening herself to this stranger, but he was as vulnerable as she was.

It came down, she realized, to a decision to trust. And that was less a decision than a gamble. A spin of the roulette wheel. She had put all of her chips on Stony. Had he as much riding on her? The answer came to her like another revelation; joy reached into her soul like fingers of sunlight. Long before the wheel had stopped spinning she knew that she—that *this* was right.

Relaxed and drowsy with desire, she lay on Stony's clean sheets, feeling the mattress give with his weight as he stretched himself beside her.

"You don't need that," she said, gently placing her hand over his. "I told you, I won't get pregnant. I can't."

"I know, but I thought—" He raised himself on one elbow to look down at her. "Are you sure?"

"Very sure." She reached for him, and he sighed as he leaned down to kiss her.

Yet there were doubts when she felt his weight shift, the rough and unfamiliar pressure of his body, moments akin to panic. Would she be too dry? Would he hurt her? And then his big, strong hands were moving her legs apart, finding the soft and throbbing part of her, stroking her to readiness with a touch so gentle and sure it left her gasping, squirming mindlessly against the pressure, wanting more. Still holding her, still stroking her, he moved into position, guiding himself, distracting her with kisses. And when he slid at last into her warmth it was so easy. Wonderfully, gloriously, beautifully easy.

Stony smiled down at her, stroking her forehead as he adjusted his body to hers. He whispered, "Toby..." and lowered his head to kiss her. "You okay?"

"Mmm-hmm!" She sighed and moved her hips against his. "You feel...so good."

"Believe me." His voice was ragged and fervent. "So do you." His hand moved along the outside of her thigh, hooked her knee and lifted. Without the slightest hesitation she obeyed his gentle command, bringing her legs around him, arching sinuously as he stroked her. His hand traveled upward, following the curves of hip and waist, breast and underarm, catching her arm and drawing it up, up, lacing his fingers through hers. He smiled at her. "How's that?"

Her eyelids fluttered down as she murmured, "You're right, it's like...riding a bicycle."

The bump of Stony's laughter was a new sensation to her. Joy ran through her like a crystal river. In all the cold and lonely places within her she felt things blossoming, stirring, growing lush and verdant. And as he began to move, slowly at first, but with gathering intensity, she wondered why she had ever been afraid.

"Toby," Stony said wonderingly in the aftermath, "are you laughing or crying?"

"Both," she whispered, sniffling a little.

"I thought so." Braced on his elbows, he bent down to kiss her, each wet eyelid first and then her drenched and quivering mouth. He wiped the moisture from her cheeks and framed her face in his hands. Smiling down at her, he asked, "Okay now?"

She nodded. "I just can't believe it turned out so well." Laughter rocked his weight against her. She held him impulsively tighter. "I thought—the first time..."

"I know." He cleared the gravel from his throat and whispered, "You are one very special lady, you know that?"

It was the way he said it, with that slight huskiness in his voice, his face so grave. Fresh tears sprang to her eyes. "So are you," she whispered back, laying her hands on his face, smoothing the care lines around his mouth with her thumbs.

For a long time they were silent, looking into each other's eyes, puzzling, asking questions and shying away from the answers.

Finally Stony coughed and muttered, "Yeah, well, we're just a couple of special people. Here, this has got to be uncomfortable for you."

She made a wordless sound of protest, unable to bear the thought of separating from him.

"It's okay," he said with a tender indulgence as he lifted himself to allow her legs a more natural alignment, "I'm not goin' anywhere. I just want to hold you for a while without crippling you, that's all."

New wonder burgeoned inside her. Somehow, she must have stumbled into heaven. "You do?"

"There, that's better." When she was settled comfortably, half draped across his chest and thighs, Stony raised his head to frown at her. "Why do you say it like that? Don't you like to be held?"

"Oh yes," she said, her throat tightening. "I love to be held. It's just...it's been a long time since anybody has."

There was a long silence. Stony's fingers played slowly up and down her spine. "Toby? Can I ask you a question?" She could hear the frown in his voice as he went on without waiting for her reply. "Your husband died...what, six months ago? That's not all that long. So why do I keep feeling as though I'm seducing a virgin?'' She couldn't answer. His voice took on that roughness she was beginning to recognize as a sign of deep emotion.

''How long has it been, Toby?''

Seconds ticked by. She counted them and finally drew a quivering breath and told him. ''Five years.''

He swore with a quiet and deadly vehemence that Toby hardly noticed. She continued matter-of-factly, ''He'd lost interest in me way before that, only a few years after we were married, actually. But five years ago was when it really...stopped. He told me it was because of his age, but looking back now, I think he was probably having affairs.''

''Geez, Toby!'' Stony rolled away from her and sat up. ''And you stayed married to him? Why?''

She put her hand on his back and found it rigid as stone. Obscurely frightened because she couldn't understand why it mattered to him, she whispered, ''I didn't think I had any reason not to. He was just... my husband. He was good to me. In a way, as much as he was capable of it, I think he even loved me. He saw to it that I had everything I could possibly want.''

''Everything?'' Stony said softly. He turned to her, his eyes glittering with a strange light. ''Yeah, he did everything—except dance with you or make love to you and hold you afterward or give you children—''

''That was my fault!''

''My God, Toby, you could have adopted.''

''Arthur didn't—''

''Arthur didn't! What about you? What did you want?''

She turned her face from him, furious with him for making her hurt again in ways she'd forgotten. ''What does it matter?'' she said irritably. ''It's over and done with now.''

There was a long silence. Stony muttered something under his breath. "What?" Toby asked in a resentful whisper.

He drew an uneven breath. "I said, what a waste. Twenty years of your life—"

"No!" She sat up abruptly, folding her arms across her nakedness. And then said it again more quietly, no longer angry, recognizing the truth as it formed in her mind. "No. It wasn't a waste. Don't you see? It was what it took to get me to where I am now, that's all. Everything that's happened to me in my life, good and bad—that's the path I had to take to bring me here. And I like where I am now, Stony." She drew her knees up and wrapped her arms around them, trembling with the wonder of her discovery. "Do you know what I feel like? I feel...like a girl again. I don't feel like I'm middle-aged, I feel like I'm starting all over again, with my whole life ahead of me. It's scary, and it's so exciting. There are so many possibilities. I can do anything—get my masters, maybe even my doctorate, have a career. I could even get married again." She paused, chewing pensively on her lip. "But only if I fall madly in love."

"Well, that's the only good reason I can think of for getting married," Stony said dryly.

Toby's chin rose. "Well, I'll never settle for less than that again," she said positively. "No matter what. Never, never again."

As Stony sat gazing at her, he felt his smile grow crooked. After a moment he fingered a floating wisp of her hair away from her face and said softly, "You're one in a million, you know that?"

She gave a low, throaty chuckle that was new to him and, he was almost certain, to her, as well. "I'm not, but it feels very good to have you say so." He trailed his fingers down the side of her face, tracing her hairline. She moved her head a little, rubbing against the caress like a cat being petted. "Mmm, and that feels good, too."

Emotion tightened his chest and roughened his voice. "You're hungry for touching, aren't you?"

Toby answered simply, "Yes." And then she sighed and turned her head to press her lips into his palm. "At least... the way you touch me. I've never been touched like that before." She gave a little shiver. He moved his hand to her neck, curving it around the vibrant column, feeling the ripple of her swallow. "It's all so new to me, the way you make me feel."

"How's that?" he whispered. "Tell me."

"Hot and cold," she mumbled. "Both at the same time. Full of shivers inside. Like I'm going to explode. I don't know—" She gave a shaken laugh. "I don't think I can explain, but it's... wonderful."

"A sexual fantasy come true, that's what you are," Stony murmured, dazed by the explosions of desire within him. Surely, it must be every man's fantasy—a beautiful woman, fully responsive and experienced, but in so many ways untouched.

Her eyes darkened but didn't close as he leaned toward her. Locking her gaze with his, he whispered, "Do you know what I'm going to do?" The movement of her head was unconscious and almost imperceptible. "I'm going to touch you... like this...." He drew his thumb across the satiny pillow of her lower lip and felt the warm caress of her breath. "And this...." His lips followed where his thumb had been. "All over...." His tongue swirled into her mouth and out again. "And I'm going to take my time, all the time in the world." He smiled into her rapt, unfocused eyes. "And when I'm through, there won't be a spot anywhere on your body that I haven't kissed. The only thing I haven't decided," he said with a thoughtful frown, skimming his hand lightly down her drawn-up leg, "is where to begin. Ah, here's a spot." She gave a soft gasp as he flipped his fingers under her arch. He paused. "Ticklish?"

"No," she said weakly, "just surprised."

"Good," he said, and lifting her foot, he delicately nibbled the soft pink pads of her toes. She giggled. "Did you say something?" he asked, raising his eyebrows at her as she dropped back onto her elbows, muttering in a muffled voice.

"I said," she repeated, grumpy with embarrassment, "I'm sure glad I shaved my legs."

"If you hadn't, I guarantee I wouldn't have noticed, not unless you told me," Stony said, interrupting his sequence of kisses to skim his hands along the whole silken length of her legs. They were unfashionably pale. He could see the delicate tracings of blue veins beneath the skin. She would probably consider that a flaw. Impatiently, almost angrily, he said, "Those things aren't important, don't you know that? I don't look at you and see parts and imperfections. All I see is you, and if you have flaws, then they're just part of you. Understand? So let's get past this business of being shy and embarrassed—about anything. You look beautiful, you feel...incredible, you smell good and taste delicious. Have I forgotten anything?"

"No," Toby said, "that about covers it."

"Good. Then where were we?"

After a brief and thoughtful pause, she delighted him by pointing to a spot halfway up her thigh. "Here," she said huskily, and shuddered with pleasure when his mouth found the mark.

He knew the moment desire overtook shyness, the moment the rosy flush in her skin became passion instead of embarrassment. He felt her relax, felt her bones grow liquid and her flesh heat and soften in his mouth and in his hands. His lips touched whispers of encouragement to her skin while his fingers sought her body's softest and most secret places. And when his mouth had taken over that most intimate of caresses and her breaths came high and quick and frightened, he encouraged and praised her with his hands, stroking her, soothing her, cherishing her, drawing out her ecstasy to the last trembling, shuddering moment.

He held her while the waves rolled through her, protecting her with an almost maternal fervor, nursing her pleasure with kisses offered like life-giving water to a thirsty soul. The dry, desperate sound of her sobs and the panic in her fingers told him something, something he didn't think he could stand to hear her say. *It's been a long time.*

Or maybe even, as hard as it was to believe, *never*.

She hadn't experienced full release the first time, he knew. Her pleasure had been a quiet joy, emotional rather than physical. And that she found the cataclysm disconcerting, even frightening, was evident in the tears that squeezed from between tightly closed eyelids and the way she lay in his arms afterward, rigid as a post, resisting him. A long time or never, either way—it didn't matter, Stony vowed as he stroked and petted her and whispered tender reassurances into her feather-fine hair. Because it sure as hell wasn't going to be her last.

Adrift in a hazy state that wasn't quite sleep, Toby felt a tremor ripple beneath her cheek. Wondering at its cause, she moved her hand across Stony's broad chest, pushing her fingers through the soft furring of hair to warm skin and solid muscle and the strong, steady vibration of his heartbeat. Tipping her head back to look at his face, she saw that his eyes were open, focused on the ladder of sunbeams that slanted from the foot of the bed to the dormer window. His jaws looked tense and hard as his nickname.

But in the next moment, aware of her gaze, his face softened with a smile. "Hi there," he said in his warm raspy voice. "You look worried." His arms tightened around her; his lips pressed the top of her head. "What's the matter?"

"Nothing," she lied. Insecurity was such an unattractive emotion. It irked her that she should feel the need for some kind of verbal reassurance after what had just happened to her. To Stony it was probably just standard operating procedure—no big deal. Happened all the time. And whatever the unknown emotion that had rocked his body and hardened his jaws, it wouldn't have anything to do with her. He was so open. Hadn't he promised her that she would always know where she stood with him? "The turkey," she said. "I was wondering about the turkey."

Laughing, he pulled her onto his chest. "Forget the turkey. I'm not through nibbling yet. In fact, I've barely started. Okay, let's see, where haven't I kissed you?"

Already breathless with pleasure, the exquisite sensations produced by his varied textures diffusing like light through her skin, Toby lifted her arm and pointed to her elbow. "Here, I think."

"Hmm, yes . . . and here . . . and here."

She squirmed with delight as his mouth began a languorous journey along the sensitive inside of her arm, gasping at the brazen forays of his tongue into places she'd never dreamed could yield such pleasure. When he pushed her back a little so his lips could scale the gentle rise of her breast, she arched her back, bringing her nipple to him. Head back, hair wafting like cobwebs over his arms, she clung to his shoulders, her breath coming sharp and quick as the fierce, hot tugging pulled deep, deep inside her. Laughing, giddy as a maiden on a swing, she felt him raise himself to bury his face in the hollow of her neck:

"Let me feel you, darlin', open for me now." His hands lifted and settled her, sheathing himself in her so deeply her breath drove from her lungs in a long, openmouthed gasp.

"Yes," he growled, and covered her mouth, taking her cries into himself as he surged into her. Her body arched, wrenched from her control, rocked by waves of sensation so overwhelming all she could do was cling to him, abandoning herself to him in blind faith and absolute trust.

It was a long time before either of them thought again of the turkey.

## Chapter 8

In the soft lavender light of early morning, Toby lay awake thinking of fate and of miracles.

Against her back the biggest miracle of all heaved gently, like a mountain stirring to life. His breath gusted warmly into her hair. He muttered, "Mmm, that tickles," and then, cuddling her in cozy intimacy, blew showers of shivers into her ear with his whisper. "Are you awake?"

She laughed and wriggled closer to him. "Yes."

"Hmm. You're so quiet."

"I was just thinking...."

"What about?"

But it was too complicated to explain, especially at that hour of the morning, so she just said, "I was thinking about spring. I know it's November, but it feels like spring to me."

"That's L.A. for you," Stony said with a yawn. She felt him crane to look out the window. "It's foggy. I guess that's why. Hey—" His lips were back at her ear, playing havoc with her nerve endings. "What are we going to do today?

Are you hungry? I don't know about you, but I could use some breakfast."

"I don't suppose we could have it in bed?" Toby said hopefully. She wasn't sure she could even get out of bed. Her muscles were screaming a mixed chorus of complaints.

"Shameless wanton," Stony said fondly. "You had Thanksgiving dinner in bed. What we both need is a brisk walk. Upsy daisy." Toby gave a heartrending groan. He raised himself up on one elbow, instantly solicitous. "Sore?"

She nodded. "Muscles—a few I didn't know I had."

His frown of concern became a pleased smile. "Oh, well, a massage and a hot shower will fix you up. Or better yet—" he leaned down to kiss her "—we could work the soreness out."

"Is that possible?" she asked presently, her voice already growing faint and breathless.

"I don't know. Give me a minute and we'll find out. Or...less."

"Incredible," Toby whispered.

Stony chuckled. "Well, you know how it is in the spring..."

Some time later, when they had finally made it downstairs and were rummaging in the refrigerator for something to eat, Stony said thoughtfully, "Speaking of spring, let's go out to breakfast."

"Were we?" she asked, giving him a quizzical look as she waited for him to explain the non sequitur.

"Yeah. You've got me in a springtime mood, too." He grinned at her as he shut the refrigerator door, feeling light-headed, lighthearted, young. "You know, 'twitterpated,' like in *Bambi*. And that reminds me—I know a place where it always feels like spring. It's not far from here. I used to go there a lot. We can eat there. What do you say, want to go find spring in November?''

"Sure." Her lips were parted in laughter, her eyes enchanted as an April morning. "What should I wear? Am I okay like this?''

Okay? Didn't she know how adorable she looked with her hair in a ponytail, wearing one of his sweaters over her blouse and slacks and not even a hint of makeup? "You are beautiful," he said, kissing her, hoping she knew it wasn't something he went around saying all the time. "Just perfect." He couldn't believe the bolt of desire that shot through him every time he looked at her. Even now, after the way they'd spent the last twenty hours or so. It was like being hit in the breastbone with a sledgehammer.

"You'll need shoes," he said, trying to collect his wits. "Walking shoes. Chris should have an old pair of Reeboks around somewhere." Shaken, he went off upstairs to find some, wondering what in the world he was going to do if he fell in love.

"The zoo?" Toby's delighted laughter tinkled on the autumn air like wind chimes. "I never would have dreamed—the zoo!''

"Ever been here?" Stony asked casually, strolling along with his hands in his pockets, absurdly pleased that she was pleased.

"No. At least, I don't think so."

"I used to come here a lot when Chris was little. When she was cranky or I didn't know what else to do with her, I'd put her in her stroller and we'd kill a morning or an afternoon just walking up and down these paths. I don't know why it is . . .'' He put back his head and filled his chest with cool, crisp air, pungent with the exotic smells of animals. "It just always seems like spring in the zoo. Maybe because there are always babies of one kind or another, flowers blooming, birds singing. What?'' he asked, stopping himself in midstride, his smile slipping askew because she was staring at him and the expression on her face took away his breath.

"Nothing," she whispered, as if her own breath were in scant supply. "I'm just—you keep surprising me, that's all."

His heart stumbled, then righted itself and resumed its quickening pace. He felt fragile and precariously balanced, like a man walking on eggs.

"Once," he said, looking over her head to where a family of gorillas was drawing a crowd, "right on this very spot, I saw a miracle. There were bears here, then. Alaskan kodiaks. Huge things, ten feet tall when they stood on their hind legs. Chris loved them, especially this one who used to sit with her feet out in front of her, you know the way they do, paws on her knees, and beg for handouts.

"So, on this particular day we're watching the bear, and all of a sudden she gets up, turns around and starts nuzzling something that's lying there on the cement. This little tiny naked pink thing, no bigger than a kitten. And then, while we all watched, in a state of shock, I guess, she picked it up in her mouth and started pacing up and down, back and forth, like she didn't know what to do with it. Someone ran for a keeper, and eventually they got the bear into her cage in the back. Later, we heard she'd had two more cubs, and they rescued all three and raised 'em on bottles. Incredible, huh?'' He grinned crookedly at Toby, who was staring at him with either awe or horror, he wasn't sure which. "How many people can say they've witnessed the birth of an Alaskan kodiak bear?"

Toby shook her head in a wondering way, but didn't answer. Stony chuckled and put his arm around her, drawing her close to his side as they walked on, leaving Africa behind.

But after a while he cleared his throat and said, "Toby? Remember yesterday, when you were talking about how it's taken everything that's happened to you, good and bad, to get you to where you are now? Well, that's what I kept thinking about after the bear thing. About all the little problems and delays that happened that morning, to put me in that particular spot at that particular time. Chris deciding she didn't want to put on her shoes and throwing a fit; me discovering I'd lost a button on my shirt and having to go back and change. Things like that. If any one of those things had been different, I'd have missed it.''

He stopped walking and thrust his hands into his pockets, unable to look at her, unable to finish, hoping she might understand what it was he was trying to say. It wasn't like him to speak in parables, but he could not—he could *not*—bring himself to put into words what he knew to be the truth: that if it hadn't been for Chris's tragedy, he and Toby would never have met, except, perhaps, in the most casual of circumstances, would never have exchanged more than a few courteous phrases. Mrs. Thomas and Mr. Brand.

When she turned abruptly from him and swiped a surreptitious hand across her cheek, he thought maybe she did understand.

After a moment she cleared her throat and murmured, "About Chris..."

"It bothers you, doesn't it?" Stony said softly, moving up beside her to watch a mother hippo escort her baby into the pool, jealously screening him from the curious onlookers with her body. He took a deep breath, knowing that what he was about to say was a declaration, of sorts; or at the very least, an acknowledgment. "I'll tell her about this," he said, putting his hands on Toby's shoulders. "First chance I get. I promise." His voice roughened. "Look, I don't want to deceive anyone. And I want this to continue...between us." Oh, yes, he wanted it to continue, but in what form? His thoughts terrified him.

She relaxed against him with a little sigh. "I just don't want anything to upset her right now. She's so fragile, Stony. I'm worried about her."

"So'm I." Needing her closeness, he crisscrossed her body with his arms and lowered his head, bringing his lips to the side of her neck. "But it's not going to upset her. Chris has never had a problem with my dating. Well, except for being a busybody at times, worrying about me, things like that. In fact, she'll probably be happy about it," he said with a short, hard laugh, remembering what Chris had said to him about his aloneness. And about stepmothers.

Well, he thought bleakly, that wasn't going to happen. He couldn't let it happen. Ever again.

Catching Toby's hand, he carried it to his mouth for a quick, yearning kiss and then walked on, holding it tightly, suddenly hurting inside, fear beating in his chest like a wounded bird.

The telephone rang while they were eating dinner—turkey sandwiches—in front of the fireplace in the living room.

It zapped Stony's nerves like an electrode because he knew there were only two reasons why anyone would be calling him at eight o'clock on a Friday evening, and neither of them meant good news. He stretched an arm along the couch behind Toby's shoulders to pick it up. "Yeah," he said tersely, bracing himself.

Toby had stopped chewing and was watching him, wide-eyed and tense. When he heard his assistant's voice he looked at her and shook his head. It wasn't Chris. Chris calling home on a Friday night would have meant a crisis; Jake Riley calling him on a Friday night meant a crisis, too, but it would be one he knew how to handle.

"Yeah, Jake, what have you got?"

"I hate like hell to bother you with this, Stony, but we've got kind of a problem here. Remember Frank Randall Quaid?"

Stony pressed thumb and fingers against his eyelids. "Uh, Global Shipping, right? Freighter, Cabot Strait, five years ago."

"That's the one. Okay, last week his wife's yacht hit a reef somewhere west of New Caledonia. Everyone got off before she went down, okay, so now the boat's just sitting there on a shelf—"

"Sounds simple enough. So what's the problem?"

"The problem is, there's been a lot of volcanic activity in that area recently. That shelf happens to be right on the edge of an active fissure—"

"You're telling me—" Stony stopped, swearing under his breath. He didn't want to say the word volcano with Toby sitting there listening to him. He took a deep breath, thought for a minute, then said irritably, "Why in hell doesn't Quaid just write her off? It's going to cost him more than the price of the damn boat to bring her up."

"It's his *wife's* yacht," Jake Riley said pointedly. "The *Lillibeth*."

Stony swore some more.

"I wouldn't bother you with it," Jake said, "except that, when last heard from, Quaid was throwing heavy objects and bellowing, 'I want the best! Get me Stony Brand!' That's the problem. Otherwise I'd handle it myself. I still will, if you want me to. Say the word and I'll call him, or you can talk to him yourself."

"No, no, it's all right, I'll . . ." Stony looked at Toby and felt *himself* sinking in the quiet gray pools of her eyes.

"Stony," Jake said, "I can handle this. Why don't you sit this one out? You're due—that last job was a real—"

"I'll be there," Stony grated. Toby closed her eyes. "Tomorrow morning." He hung up the phone and dragged her hard against him, enfolding her in his arms.

"You have to go?" The words were muffled against his chest.

"Yeah," Stony said on a long sigh, stroking her hair and staring over it, into the fire. "I do." It was just as well, he thought. The way his thoughts had been going lately, he needed something like this to remind him of the way things were.

Relationships wouldn't work for him. He had to keep remembering that. His life was running off to a place nobody'd ever heard of to pluck a rich man's toy off the lip of a live volcano, where a thousand things could go wrong, and no one could say with any certainty how long it would take. A few days, a few weeks. Chances were good he'd miss another Christmas. He thought of all the Christmases he'd spent apart from Chris, in some godforsaken spot, usually colder'n hell, always lonely. Winter was the season for shipping disasters.

"Where are you going?" Toby asked.

"The South Pacific," he said shortly. "North of Australia."

"Really?" She pulled back a little to smile at him. "You know, it's springtime down there."

For a long moment he just stared at her. Then, with his hand on the back of her neck he brought her mouth against his like a starving man given food, not knowing when he'll ever eat again.

Toby Thomas. He wished he'd never met her, but he had. She was both a miracle and a calamity in his life, and he didn't know what he was going to do about her. But tonight . . . for tonight, at least, she was here, and she was his; and he would pretend that it was spring, when miracles abound and anything seems possible.

*   *   *

Toby had never been busier than she was in the weeks between Thanksgiving and Christmas break, or more lonely. There were quarter finals, of course, and Greek Festival and the Winter Formal, not to mention all the details involved in closing down the house for a month, but no amount of company or activity could keep her from missing Stony with bewildering intensity. It had happened so fast, and then just as suddenly he was gone, clear to the other side of the world, beyond reach of telephones and casual missives of verification and reassurance. She felt like the victim of a hit-and-run left dazed and bleeding by the side of the road.

It felt worse because she couldn't talk to anyone about it, which was strange, because she'd never confided in anyone before. In her youth she'd always been the one who listened to other people's problems. And during her marriage she'd been so isolated. She'd had no close friends, only Arthur's business associates and casual acquaintances, and she'd kept her feelings buried deeply, carefully hidden, even, most especially from herself.

But now she wanted to talk about what had happened to her so badly she felt as if she would explode. Who could she tell? Certainly not the girls who came with their cocoa and confidences to sit cross-legged on the foot of her bed, though it was tempting. They seemed so much more experienced than she was, so much more in control. So open-minded, unflappable and matter-of-fact about sex. But how would they feel about their housemother having an affair? Worse, an affair with one of their fathers? No, it was impossible. The very thought of their knowing made Toby's stomach writhe.

She came close to telling Malcolm. He was worldly and wise about the ways of men and women, and he had become her friend. But he was a man, and Toby was new to the experience of platonic friendship with members of the opposite sex. She was still a long way from being able to share something as personal as her feelings for Stony.

As a last resort, she wrote to her sister. Japan seemed far enough away to be safe, and besides, Margie's kids kept her so busy, there wasn't a chance in the world she'd have time to answer.

On her office computer she wrote:

Dear Margie,

You'll never guess what's happened. I've met someone. A man, actually—and I'm having an affair with him. Yes, that's right—me, your own big sister. At least I think I am. We spent Thanksgiving together, and then he had to go away and I haven't heard from him since. And I know what you're thinking, but it isn't like that at all. He's at sea, somewhere in the South Pacific. It's a long story. But I miss him so badly that sometimes I feel physically ill. Is that possible? I can't eat, and I don't feel like doing anything, all I want to do is sleep. Is it possible for a modern woman to pine?

I know it's only been seven months since Arthur died, and I should feel guilty, but I don't. I don't really know what I feel. There's so much going on inside me right now, I just can't sort it all out. I do know that I've never felt like this before in my life. Could I be in love, do you think? I hope not, because if I am, then that means it's happening to me for the first time at nearly forty, and that seems just plain ridiculous to me! People don't fall in love for the first time at my age. It's probably just sex. I guess I never missed it before because I didn't know what it could be like. (I'm blushing as I write this!)

Enough of that. The housemom's job is going well. Finals are almost over—mine were a moderate success, a B and an A−, which wasn't as good as I'd hoped to do this first quarter, but considering the distractions, I'm not too disappointed. The girls are clearing out gradually. The house closes officially for winter break this weekend. I don't know yet what I'm going to do for Christmas. The people who got me this job—Michael Snow, Arthur's old lawyer, remember him?—and his wife have invited me for Christmas dinner, and I may take them up on it. They've become unexpected friends. But in any case, if Stony doesn't get back from the South Seas, it promises to be a very lonely Christmas.

Speaking of which, your box in is the mail. Hope it arrives before next Easter. Give my love to Kenji and the kids. I miss you.

Love,
Toby

It was raining, a cold, misty winter rain that dropped the snow level to within visual range of the Los Angeles basin. It would no doubt gladden the hearts of ski enthusiasts and resort owners throughout Southern California, but it depressed Toby. Cozily enswathed in bathrobe and blankets on the couch in the parlor of the Gamma Pi house, she watched weather reports on television and thought of Chris, skiing in Tahoe with a group of Gee Pi's and their fraternity "big brothers." They'd be grounded today, with a blizzard howling through the Sierras, a wind chill of forty below and visibility near zero. Toby shuddered. She'd always hated cold weather and snow and especially skiing.

She was feeling very grumpy and sorry for herself. It was the height of the Christmas holidays, she was alone, it was raining, she hadn't heard a word from Stony and, to top it off, she was almost certain she was coming down with the flu. She didn't understand it. She was never sick. But she'd been feeling so tired and run-down lately, a belated reaction to stress, she supposed, and in that weakened state had managed to fall prey to an intestinal bug of some sort. Her stomach had been upset all morning.

However, at the moment, perversely, she was feeling ravenous. Taking that as an encouraging sign that the bug, whatever it was, had been of the mild, twenty-four-hour variety, she went to the kitchen and opened a can of chicken noodle soup. While that was heating in the microwave, she got a box of crackers out of the storage pantry and poured herself a glass of milk. She was on her way back to her nest on the couch, juggling all three, when the telephone rang.

Adrenaline zapped through her like a lightning bolt. The box of crackers dropped to the floor and hot soup slopped onto her hand. She bent over and placed the bowl and milk glass carefully on the floor, then tottered on wet-spaghetti legs to the alcove and picked up the receiver.

"Gamma Pi house," she said, in a voice like cracked glass.

A thin, hesitant voice said, "Mrs. Thomas?"

Toby sagged against the wall. "Yes?" And then she came bolt upright again, her body icy cold. "Chris? Is that you?"

"I didn't know who else to call...." She was crying, sobbing uncontrollably.

Through jaws paralyzed by fear, Toby rasped, "Chris, what is it? Where are you? What's happened?" It had to be Stony. Something must have happened to Stony. Chris wouldn't cry like that unless—

"I couldn't reach my dad—I didn't know who else..."

Toby's legs gave out. She slid slowly down the wall and sat on the floor. "It's all right," she heard herself say through the ringing in her ears. "It's all right, Chris. Tell me what's wrong. Where are you?"

"I'm, uh, at the police station."

"The *what*? The police—*where*? In Tahoe?"

"No, I'm in L.A. Umm, do you think you could come and get me? I know it's a lot to ask. I couldn't think of anybody else. Dad's gone, and Jake's not there, either. I'm sorry. . . ."

There were a dozen questions Toby wanted to ask, but since it was obvious Chris wasn't up to answering most of them at the moment, she limited herself to one. "Chris, honey, which police station are you in?"

"Umm, I don't know. Just a minute, I'll ask, okay?" She was gone for several minutes, and when she came back it was obvious she was trying to speak more calmly. "It's the one right downtown. I'll give you the address. . . ."

Toby repeated it, then said firmly and calmly, "All right, I'll be right there. You just sit down and wait for me, and try to relax, okay?"

"Okay," Chris said with a sniff, sounding like a very small and frightened child.

"Christine Brand?" The desk sergeant glanced up at Toby and pointed with the pencil. "Right over there."

The butterflies in Toby's stomach quieted a little as she located the forlorn figure in blue ski jacket and jeans sitting on a bench against a far wall, hugging a backpack to her chest.

Raising her voice above the bedlam, Toby said, "Is it okay if she—do I just . . ." and floundered to a halt. She'd never been in a police station before and wasn't sure of the procedure. "Is she free to go?"

"Yes," the sergeant said patiently, "she's free to go. She's not under arrest."

That, of course, had been one of the possibilities that had gone through Toby's mind on the harrowing drive through rainy twilight and rush-hour traffic. She had almost preferred it to some of the other explanations for why Chris should be in a police station in downtown Los Angeles instead of a Lake Tahoe ski resort.

Taking a bolstering breath and a good grip on the sergeant's desk, she said, "Then what happened to her? Why is she here?"

The sergeant, who had gone back to his paperwork, gave her a harassed look and called over his shoulder, "Washington."

From somewhere in the chaos a deep voice answered, "Yo!"

"You and Cruz brought the Brand girl in, right? You wanna come talk to this lady?"

A tall, black uniformed officer came strolling up to the desk, carrying a disposable cup of coffee. Dark, watchful eyes regarded Toby through the steam. "Are you her mother?"

"No, I'm her...friend." Housemother would require explanations she didn't feel like making.

"My partner and I picked her up in the downtown bus depot," the officer said in that faintly accusatory manner all law enforcement officers seem to adopt that can manage to instill guilt feelings in a saint. "Judging by her behavior, we took her to be a juvenile, probably a runaway, possibly under the influence of a controlled substance—"

"Please," Toby said, closing her eyes and fighting for calm, "can't you just tell me in plain old ordinary language? What was she doing?"

"Crying," the cop said with a shrug. "Hysterical. Wouldn't let anybody near her. We figured her for a nut case or on some bad stuff and were all set to take her down to County General, but soon as we got her in the unit and she'd calmed down a little, we could see she was just plain scared to death. Wouldn't tell us why." He drank coffee, giving Toby a piercing look over the cup.

"She was attacked a couple of months ago," she said, feeling compelled to explain.

"Ah," the cop said, nodding as he crushed the cup and chucked it into the sergeant's wastepaper basket. "Well, maybe you ought to think about getting her some help. Looks to me like she's not handling it too well."

"I will. Thank you," Toby murmured as the cop wandered off into the confusion of desks and compartments, mingled voices and ringing telephones.

She walked over to where Chris sat hunched and defensive in her corner, tangled hair almost covering her face. When Toby touched the sleeve of the ski jacket, Chris jerked and gave her a look of terror that almost instantly dissolved into recognition and a fresh flood of tears.

"Oh, God—Mrs. Thomas," she sobbed as she jumped up and threw her arms around Toby's neck. "Oh, I'm so glad you're here!"

"Nothing happened, really," Chris said, evading Toby's eyes as she sipped her cocoa. "I don't know why I flipped out like that." She was propped up in Toby's bed, wearing one of Toby's nightgowns, her hair still damp from the shower. Toby was sitting on the foot of the bed, wearing the slacks and sweater she'd put on for the run to the police station.

"Why did you leave Tahoe?" she asked quietly.

Chris shrugged. "I just wanted to come home." After a moment she took a breath and said, "It wasn't like it was with Kim's family. That was *family*, you know? This time it was just all these kids, guy and girls, all in this one big condo. It was like one big continuous party. And I . . . got tired of it, and I decided I wanted to come home. So I took off. It was snowing pretty hard, but I walked to a gas station, and then I called a cab and had him take me to the bus station. The bus to L.A. was really crowded. There were a

lot of people traveling—I guess because of the holidays—
and the bus kept stopping in all these little towns, so it took
a long time to get here. At first it wasn't too bad. This
woman was sitting next to me with a little baby. But then she
got off and this man sat down.'' She looked away, and Toby
saw her throat move. ''He...made me nervous. And then
we got to L.A., and the bus depot was huge. I—I guess I got
confused. These...people kept coming up to me and asking for money. I don't think they meant any harm—they
were homeless, I guess—but it...upset me. There were just
so many people, and I don't know what happened, I just
overreacted, that's all.'' She spoke very softly, smoothing
the bedspread over her legs with her hand. ''It was childish
and I feel like an idiot.''

''You weren't an idiot,'' Toby said quietly, ''You were
scared. Weren't you?''

For a long time Chris didn't say anything, just stared
down at her hands, smoothing the bedspread. Then suddenly she pulled her legs up, wrapped her arms around them
and laid her forehead against her knees. Her voice came
muffled, a shaken whisper. ''Yes. I'm scared. Oh, God,
Mrs. Thomas, I'm so scared. I've been scared ever since it
happened. I keep waiting for it to get better, but it never
does. It seems like I'm scared all the time. I used to like
going places, being with people. Now I'm afraid to go anywhere. People—strangers—look ugly to me. Everything
looks ugly. I was so happy, before. And now...'' Her
shoulders began to shake.

Aching with sympathy, Toby leaned forward to rescue the
cocoa mug. ''Chris,'' she began, taking her hands.

But Chris pulled her hands free and used them instead to
hold her hair away from her face. ''That's what really gets
me, you know?'' She lifted streaming eyes to Toby, eyes as
blue and bright as sapphires, drowned in pain and rage. ''I
thought...I really thought the world—my part of it, any-

way—was beautiful. I really thought people—most of them—were kind and good. When it...happened, you know what I felt most? I felt betrayed. Like everyone had been lying to me. Why hadn't anyone told me I could be hurt like that? Toby, Mrs. Thomas, he hit me. He hit me...."

"Shh," Toby whispered, and putting her arms around Chris, rocked her like a child. She'd seen that same look on her face before, the night of the rape. That heart-wrenching look of bitter reproach.

"I was so angry," Chris whispered. "I was even angry at my dad for making my life so happy. For making me feel so safe. And it was a lie, all a lie. He should have prepared me..."

Toby, not knowing what to say to her, just listened and held her and stroked the hair back from her forehead while she poured out her pain and anger and fear. After a while, when the words had begun to slur and eyelids grew heavy, she stood up, smoothed and tucked the covers and whispered, "Good night, Chris." And then, impulsively bent down and kissed the girl's damp cheek and murmured, "Sleep tight," the way her mother used to do when she was little.

Out in the hallway, she listened to the clock on the mantel in the parlor strike the hour. Good heavens, she thought, counting. Only ten o'clock? It seemed later.

*Stony, I need you. Where are you?*

The loud pounding on the front door shocked her, coming as it did in the profound silence that followed the clock's last chime. For an instant she stood motionless, awash in a shower of cold prickles, and then she ran, heart pounding, knowing there was only one person in the world who would bang like that on the door of a supposedly closed sorority house at ten o'clock at night. His name was on her lips as she threw open the door.

"Stony."

He blew in like a gale, cold and wet and smelling of the sea. Rain darkened the shoulders of his jacket and clung in fine droplets to his hair and a half-inch growth of beard.

"Toby," he rasped in a voice like sand, clutching at her arms, "Chris is gone—missing. Is she here? Have you heard from her?"

"Yes," Toby said, emotions tumbling through her, shaking her body with joyous laughter. "Yes, it's all right. She's here."

"Here? She's *here*?" For a moment his eyes lashed her, heedless and wild. Then he closed them and groaned, "God, Toby," as he caught her up in his arms.

His strong arms crushed her to him; his mouth, impatient and greedy, found hers. His tastes, smells, textures engulfed her; salt and rain, wet wool and warm masculinity, the unfamiliar prickle of a beard on her face and lips. Her mouth opened to him in laughter, wet with her own tears.

"Stony—"

"Hush, let me kiss you."

The wind roared in her ears, the earth tilted, but it could have turned over completely, and she wouldn't have cared. Stony was back, and she was in his arms, and nothing else mattered. Nothing.

Except . . . from far, far away, a voice, breathless and young, crying, "Dad? *Dad!* I thought I heard— Mrs. Thomas! What's going on?"

# Chapter 9

Toby's body went rigid; Stony's arms tightened and his mind cried out in silent protest, No, don't go! Don't go.

His own body was pulsing with excess hormones, the natural product of long abstinence and some intensely frustrating fantasies. But he'd managed to keep them pretty much under control on the long trip home, in spite of the anticipation that kept him balanced on a razor's edge for days and a need that gnawed at him like a toothache. He'd meant to be a lot cooler about this—maybe a Clark Gable grin and a suave, "Hi there, darlin', miss me?"

What had done him in, he thought, was the sudden release of tension after the terrible worry over Chris. There was Toby, standing there with her hair long and loose, wafting around her face like a cloud of black smoke, and her smile and her words telling him that Chris was all right. Something had snapped. The dam had burst. Now here he was, holding on to Toby for dear life to keep her from jumping out of his arms, shaking like a wet puppy and trying his best to remember that he was a father and to absorb the fact that the daughter who'd been missing for the last twenty-four hours was standing right there in front of him in bare feet and nightgown.

"Chris," he muttered, the best he could do, under the circumstances.

Chris didn't say anything. She just stood there, looking from him to Toby and back again with her head tilted a little bit to one side. Stony wished he could read her, but he couldn't. She looked guarded. Finally she said quietly, "Why didn't you tell me?"

At his side, Toby made a sound. He gave her shoulders a squeeze and cut in, "Hey, there wasn't anything to tell until Thanksgiving, and you were out of town, and I left before you got back. I was going to tell you."

"Your 'date,'" Chris said with an odd little smile. "That was it, wasn't it? You and Mrs. Thomas. You went out—"

"Now look here," Stony bellowed, "my love life is beside the point. Where in the hell have you been?" Now that he was on firm parental footing, he let go of Toby and advanced upon his daughter. "Do you know how worried I've been? I've been going out of my mind!"

"Dad, you're shout—"

"You're goddamn right I'm shouting! How do you think I felt when I called Tahoe from Honolulu to tell you I was going to make it for Christmas, after all, and they told me you were missing? Huh? And then I called home, and you weren't there, either, and I called here and nobody answered, not even the blasted machine?"

Behind him, Toby made another small sound—a gulp. "I must have forgotten to turn it on when I went to pick up Chris at the police station. I'm sorry."

"It wouldn't have made any—did you say, *police station*?" All the air ran out of him and his voice got quiet. He saw Chris throw Toby a look of silent appeal.

"It's not what you're thinking, Dad," she said in that bright, bouncy little voice she always used when she was hiding something from him. "I just got sick of Lake Tahoe and decided to come home, that's all. I know I should have told someone I was going, and I'm really sorry I worried you. But anyway, I took a bus to downtown L.A., and when I got off, I was lost. You know what it's like down there, Daddy. So I...went to the police station and I called Toby— Mrs. Thomas—and she came and got me and brought me here, because it was raining and late. I'm sorry I inconvenienced everyone. But as you can see, I'm all right. Really."

"Hmm," Stony said, scowling at his offspring. He didn't think she was lying to him, not technically. But he knew good and well there was more to it than that, and he wondered who he'd have better luck getting it out of—Chris or Toby. Chris would keep things from him to protect him, and Toby probably wouldn't want to get in the middle of a father-daughter thing. And she was right. It was going to have to be Chris. And this time he didn't intend to let her get away with, "I'm okay, Dad, really."

But that was for later. For now, he was just damn glad to see her safe and sound. Letting his breath out long and slow, he hauled her into a hug and growled, "Okay, kitten. I'm just glad you're all right."

"I'm glad you're all right, too, Dad." She sounded like she had when she was a little girl. "I'm glad you're home."

After a moment Stony coughed and put her away from him. "Hey, why don't you go put some clothes on, and I'll take you home."

"Okay." She turned away, wiping surreptitiously at her cheeks.

Stony watched her until she turned a corner, feeling pretty choked up himself. Then he caught Toby by the arm and hauled her through the nearest doorway.

"God," he whispered as the softness of her breasts came against him, "do you have any idea how much I've missed you? How much I want you?" There was something about the way she felt.... Shoving his hands under her sweater, he met only the smooth warm flesh of her back. He groaned aloud. "Right . . . now."

"Me, too." She sounded drunk. He could feel her body shaking beneath his hands.

"I want to feel you against my skin," he murmured into her hair, searching for and finding her beaded nipples with his thumbs. His need for her was a fire in his belly. "I want to taste you with my mouth . . . here . . . everywhere."

She made a little whimpering sound and caught at his wrists with frantic fingers, pulling his hands away. "Stony, we can't—what if Chris—"

"Ah, geez." He smoothed her sweater down and folded her close, not knowing whether to laugh, cry or swear like a sailor. After a moment he started to laugh. "This is weird, you know that? This is backwards. It's supposed to be the kid sneaking around, hiding things like this from the parents. Why do I feel like a forty-five-year-old adolescent?"

"I know." Toby was shaking with laughter now, too, as she pulled away from him a little, wiping her eyes.

He caught her face between his hands and stared down at it, burning it into his consciousness. It struck him suddenly, with an unfamiliar little pang, that she looked as if she'd lost weight. She was paler than he remembered and her eyes looked smudged. But, he reassured himself, she sure hadn't felt thinner. Her body was even more lush and sexy than he remembered, and that was saying something.

"I hate like hell to leave you," he said in a gravelly whisper, "but I have to talk to her."

"Yes," she said pointedly, "you do."

"Save my place," he murmured huskily as Chris came into the room.

* * *

The drive home was silent, at first. Stony concentrated on his driving and on calming his rampaging hormones, while Chris stared out the rain-spattered windows at the swirl and shimmer of Christmas lights reflecting off wet pavement, shielding her thoughts from him.

He glanced over at her once or twice, at her clean, young profile silhouetted against the kaleidoscope of colors. It struck him, not for the first time, that his little girl had grown into a beautiful woman, a fact that never ceased to amaze him. She sure hadn't gotten it from him. He had a face like a shipwreck, and he knew it. From her mother, then. But when he tried to compare his daughter's face with her mother's, he realized with another of those odd little pangs that he couldn't remember clearly what his wife had looked like. The only face he could bring to his mind was Toby's.

"Dad?" Chris said as they left the Village behind and turned onto Wilshire. "If I hadn't been there, would you have stayed with her?"

Stony gave a surprised little laugh. For a moment or two he thought about lying to her, and then he said quietly, "Yeah, I would have."

"Are you in love with her?"

He didn't know how to answer that, even to himself. "It's too soon to tell," he said. "I like her a lot. I like being with her."

"I like her, too," Chris said. "Just in case you wanted to know that." Several blocks flashed by to the steady thump of windshield wipers before she added, "You could always drop me off and go back, you know. I don't need a baby-sitter."

Stony gave a short bark of laughter. "Look, kiddo, I don't need you to run my love life for me, okay? Besides, young lady—" he stopped for a red light and turned to her, all the laughter gone from his voice "—you and I have some talking to do. I want to know what the hell happened to you, and I want the whole story. None of this 'I'm okay, everything's fine' crap, you understand?"

There was a long silence before her reply came, perilously balanced on a sob. "Okay, Daddy."

By the time the parlor clock struck midnight, Toby had given up all overt attempts to induce sleep and was propped up on pillows with an Agatha Christie paperback. Ordinarily the early stages of a murder mystery were a sure bet to put her to sleep, and, of course, had the additional advantage of being utterly devoid of sex. Tonight, however, she kept being distracted by the staccato rattle of rain against her window and by the fire inside her that refused to die down.

Though the throbbing, insistent demands of her body disconcerted and dismayed her—there was still enough of the fifties influence left in her to make her wonder whether "nice girls" really ought to feel this way—on a much more primitive level, she felt pleased. Self-confident. Even proud. Why not? Her body was young, vital, capable of giving and receiving unimaginable pleasure. It must be a uniquely feminine feeling, she thought, languorously stretching.

The tapping didn't register, at first. In her dreamy, distracted state, she thought it was just the rain. When it came again, heavier and much more insistently, she sat bolt upright in quivering, heart-thumping terror, staring at the wavering, distorted face in her window.

"Oh, God," she gasped as she jumped out of bed and ran on weak legs to crank open the window. "Stony, what are you doing here?"

"Saving your reputation," Stony grunted, wiping rain off of his face. "What would your neighbors think if they saw a strange man on your front doorstep at this hour? What

were you smiling at, by the way? You looked like the Mona
Lisa."

"What will my neighbors think if they see a strange man
at my window at this hour?" Toby whispered hoarsely,
giddy with adrenaline and laughter. "I'd better let you in
before somebody calls the police—no, not here! Go around
to the back, I'll let you in through the kitchen."

Still shaking like a leaf, she cranked the window shut and
ran down the hallway to the kitchen. Without stopping to
turn on a light, she skirted the worktable and salad bar,
fumbled with the dead bolt and threw open the door. Stony
slipped through it, brushing raindrops from his hair and
shoulders.

"Idiot," Toby murmured as his warmth engulfed her,
overflowing with feelings she didn't dare name. "You *are* a
forty-five-year-old adolescent!"

"Mmm," he growled into her neck, "tell me about it.
Complete with adolescent glands, too. Hey, you're shaking, you know that?"

"So are you."

"Yeah, but I'm soaking wet."

"Well, so am I, now." They were laughing, whispering,
breathless as children engaging in secret mischief.

"I can fix that," Stony said, shrugging out of his coat.
"Here, what are you wearing?" He reached for her, haul-
ing up her nightgown, his big hands roving greedily over her
pliant flesh, his mouth searching through nylon folds for her
eager, lifting breasts.

"Stony," she gasped, awed by the feel of his cool, wet hair
on her skin, and then cried out as his mouth closed hungrily on one tender nipple. Her knees buckled. Desire
flooded swiftly through her, making her head swim. She
pushed unthinkingly into his mouth, clutching his shoulders, breathing in shallow little pants. Oh, how she wanted
to let go, to give in completely to the black waves of pas-

sion that were engulfing her, but there was something . . . there were things she needed . . .

"Stony!" she cried, her voice high with panic, unable to remember what it was she had to ask him.

"Sorry," he said roughly, lifting his head and folding her close. She could feel his heart knocking against her. "I just want you so badly. I want to make love to you. I want to go to bed with you, sleep with you, wake up with you, make love to you some more."

"So do I," Toby whispered, breathing through a thick gauze of passion, "all of the above. But we can't. Not here." She drew back a little, hoping he would understand, and encountered a quizzical look. Laughing, she murmured huskily, "If you think my neighbors would wonder about a strange man arriving at this hour of the night, imagine what they'd think about one leaving in the morning."

"Hmm. Would they really notice? What if I left early?"

"Mrs. Lubin at Tri-Delt next door comes out for her paper at six o'clock, sharp. The Alpha Sigs' Mrs. Fenstermaker jogs. And you know very well you won't want to leave early."

"You got that right," Stony said fervently, heaving a big sigh. "All right. Let me think a minute here. We can't go to my place, Chris is there."

That was it, the other thing she'd wanted to ask. "How is she?" Toby broke in. "About . . . us, I mean."

"Fine," Stony said shortly. "She's the one who suggested I come back here tonight." His hands moved restlessly over her back and tightened on her shoulders. "You know, of course," he said peevishly, "that this is supposed to be strictly an adolescent's problem? Fortunately, however—" he put her reluctantly away from him and bent to pick up his coat "—I have resources most adolescents don't have. Go put on a coat or something and let's get out of here. Don't bother with clothes, I'll just have to tear them off you."

Growing weak-kneed at the thought, Toby asked breathlessly, "Where are we going, to a motel?"

"Nah, I can do better than that. Don't waste time with questions, woman! Get a move on, before I'm forced to ravish you on the kitchen table!"

"I had a talk with Chris," Stony said as they drove west through a steady downpour. The atmosphere in the car was heavy and humid; the fires of passion were only banked. "She told me what happened."

"Did she?" Toby said quietly. "I'm glad."

"She told me other things, too. And she's agreed to talk to a counselor. She wants to take some kind of self-defense course, too." He was silent for a long time while Toby waited, studying his craggy profile in the shifting light. She saw his lips pull back in a grimace of pain. "Goddammit," he said harshly, bringing his open hand down hard on the steering wheel, "why didn't she tell me? Why didn't she let me know how she was hurting? She tries to protect me, you know. Doesn't want me to worry. *Worry?* Geez." His laugh was pain wracked. "Isn't that all a parent does?" He was silent again, shaking his head. Toby didn't reply, knowing it wasn't necessary to do anything but listen.

"I should have been there," he said after a while. "Just one more time I wasn't there when she needed me. Damn." He swore softly and with anguish.

"You're here now," Toby said, putting her hand on his thigh. "You've been there more than you think you have."

"Yeah?" The look he threw her was angry, but she knew it wasn't directed at her. "You just don't know...."

They didn't talk any more after that, until Toby, recognizing her surroundings, straightened and said, "This is the marina. Are we going to a boat?"

He flashed her a grin. "Yep."

"Really? Is it yours?" She'd never been on a boat before. Arthur had suffered from a deep and abiding fear of water.

"Yes," Stony said, chuckling, "it's mine. Silly, isn't it? Talk about your busman's holidays. Haven't used it much lately, but my assistant, Jake Riley, looks after it for me, so everything should be in good shape."

Even with delight and excitement fanning the embers of her desire, Toby heard the quietness in his voice, the residue of pain. Combating it the only way she knew how, she slid her hand upward on his thigh and murmured, "I've never made love on a boat before."

"No!" He caught her hand and pressed it briefly against hard muscle before carrying it to his mouth. "Now there's a surprise," he murmured, tickling her palm with his husky laughter.

A pleasure-boat marina on a stormy night. It seemed an odd place for...a tryst, Toby thought, remembering their first—and how nervous she'd been—with a soft, inner smile. There was something alien and exciting about it— boats heaving gently on dark swells, haloed lights reflecting in slippery patterns like oil on the water and the night alive with the sounds of creaking wood and clanking rigging and the rhythmic rush and sigh of rain. It filled her with a strange, wild exhilaration. She felt wanton, free.

She waited, trembling with excitement more than cold, while Stony uncovered the hatch, holding his jacket over both of them like an umbrella.

"Okay, in you go—watch your step," he said, handing her in first. He followed her, pulling the hatch closed behind him. The darkness seemed absolute.

When she heard him drop with a soft thud to the floor of the cabin, she reached for him blindly, lifting her arms to his neck and gasping at the shock of his cold hands on her fevered skin.

He laughed as he caught her to him, but almost immediately turned to fumble in the darkness, muttering, "I'll get some heat going. We should be hooked up to the electricity. Just a minute, darlin', I want some light."

Golden light flooded the tiny cabin. It gave his eyes a feral glow, his bearded face a savage, untamed look that called to the wildness within her. Her breath caught.

"That's more like it," he said, his voice a deep-throated purr that shivered across her nerves like demanding fingers. "I want to see you...."

Without a word she unbuttoned her coat, feeling no shyness at all as he pushed it over her shoulders, lifting her arms willingly as he drew her nightgown over her head. She shook her damp hair down around her bare shoulders and then watched him, languorous as a cat, feeling her body grow humid and heavy under the burning touch of his eyes.

"Beautiful."

She moistened her dry lips with her tongue and whispered, "I want to see you, too."

Her avid eyes followed his hands down the front of his shirt, lids becoming weighted and slumberous, the rise and fall of her chest accelerating as his clothing joined hers on the cabin floor. Naked, they faced each other, smiling a little, their fingers touching lightly, reverently. And then Toby put her hands on his hips and with a sigh, moved close, sliding her body against his silken heat. He made a sound— a cry, a groan, torn from the depths of his being, a sound of pure animal need—and took her mouth with a fierce and savage hunger.

Their joining was violent and sweet, so intense that she cried out. But there was something else, too, and it wasn't until the tender, trembling aftermath that she realized Stony had made love to her with a kind of urgency that bordered on despair. And just before she drifted off to sleep in his arms, she felt a small, cold frisson of fear.

Stony woke alone in the triangular-shaped bed in the forward stateroom. Feeling obscurely abandoned, he reached for Toby, then went cold and still. He could hear her, in the head.

When she came out he was waiting for her, sitting up with his arms resting on his drawn-up knees. "Good morning," he said with gentle irony.

She mumbled a peevish response and lurched toward the bed, collapsing near his feet. "Oh, God," she groaned, "I think I'm seasick."

"How can you be seasick? We're tied to the dock."

"I don't know, but I am. The boat's moving. I can feel it."

"It was moving even more last night."

"Hmm, but that was different."

She snuggled next to him with a complacent little sigh and the next thing he knew she was purring rhythmically, like a kitten, sound asleep, so he knew there couldn't be too much wrong with her. But he lay for a long time, stroking her hair while the boat heaved gently beneath him, thinking about what ifs. What if something were wrong with her? What if something happened to her? What if she wasn't in his life anymore?

The sickening upsurge he felt in his belly had nothing to do with the boat.

But later, when he'd found a pair of Chris's jeans and one of his sweatshirts for her to wear so they could head for home, she announced that she was starving. They stopped in Santa Monica for breakfast, where she ate a meal that would have stuffed a lumberjack. That, plus the sparkle in her eyes and the color in her cheeks when he teased her about it, pretty much put an end to his fears about her health.

When he dropped her at the sorority house, though, he noticed something else that bothered him. She didn't have a Christmas tree.

"They never get one," she said with a shrug when he asked her about it. "The house closes for winter break so early in December because of the quarter system, there's really no reason to. And for just me, it would be too much trouble. There wouldn't be any decorations around here, I'd have to buy everything, and it's too much bother. But look, I have my decorations, see?"

What she had were two poinsettia plants and a few small wrapped gifts nicely arranged on the mantel. It was pretty, but she seemed kind of embarrassed about it, and Stony had an idea from the way her eyes had slid away from his when she'd mentioned it, that it was the "buying everything" that was the problem. It was funny, the things he took for granted, like boxes of glass balls and tinsel garlands and snarled strings of lights tucked away somewhere in a closet, boxes of treasures made by a little girl's hands out of plaster of paris and papier-mâché and bread dough and clay, tunafish cans and wooden clothespins and cotton balls and yarn.

It would be no small expense, he realized, to buy a tree and all the decorations and lights she'd need, from scratch. It would probably take a sizeable chunk out of what a person would make as a housemother for a sorority. Once again, Stony wondered what in the hell had happened to all of Toby's late husband's money. There was something about her—pride, independence, a certain natural reserve—that made it impossible to ask, even for him.

He kissed her long and hard and left her, promising he'd be back. Then he went straight home to pick up Chris. Somewhere in this town, he thought, even three days before Christmas, there ought to be a place where he could still buy a Christmas tree. Two trees, as a matter of fact. It had just occurred to him that he didn't have one, either.

The next morning Toby's flu bug was back. The moment she opened her eyes, she knew that if she got out of bed she was going to throw up. She lay there for a while trying to decide whether to fight it or to get up and get it over with, and eventually decided on the latter course. Afterward, cranky and dispirited, she dragged herself out to the kitchen to make a cup of tea.

How depressing it was being sick, now of all possible times, when Stony was back and it was Christmas and she should have been so happy. And there was a niggling little fear in the back of her mind, too. What could possibly be the matter with her? She was never sick.

She was shuffling back to her bedroom with a cup of hot tea and a box of crackers when the front doorbell rang.

It was Stony, of course, it had to be. Her feelings were a bewildering mix of joy and dismay. She couldn't let him see her looking like this. But then, remembering what he'd said about her flaws not being noticeable to him, she gave a sigh of resignation and went to open the door. She would remind Stony of that little speech, too, if he said one word.

"Mornin', darlin', Merry Christmas."

"Merry Christmas, Mrs. Thomas!"

"Oh," Toby said faintly, "my goodness."

Stony stood on her doorstep, Chris at his side. Both of them were laden down with bags and boxes and grinning from ear to ear. Trailing behind them down the steps was an enormous, though slightly bedraggled Christmas tree.

"Don't panic, all this stuff was on sale," Chris said, puffing a little as she dumped her armload on the parlor floor. "You wouldn't believe it—stores have their half-price sales before Christmas now. And the tree—we got such a deal—boy, were we lucky! We got to this one lot just as they were loading all the leftover trees on a truck to take to the dump. Can you believe it? We got one, too. This is the biggest—I thought it should go in here because of the high ceiling. What do you think of it? Isn't it great?''

Toby murmured some sort of dazed affirmation. Stony gave her a long, hard look as he was dragging the tree through the doorway, but all he said was, "It's a little dry, but it should be okay through Christmas. We can take it down right afterward."

He set the tree upright near the front windows and turned to her, rubbing at some pitch on the heel of his hand and trying to look as endearing as possible, like a small boy with his hands full of wildflowers and mud on his shoes.

"Look, I know you said you didn't want the bother," he said in a low voice, glancing at Chris, who was on the other side of the room unloading bags and boxes. "But she just couldn't stand the idea of you not having a tree. And she was so bent on surprising you, I just couldn't disappoint her."

He was a very bad liar, Toby thought, but it didn't matter. She'd forgive him anything if he looked at her like that.

"We'll help you put it up and take it down," Stony said beseechingly.

"It's all right," Toby said, moist-eyed and laughing. "It was very sweet of you." She touched his face and whispered, "Your beard's gone."

"Yeah." He rubbed his jaw. "I get out of the shaving habit when I'm on a job."

"I sort of liked it."

"I'll sort of grow it back."

"I think I'd better go get dressed."

"I'll help," Stony whispered, with a quick glance at Chris.

"What about—" Toby hissed as he slipped into her room after her and closed the door behind him.

"Hush—she's a big girl. I just want to kiss you properly, that's all." He did so, then framed her face with his hands, brushing the fragile skin under her eyes with his thumbs. His eyes were narrowed and thoughtful.

She noticed the care lines in his face, the ones she'd found so appealing the very first time she saw him.

"You look like hell. You've been throwing up again, haven't you?" he said with his usual lack of tact.

Toby nodded and leaned her forehead on his chest. "Yeah," she sighed, "I think I've picked up a bug. It makes me so mad—right at Christmastime."

"Maybe you should see a doctor."

"Oh, I really don't think it's anything serious. I'll probably be over it by the time I could get an appointment. Maybe if I'm still feeling bad after the holidays..."

"So what are you going to do, feel lousy all through Christmas? Why wait? I'll bet if you called a G.P. or a clinic, they could get you in right away. Maybe you can get something to make you feel better—antibiotics or something, I don't know."

"I suppose you're right."

"Of course I'm right. So promise me you'll call somebody. Do it today."

Toby didn't understand his urgency, but because it was pretty much what she'd planned to do anyway, she agreed. And then she was having such a wonderful time with Stony and Chris, decorating the tree, making popcorn, playing Christmas songs for them on her guitar and, afterward, driving down to the beach to see what interesting debris the storm had washed up, that she forgot all about feeling sick and consequently, about calling the doctor.

She remembered the next morning. Cross and exhausted, both ravenous and revolted by the very thought of food, she dragged herself into her office and managed to locate her old telephone address book. She decided against calling her own doctor—a gynecologist, she thought, wouldn't be much help with a flu virus. Instead she called Arthur's doctor, an old-fashioned general practitioner who still maintained his offices in a one-story duplex in Culver City. She'd known Dr. Morrisset for twenty years. She was sure he'd manage to squeeze her in.

The nurse who answered the phone was one Toby recognized. Her voice was warm and cheerful. "Yes, Mrs. Thomas, how may we help you?"

"Umm, I'm not sure," Toby said, nervously rubbing her forehead. It had been years since she'd been to a doctor. "I haven't been feeling well lately, nothing serious, just some nausea, and I seem to be tired a lot more than I should, but I was wondering if Dr. Morrisset could squeeze me in for a checkup, either today or tomorrow. I know it's short notice—"

"Doctor can see you today at eleven," the nurse said briskly. "How would that be?"

"Fine," Toby gulped. "That will be fine." She hung up the phone and blew out the breath she'd been holding. Doctors gave her butterflies.

She still had the butterflies at noon, fidgeting nervously on a paper-covered examining table, wearing nothing but a paper gown. They all took flight at once at the discreet knock on the door, making her lurch violently upright as if she'd been jabbed in the spine.

The door opened and the doctor came in, carrying a clipboard. Dr. Morrisset was originally from Texas. He had a fine head of thick white hair of which he was very proud and called all females "honey."

"Well, Toby, honey," he said with a great big smile, peering at her benignly over the tops of his glasses, "I've got some good news for you."

"Oh," Toby said, rubbing her damp palms on her paper-covered thighs. She smiled back at him. "Well, that's good. So, it's nothing serious?"

The doctor chuckled. "Well, I suppose that depends on how you look at it." He frowned down at the clipboard. "Course, now, most of your test results won't be back for a couple of days, but as far as I can see, you're healthy as a horse. No reason in the world why you shouldn't come through this just fine. You're probably gonna want to see your own doctor—who'd that be? Dr. Schmidt, wasn't it?— and you should do that as soon as possible. We like to get you started off right—"

"Dr. Schmidt?" Toby said, puzzled. "Why do I need to see Dr. Schmidt?"

"Well, you don't have to, of course. I'd be tickled to death to see this through with you, if you want me to."

"See what through?" Toby asked through jaws that seemed to have locked. Surgery. That's what it was. She was going to have to have surgery. Oh, God.

Dr. Morrisset was shaking his head, silently laughing. "Honey," he said, leaning over to tap her thigh with the clipboard, "you're not sick. What you are is pregnant. You're goin' to have a baby."

# Chapter 10

It simply didn't register at first. The words had no meaning for Toby, as if the doctor had said something to her in a foreign language. But he was sitting there, obviously waiting for her to respond, so she shook her head and said, "I beg your pardon?"

"That's right," the doctor said, beaming at her like a proud grandpa. "You're just pregnant, honey, that's all."

Toby laughed. Obviously, dear old Dr. Morrisset was slipping a bit. Relieved that there was so simple an explanation, she said kindly, "I'm sorry, but there's been a mistake. You know I can't possibly be pregnant."

Dr. Morrisset reared back in mock alarm. "Now why would I know a thing like that?"

"Well, I—because I can't be," Toby floundered, uncertain how to proceed without insulting him or hurting his feelings. And she was beginning to feel confused, like Alice. "Because . . . I couldn't, all those years. I tried and I never could. I can't—"

"Well, you sure couldn't as long as you were married to Arthur," the doctor said briskly, putting the clipboard down on the desk with a clatter. His gaze was suddenly very intent. "Not unless you wanted to give him grounds for divorce. Toby, honey—" He stood up and took her limp hands in his. "When you were tryin' to get pregnant, did you see a doctor?" She nodded, feeling numb. "And what did the doctor say?"

"That I was—" She swallowed and tried again. "That he couldn't find anything wrong with me. He said he couldn't find any medical reason why I shouldn't be able to conceive. But he also said there was still a lot they didn't know and that sometimes..." She waited, then finished in a whisper. "The point is, I never did get pregnant, and it had to be my fault, because Arthur already had two children."

Dr. Morrisset was shaking his head, muttering under his breath. He took off his glasses and rubbed his eyes then sat down at the desk. Toby gripped the edge of the examination table and rocked herself slowly, back and forth, back and forth.

"That old son of a so-and-so," he said finally, putting his glasses back on. "I just can't believe he didn't tell you. If I'd had any idea..." He leaned toward her suddenly, his hands clasped together between his knees. "Listen here, hon', I'm gonna tell you something—maybe I shouldn't, but I'm goin' to. Arthur was my patient, but he'd dead and I don't think it makes any difference to him where he is now, one way or the other. The only reason why you never conceived a child is because your husband had a vasectomy before he ever married you. That's a fact, and I know it's a fact because I performed the surgery myself, right here in this office. He did a terrible thing, not telling you about it, but that's in the past, now, and there's not a thing you can do about it. What's important is right now. And I'll tell you, I may be just an old-fashioned sawbones, but I've delivered enough babies in my time to know pregnant when I see it—even without these new-fangled tests—" he thumped the clipboard with his knuckle "—which, by the way, are very seldom wrong. Honey, sure as I'm sittin' here, you are pregnant."

*Pregnant.*

Something strange was happening to Toby. She was still sitting on the table and Dr. Morrisset was still at his desk, but he seemed to be sliding away from her, faster and faster, becoming tinier and tinier, his voice coming from far, far away. She heard a rushing sound, like wind . . .

The next thing she knew, she was doubled over with her head between her knees and something heavy pushing on the back of her neck.

"Here, now," Dr. Morrisset's voice came from nearby once again, "we can't have you faintin'— Keep your head down, take a couple nice deep breaths . . . there you go. Feel better?"

Toby nodded, though she still felt cold and clammy. She heard herself mumble, "It's just . . . sort of a surprise."

"I can see that," the doctor said with a kindly chuckle, rubbing the back of Toby's neck. "Listen, I want you to sit here and talk to me until you get to feelin' okay about this, you understand? Talk to me—ask me any questions you want. You've probably got a bunch of 'em."

"I'm almost forty," Toby said faintly. "Will it . . . will it be all right?"

"That's a little older than we like to see, for a first-timer," the doctor admitted, "but it's not that uncommon nowadays. Awful lot of women puttin' off motherhood until the last minute. Like I said, you're strong and healthy—no reason why everything shouldn't be just fine."

"Will the baby be all right? I know there's more chance of something being wrong. . . ."

"We're going to want to monitor you pretty closely, just to be on the safe side, but I don't want you to worry. The odds are overwhelmingly in favor of you havin' a healthy baby. And we'll see you have all available tests."

The cost of which was going to be staggering, Toby realized. And she didn't have any medical insurance. But she couldn't think about that right now. She couldn't think at all. She didn't dare.

"Okay," Dr. Morrisset said, tipping her chin up and studying her face clinically through his bifocals. "Your color's improving. I'm going to have my nurse come in and give you some readin' material—some pamphlets on pregnancy, some suggestions that might help with the nausea, important do's and don'ts, things like that. She'll give you a prescription for some vitamins, too—we'll want you to get started on those right away. And then as soon as you've had a chance to think it over, you need to get in touch with either Dr. Schmidt or me or whoever you decide, and get started on your regular prenatal program. Okay?" He gave her shoulder a squeeze. "You call me if you have any questions, now, you hear?"

After he had gone, Toby sat, cold and motionless on the exam table, her mind like a blank wall. After a while she slid off the table and began to dress herself, moving slowly and stiffly, feeling a little like a windup toy whose joints had rusted. The nurse came in, bustling and cheerful, with her hands full of papers and little foil sample packets of vitamin pills. Toby listened to everything she said and nodded her head, but all she heard was gibberish. Alone again, she looked around for some place to put all those pamphlets and pills, but the problem defeated her. Finally she just gathered up her purse and coat and walked out of the office, carrying everything in her hands.

In her car, she inserted the key in the ignition and then sat motionless, frowning at the dashboard. *Pregnant*. She said the word in her mind, trying it out, then shook her head, puzzled. She ought to be having some sort of reaction, she knew, but she felt nothing—nothing at all. She wondered when it would hit her.

She turned on the engine and pulled carefully out of the parking lot, driving aimlessly, or so she thought, until she found herself on Pacific Coast Highway with the ocean on her left, glittering in the bright December sun. Strange, she thought, that people in crisis so often seem to be drawn to the edge of the earth.

Far up the coast, beyond the shopping centers and beach colonies, she found a turnout overlooking the water and pulled into it. She turned off the engine and sat holding the steering wheel, staring through the windshield, listening to the sound of the waves crashing on rocks.

*Pregnant.*

She was going to have a baby. A *baby*.

She shook her head, smiling. It was ridiculous. She was almost forty years old. She chuckled, then began to laugh. Before she knew what was happening, the laughter somehow became mixed up with sobs, and she was shaking and hanging on to the steering wheel for dear life, laughing wildly while tears ran down her cheeks in warm, salty streams.

It was late by the time Toby got back to the Gamma Pi house, almost sundown on one of the year's shortest days. The place looked familiar, unchanged, and yet it seemed strange to her, as if she were returning home after a long, long journey. The house was the same. It was she who had changed.

The thirties mansion with its pink stucco walls and red tiled roof and wrought-iron embellishments was her home. But for how long? Oh, Lord—it suddenly struck her—this house, her job, her classes—how long could she keep them?

What sorority would want as its "front person" and role model a forty-year-old unwed mother? Her whole future—how could she finish school? How could she work and raise a child? How would she *live*?

Her stomach heaved. Cold and shaking, more frightened than she had ever been in her life, she gathered up her things, locked the car and walked up the steps to the house.

There was salvation, she discovered, in routine: check the mailbox, gather the mail and carry it into her office; drop coat and purse on the chair, put the mail on her desk; check the answering machine for messages. The light was blinking. She pressed the button and glanced at the mail while the tape whistled through its rewind. The gas bill, some junk mail and a letter from her sister. She picked up the letter and was thinking about opening it when she heard Stony's voice. And suddenly her hands were just so much Silly Putty; her knees gave way and she sank into the chair, oblivious to the purse and coat already occupying it.

Stony.

"Hi, darlin', it's me. I hope this means you've gone to the doctor. I'm calling from my office—Jake's been on my tail ever since I got back, so I finally figured I'd better get crackin' on some year-end paperwork—but I'll be leaving here early, since tonight's Christmas Eve—about four, I guess, and I . . . well, I was wondering how you'd feel about spending Christmas with Chris and me. We never really talked about it, and...uh, well, hell, you know I want to be with you in the worst way—and every other way we might happen to come up with. Ahem—anyway, you can call me here before four, or call Chris at the house. I was thinking maybe I could just swing by there and pick you up, but if I don't hear from you before four, I'll probably just go on home. My office is in San Pedro, so it'll take a while. So, one way or another, I'll talk to you later, I guess. I'll be want-

ing to hear how your visit to the doctor went. Hope everything's okay."

The machine beeped loudly and went on to broadcast the
hiss of empty tape. Toby listened to it for a while and then
punched the button and covered her face with her hands.

Stony. How would she ever tell him?

She could see his face so clearly, the pain in his eyes. She
could hear the anguish in his voice when he'd said, "Never
again." She remembered how concerned he'd been about
using protection, and her own assurances that it wasn't
necessary.

A sharp little cry escaped her, half sob and half laughter.
Appalled, she clapped her hand over her mouth to stifle it.
Stony would never forgive her for this, never. He'd made it
so clear that he never wanted to become a father again or
marry again—

Marry! Toby's already precarious stomach turned over
one too many times. She ran for the bathroom.

It isn't supposed to be like this, she thought, sitting exhausted and clammy on the bathroom floor. Pictures
flashed through her mind like snapshots in an album—her
sister's children, dark-haired, dark-eyed children with ap-
ple cheeks, their happy smiles captured on film over and
over again by their doting daddy's camera; a little girl with
blond curls, her laughing face framed in the window of the
playhouse her daddy had built for her; Stony, pushing his
cranky toddler in her stroller, holding her up to see the
bears.

But *she*—she was alone. She would have to do this all
alone.

Marrying Stony was impossible. Out of the question. He
was going to hate her for doing this to him. Even if he did
offer to marry her, it would only be to give his child legiti-
macy, and once again she would be trapped in a marriage
without love.

No! Her mind recoiled from the thought. Never again. Half a lifetime was enough. Yes, a child needed two parents, but *she* needed something, too. She wanted—she *deserved* to be loved, cherished, desired. And she wanted to fall in love herself—wildly, head over heels in love. She wanted to feel her heart leap at the sound of someone's voice, grow weak at his touch, feel the sun rise when he walked into a room, be happy just to be near him. She'd have that, she vowed, or she'd never marry at all. She didn't have to—these days, it was almost stylish to have a baby without getting married. She didn't need anybody.

She didn't need Stony.

*Oh, Stony, please don't hate me.* Pain lanced through her; she pulled her knees up and hugged them tightly, curling her body against it, riding it out, gently rocking.

Somehow, she'd have to find a way to tell him. But not yet, not tonight. She wasn't strong enough. She was too fragile, too overwhelmed, there were too many things going on inside her that she'd have to deal with first. She'd have to call him and make excuses about Christmas. She couldn't possibly face him tonight; she wasn't a good enough actress to keep something like this from him. He'd take one look at her and know.

"Hi, this is Toby. I'm sorry you're not there. I wanted to tell you how sorry I am that I won't be able to spend Christmas with you. I guess I forgot to mention that I already had plans. But I did want you to know how much I appreciated the invitation and the tree and . . . everything. I wish I could be with you on Christmas Day, but since I can't . . . Merry Christmas, and I'll see you . . . later, I guess. Bye."

"See what I mean?" Chris said as she switched off the machine. "Don't you think she sounds . . . I don't know, kind of strange?"

"Yeah," Stony said. She sounded strange because she was lying, he was sure of that. The only thing he didn't know was why.

"I wish I'd been here when she called," Chris sighed. "I was just next door, taking Mrs. Kelsey some cookies. Do you think maybe she's afraid she'll be intruding? Some people get weird about Christmas—you know, the family thing."

"I don't know," Stony said, frowning. "Did you try calling her?"

"Yeah, but her line was busy. You could try her again now."

Toby's line was still busy. Either that, or she had it off the hook, Stony thought grimly as he replaced the receiver on its cradle. Dammit, she was ducking him, that's what she was doing. Now why in hell—

Fear crawled through his belly. The doctor. Of course. That had to be it. She'd gone to see the doctor today.

Wiping sweaty palms on his thighs, he snatched up his car keys and gave Chris a quick kiss. "I'm going over there and see if I can get to the bottom of this. Hold down the fort, okay, kitten?"

Chris grinned at him and patted his cheek. "Sure, Dad. Bring her back, even if you have to throw her over your shoulder. I don't want to have to look at this face all through Christmas."

"What the hell's that supposed to mean? I'm just concerned about her, that's all."

"And disappointed, I can tell."

"Well, sure I'm disappointed, a little. You know I like Toby."

"A lot."

"Okay," Stony growled on his way out the door, "a lot. Satisfied?"

"Well, for now." Chris grinned smugly and said, "Hurry back, Dad."

It was a beautiful Christmas Eve, moonless and still. There would be frost warnings for the colder inland valleys tonight. In the Gamma Pi house, all the lights in the parlor were off except for the ones on the Christmas tree. In their gentle glow, Toby sat cross-legged in the center of the sofa with her guitar across her lap, her hands resting on its silent strings. Her head was back on the cushions; her eyes gazed, unfocused, at the colored lights; her mind drifted.

She'd never spent a Christmas alone before, although there had been times when she'd felt lonely. In actuality, of course, she didn't have to be alone. She'd been invited to have dinner Christmas Day with Professor and Mrs. Wu and the Snows. The two potted poinsettias on the mantel were for them, as well as the two wrapped gift boxes of nuts—pistachios for the Wus, unsalted, dry-roasted peanuts for Michael and Brady, who were very health conscious. She'd canceled after calling Stony.... But she could always un-cancel; they would probably be delighted. Maybe, she thought, she would drop by the Snows' house tomorrow afternoon, just to drop off the presents.

The other two packages on the mantel she didn't know quite what to do about. One, the smaller, was for Chris. Toby had gotten her a pair of faux-pearl-and-rhinestone earrings, because she'd remembered that Chris had had to borrow some to wear on Presents Night. Stony's gift had been more difficult. It was hard to know what to get when she wasn't exactly sure what sort of relationship they had. They'd become intimate very quickly, and yet, she realized, she didn't really know him all that well.

She had found the little bronze in a gallery she'd had no business even being in because it was much too expensive for her in her new life, but she'd known the minute she'd laid eyes on the sculpture that she had to have it for Stony. It was a sailor at the helm of a ship, facing into a gale—hands strong on the wheel, jaw thrust pugnaciously forward, lips drawn back in a wild, exultant grin. It was...Stony.

The knock on the door didn't startle her. She had been expecting it. Maybe, she thought bleakly, if she sat very quietly here in the dark, he would give up and go away.

Fat chance—this was Stony. The knocking became a furious pounding. "Toby," he thundered, "I know you're in there, dammit! Come on, open up or I'm going to stand here and bang on the door until you do. Unless you want your neighbors to really get an earful, you're going to have to let me in!"

Toby sighed, laid the guitar carefully on the couch and untangled her legs. Stony had so often reminded her of a gale wind, but never had the comparison seemed more apt than it did now. Storms couldn't be controlled, prevented or diverted. There was just nothing to be done about a storm, she thought resignedly as she went to unlock the door, except batten down and ride it out.

"Toby, goddammit—" Stony was raising his fist for another assault on the door when it suddenly opened.

"Heavens, what a racket," Toby said, standing there looking calm and serene. "Do come in, and Merry Christmas to you, too."

She was wearing her nightgown, something blue and soft, molded to her breasts but loose and flowing everywhere else. Her hair was loose, too, brushed back and away from her face and hanging down her back like a schoolgirl's. She had a scrubbed, shiny look that made her seem fragile as porcelain, breakable as blown glass, and it may have been that, or something else, that kept Stony from reaching for her and pulling her into his arms.

Whatever the reason, instead of touching her as everything in him was yearning to do, he braced one hand on the door frame above her head and growled, "Where the hell have you been?"

She lifted one eyebrow and said evenly, "I was in the bathroom."

"Oh," Stony said. His stomach gave a lurch. "Doing what?" he asked with an unpardonable absence of tact. She gave him a funny look, so he cleared his throat and qualified, "I mean, you weren't throwing up again, were you? Did you see the doctor?"

"Yes," she said softly, with an odd little half smile, "I saw the doctor, and no, I'm not sick. I'm fine. Stony, would you like to come in? I'm really not dressed to stand here and talk in the doorway."

"Oh. Yeah, sure," he muttered, stepping into the entry and pulling the door shut behind him. Something about the way she was acting made him feel as if he ought to wipe his feet.

Toby seemed to float ahead of him down the hallway, her nightgown fluttering behind her, bare feet making no sound on the carpeted floor. Stony frowned as he followed her, feeling that inexplicable awkwardness. And feeling puzzled—something was wrong here. She seemed a million miles away from him. Why wasn't she in his arms? Why wasn't he kissing the daylights out of her, telling her how much he'd been missing her, worrying about her?

"I tried to call you," he said, taking a shot at it. "Your line's been busy."

"Oh, I know, I'm sorry about that," Toby said, not looking at him. To Stony, she sounded glib and false as a three-dollar bill. "I inadvertently left the one in the alcove off the hook. I just discovered it a little while ago. I hope you weren't inconvenienced."

Inconvenienced? What the hell was going on here? She was treating him like a goddamn stranger! Tentacles of unease crawled along his nerves.

"I was worried about you," he said quietly, touching her arm.

"Were you?" She slipped away from him, her voice breathless. "You shouldn't have been. I told you, I'm perfectly fine." Without turning on the lights she crossed the parlor, and from a safe distance, standing before a cold fireplace, invited him with a gesture to sit down.

She was gracious as a duchess, Stony thought sardonically, and about as approachable.

Rather than meekly accepting her invitation, he took off his jacket and tossed it with controlled violence onto the couch. "So," he said carefully, "you're fine. And you're going to bed at eight o'clock on Christmas Eve? Your message said you had plans. What happened, they fall through?"

He watched with growing frustration as she folded her arms across her chest, an unconsciously defensive posture, shutting him out.

"That's tomorrow," she said remotely, turning her head just enough so that her face was in deep shadow. "Tonight, I—I have kind of a headache, and I thought I'd go to bed early so I'd be nice and rested for Christmas. As you said, it wouldn't be much fun to be sick on Christmas."

"Toby..." He let his breath out in an exasperated gust, thinking that she sure was a lousy liar. He started toward her, but she shrank away from him, almost, he thought, as if she were afraid. Afraid...of him? The idea shocked Stony so much he halted, an ominous little pulse beginning to throb in his belly.

"Toby, what the hell's wrong?" His voice came out harsh and angry sounding, which wasn't the way he felt at all. He felt helpless and confused, a lot like he had when he'd faced Chris in the hospital after hearing that she'd been raped. "What is it," he demanded, determined not to let go of it until he had some answers, "something the doctor said? Or is it me—something I said?"

"No!" It sounded like a cry of pain.

His natural response to her distress was stymied by the walls she'd thrown up between them. He lifted his hands toward her but didn't touch her. "What, then? Please, tell me." And then, eagerly, remembering what Chris had said, "Are you afraid of intruding on our holiday? On Chris and me? Is that it?"

She shook her head and opened her mouth to say something but before she could, inspiration struck Stony. It was what Chris had said about some people having a thing about holidays. He didn't know why he hadn't thought of it sooner. He was an insensitive clod, he berated himself, gazing up at the ceiling and softly swearing. A total jerk. An idiot.

He scrubbed a hand over his face, took a deep breath and said gently, "Toby, listen, I'm sorry. I just wasn't thinking. I completely forgot that this is the first Christmas since your husband died. I know how hard it is." He took her by the arms and found that she was shaking. Waves of tremors were coursing through her body. She's wound up tighter than a drum, Stony thought with burgeoning compassion and tenderness and, bent only on comforting, he tried to draw her into his arms.

"No!" Her hands came up to brace against his chest, as with a choked cry she tore herself from his grasp. "Please, don't . . . touch me."

Her rejection jolted him like a hard right cross. "Don't touch you?" He shook his head, dazed. "Don't touch you—Toby, night before last you were in my arms, in my bed, making love with me in just about every conceivable way—" She made a strangled sound, clapped a hand over her mouth and turned her back to him. Her shoulders shook, and he thought for one horrible moment that she was laughing. "And I don't recall anybody forcing you. In fact, I've never had a woman respond to me with such...abandon in my entire life."

He took another deep breath, trying hard to stabilize his heartbeat and respiration. All his nerves were jumping and glowing like St. Elmo's fire. "Look, I told you once that you'd always know where you stand with me. That's just how I am. But I need the same from you." He reached out and touched her shoulder, and this time she didn't shrink away from his touch. Gently and fearfully he turned her. "Toby, I thought we had something pretty good going here. At least we'd gotten a pretty damn good start. Now, if something's happened to change that for you, then I need to know about it."

She was crying. Above the hand that still covered the lower half of her face, her eyes were dark and rain drenched. Stony's heart swelled. It was the first time he'd ever seen her cry, except for the few times she had at the climax of their loving. That had moved him, too, in a different way, but this...this was more than he could stand.

"Toby," he croaked, wracked by bewildering pain, "for God's sake, tell me."

She shook her head and whispered, "I can't."

Inside Stony there was a great stillness, an emptiness that slowly filled up with the absolute certainty that there was something very, very wrong with Toby. "You're lying to me, aren't you?" he said, hearing his own voice from a great distance. "The doctor told you something."

Her eyes slowly closed, giving him all the confirmation he needed.

In the vast stillness inside him, his words sounded like drumbeats. "Tell me."

Suddenly she wasn't crying anymore. She moved away, widening the gulf between them, then wiped her cheeks with both hands, took a deep breath and drew herself up straight and tall. She looked like a duchess bravely facing the guillotine.

"I didn't lie," she said bluntly, almost angrily. "I'm not sick. I'm pregnant."

## Chapter 11

He didn't repeat it or ask her to. He knew exactly what she'd said.

*Pregnant.*

The word entered his mind like a bullet through a plate-glass window. He didn't know how long he stood there stunned, listening to the shattered fragments of the fragile and lovely thing they'd shared crashing around him in a tinkling crystalline rain.

He put back his head and swore softly at the ceiling.

"Ah, damn," he breathed, shaking his head, "I can't believe I fell for it." It was the first thought to struggle out of the wreckage in his mind—that she'd lied to him. Deliberately deceived him. The oldest con in the book. His mouth twisted in an ironic travesty of a smile. "You'd think, at my age, I'd know better."

"What do you mean?" Her voice was breathless and very faint.

He gave a harsh and bitter laugh. "You lied to me."

She closed her eyes and turned her face away from him as if he'd slapped her. Barely loudly enough for him to hear she whispered, "I knew you'd think that."

Oh, he didn't, not really, not deep down. But for the moment he clung doggedly to the idea because, of all the emotions crashing around inside him, anger was the easiest.

"What the hell am I supposed to think?" he lashed at her, his own pain blinding him to hers, making him brutal. "You told me you couldn't get pregnant. Now you tell me you're pregnant. There's a lie in there somewhere, lady! So tell me, what did you hope to accomplish with this, huh? Did you think I'd marry you, is that it?"

"No!" Her head jerked around and her eyes homed in on his, brimming with liquid fire. "No, I don't—"

"Because I've got news for you—I won't do that. I can't do that. I made it perfectly clear to you how I felt about marrying again. And you sure as hell know how I feel about having kids! I won't go through that again, I told you that."

"I don't want anything from you!" Toby shouted, dashing furiously at her eyes with shaking fingers. "Do you understand? Nothing. This is my baby—mine."

Stony stared at her. His own emotions had left him flayed, wide open; hers scored him like saltwater in an open wound. He couldn't breathe, he couldn't think, he couldn't cry. So he turned his back to her, and, as he often did when he didn't know what else to do, looked up at the ceiling, hoping, perhaps, for divine guidance.

Toby. Ah, geez, Toby. The anger drained out of him, leaving only the pain.

After a long time he heard her whisper, "I didn't lie to you. At least—"

"I know that." He jerked one shoulder impatiently, as if shaking off an unwelcome touch.

"Then why did you—"

"Because I was in shock, damn it." His breath expired in a hiss as he turned to face her. "How clearly were you thinking when you first heard the news? Hell, you're the world's worst liar. You couldn't possibly have fooled me about something like this."

Her eyes closed briefly, and a small spasm compressed her lips as she whispered an ironic "Thank you." And then her spine straightened, her chin lifted. "There's an explanation, if you want it."

Even from where he stood, he could see that she was shaking. Damn her. Everything about her—drowned eyes and crushed mouth, fragile, spiky lashes and tear-scrubbed cheeks, schoolgirl hair and woman's body—was an appeal to some soft, mushy corner of his heart. Longing and anguish filled him as he looked at her. Part of him wanted to be holding her, kissing that lush and vulnerable mouth, burying his hands in her hair, nesting her breasts against his chest and losing himself in the embrace of her long, silky legs. This disaster was a rack, pulling him apart. Because another part of him was already grieving for the loss of what they'd had—the sweetness, the joy, the laughter and, in a strange way, the innocence. And grieving for something else, too, the more poignant because he'd never even had a chance to know just what it was he'd lost.

"Of course I want to hear it," he said softly.

"I really thought I couldn't have children," Toby whispered, suddenly looking bleak and lost. Her voice quivered. "I thought so all those years. The doctors said they couldn't find anything wrong with me, but that was before all the wonderful things they do now—the fertility drugs and in vitro stuff—and Arthur didn't want to pursue it any further. He always said if it was meant to happen, it would, and after a while I guess I . . . just accepted it. Today I found out—" She paused as if she'd choked on something, swallowed hard and went on. "I found out Arthur had had a vasectomy before we were married. All those years I thought I was barren, and it was Arthur.''

A strange, cold rage clutched at Stony's belly, unusual for him, to whom anger always came in hot, purging explosions. He clamped his jaws tightly together, knowing he had to control it, knowing her control was so tenuous that if he said anything, anything at all, she might shatter. He wondered if it had even hit her, yet, how cruelly she'd been cheated by the man who'd promised to protect her, the man who'd been so "good to her," the man who had "given her everything." The blows she'd received were incalculable. Stony couldn't even begin to imagine what she must be going through. He admired her composure, he ached for her, and if that husband of hers weren't already dead, he'd kill for her. But he just couldn't comfort her, not when he was still mentally walking in dazed circles himself.

"Have you decided what you're going to do?" he finally asked her, picking words carefully out of the chaos in his mind.

"Do?" Her eyes were dark and uncomprehending.

"Are you going to go through with the pregnancy? There are other options."

Her hands curled, white-knuckled, in the fabric of her nightgown. "Are you suggesting I have an abortion?" Revulsion coated her calm voice like frost.

Stony's face hurt. His eyes burned. "Toby," he said, rubbing them with his hand, "I'm not suggesting anything. It's your choice. I just want you to know that . . . whatever you decide, I'll help you, that's all."

She folded her arms across her body, not so much a defense this time, but as if it were necessary to keep herself from flying apart. Breathing in shallow sips between words, like someone who couldn't seem to get enough oxygen, she said, "There was a time . . . when I wanted a baby . . . more than anything in the world. And . . . I had to accept the fact that I would never have one. It was...hard. And now...I'm being given a chance I thought I'd never have. I...am going to have this baby. And I'm going to keep it. And nothing...is going to stop me. *Nothing.*"

Her face had a fierce, protective radiance, so beautiful it was a torment to look at her. Stony lifted his hands toward her, then let them drop to his sides, knowing he couldn't allow himself to touch her, knowing that if he did he might say things he couldn't allow himself to say. His voice cracked, betraying his anguish. "Toby, I'm not trying to stop you. I'd never try to stop you. I told you, whatever you decide, I'll help you. I'll pay your expenses."

"You don't have to do that," she said stiffly. "It's not your responsibility."

"What are you talking about?" Stony shouted. "Of course it's my responsibility. It's my child, too, isn't it?"

The words hung in the supercharged air, crackling like a rack of fireworks. After what seemed eternity, Toby took a deep breath and with memory darkening her eyes, whispered the acknowledgement of everything that had been between them that weekend of Thanksgiving and springtime miracles. "Yes, it's your child."

His child. His and Toby's child. Deep, deep inside him, something stirred. No matter how hard he tried to smother it, it sprang to life anyway, a tiny, warming flame. His child.

He caught in a breath and whoofed it out. "All right, then." They looked at each other in silence, her face a reflection of the turmoil inside him. Finally Stony said, "I don't suppose you feel much like discussing this now, do you?"

She shook her head, her lips silently forming the word, *No.*

"Yeah, well, I don't think I can, either. Not right now." He frowned, struggling to think logically, rationally. "Listen..." he began. *I'll call you.* And then, realizing that it might sound to her like the old tried and true cop-out, he tried to soften it. "I can't think right now, Toby. I'll call you soon, though, because we need to talk about this some more, figure out where we go from here."

She nodded and whispered, "Okay."

Stony heard himself say, "Well, I guess I'll be going, then." His body didn't feel real, didn't feel as if it belonged to him. He felt himself frown. "Are you going to be okay?"

She nodded again. So did he.

"Okay, I'll see you then. I'll call you."

The next thing he knew he was outside, the door a solid reality against his back, the night air cold in his lungs. He drew in great gulps of it, hurting in every part of his body and shaking uncontrollably, as if suffering withdrawal from some powerful addictive drug.

*Where* do *we go from here?*

He got all the way down to his car before his brain started functioning again. He sat there with the motor running and the heater blowing frigid air into his face and thought about possible answers to that question. And the more he thought about it, the more he realized that none of the answers made sense—except one.

The idea of not having Toby in his life anymore was intolerable. And the only way he could think of to keep her in his life—the way he wanted her, the way she'd been that Thanksgiving weekend, bringing joy and laughter and spring into his life—was to marry her.

Marry her. With his head cocked to one side, Stony listened to the words play over and over again in his mind, wondering why the sound of them didn't frighten him now as much as they had in the past. Marriage wouldn't work for him, hadn't he always said that? He'd been that route and it just didn't work.

But marry Toby? He took a deep breath. His heart began to lift, like a balloon slowly filling with hot air. Of course. He'd been an idiot.

Funny, he thought, smiling into the darkness. He remembered thinking about Toby that when it came down to basics, sex and hunger would usually outweigh fear. Now it seemed that the same could be said of love.

It would be different this time, he told himself. He would make it different. It was up to him to make it work, and he'd do whatever it took. He'd been lonely too damn long.

Toby didn't seem surprised to see him when she answered his knock. She was holding his jacket in one hand and clutching a couple of Christmas presents to her chest with the other.

"Toby, I—"

"It's right here," she interrupted breathlessly. "And I forgot to give you these." She thrust the jacket and presents at him, filling up his arms so that he couldn't do what he wanted to do, which was fill them up with her. "The little one's for Chris. I thought—since I won't see you tomorrow—please, tell her I'm sorry—"

She started to close the door. Stony barged through it and past her, into the dark hallway. "Toby," he blurted, "I've got to talk to you. I've been a jerk. There's only one solution to this that makes any sense. I wasn't thinking clearly. It was kind of a shock, you know?" He took a deep breath and said it. "Look, I . . . want to marry you."

It was too dark to see her face clearly, but he could see her shake her head. "Thank you for the offer," she said quietly, "but that's not necessary."

"But you don't understand," Stony said, bursting with the need to haul her into his arms and tell her how he felt. "I *want* to marry you. I really do. I—"

"No, Stony, you don't understand." Her voice was very gentle. "I don't want to get married. I told you how I felt about it, don't you remember? I spent twenty years of my life in a marriage of convenience. I'll never settle for that again."

A marriage of convenience. Stony stood absolutely still, listening to the echo of her words. Was that all it would be to her? Somehow, blinded by his own revelations, it had never occurred to him that she might not feel the same way about him.

"Stony, I know how you feel about marriage, and I know what it took for you to ask me." Her voice had a liquid sound. He had an idea she was silently crying. "But I told you—I promised myself I'd never marry again except for love, and nothing's going to make me change that. I'm almost forty years old. I deserve to be happy. Please understand."

Stony nodded; the pain in his face, in his jaws, in his throat, was unbearable. After swallowing a couple of times he managed to whisper, "I do understand. And of course you do...deserve to be happy." He cleared his throat explosively and managed to unlock his vocal chords. "Well...I guess that's it, then. I'll, umm, I'll call you after...when I—we'll work something out."

"Yes," she whispered. "All right."

"'Night," he said, and left her there. He walked to his car, got into it and drove home, protected by a blessed cocoon of shock.

In the quiet aftermath of Stony's leaving, the telephone sounded like a scream in the night. With all her nerves jerking and zapping like overloaded circuits, Toby pushed herself away from the door and went to answer it. At that hour on Christmas Eve it could only be one person.

"Hi...Mrs. Thomas?" said the young, uncertain voice. "Hi, it's Chris. Is my dad there? I'm really sorry to bother you, but it's getting kind of late and I was wondering..."

"He just left," Toby said. "He should be home soon."

"Oh. Oh, good. That's okay then. Umm, is everything all right?"

"Yes, everything's fine. I just have a little touch of the flu, and I didn't want to give it to anybody for Christmas. I'm sorry you both worried about me."

"Oh, Mrs. Thomas, I'm so sorry you're sick. What a bummer, to be sick on Christmas. Is there anything I can do?"

"No, not a thing. Except have a Merry Christmas and don't worry about me, okay?"

"Okay," Chris said reluctantly. "Would it be all right if I come over and bring you your present?"

"Maybe later on in the week," Toby said, gripping the phone more tightly. "I wouldn't want you to catch what I've got."

"Oh. Right. Okay, well, we're really going to miss you."

"Thanks," Toby whispered, "I'm going to miss you, too."

As she was hanging up, she noticed her sister's letter, lying forgotten on the desk blotter. Stifling a sniff with the back of her hand, she picked it up, tore it open and sank down in the chair to read it.

It was Margie's Christmas letter, her typewritten once-a-year update on her family's activities and accomplishments. But at the bottom of the page, there was a personal message in her neat, pretty script.

Dear Toby,

I'm thrilled to hear that you have a new man in your life. It's high time. As far as the guilt goes, what did you think you were supposed to do, throw yourself on Arthur's funeral pyre? Nobody knows when you're ready to start living again but you. And by the way, I don't think forty's too old to fall in love, so go for it!

Love,
Margie

PS I don't know whether or not a modern woman can pine, but with those symptoms, if it were me I'd probably just be pregnant!

Laughing and sniffling, Toby carried the letter into her bedroom and dropped it on her dresser. The face that stared back at her in the mirror was tear-washed and radiant, the eyes dark with pain and bewilderment.

It was true. She was pregnant. She was really going to have a baby!

And Stony was really gone.

She wondered how was it possible to feel so much joy and so much pain.

"Mrs. Thomas? Is it okay if I come in?"

"Oh, hi, of course it's okay." Toby smiled warmly as Chris came on through the kitchen's back door. "It's nice to see you."

"I took a chance you'd be here. Are you feeling better? I just wanted to bring you your Christmas present." She thrust the package she was carrying into Toby's hands, then raked back her hair with her fingers in a jerky, self-conscious gesture. "And umm, I was wondering if... Oh— hi, Malcolm." Her shoulders seemed to sag.

"Well, hi there, blondie," the cook said in his warm velvet voice, poking his head out of the pantry where he'd been taking inventory. "I wondered who that was. What you doin' here, baby? You supposed to be on vacation. You have a nice Christmas?"

"Yeah, Malcolm, I did," Chris said with a big, bright smile. "How 'bout you?"

"Can't complain," Malcolm said with one of his inscrutable smiles.

Chris laughed. "And what are you doing here? Aren't you supposed to be on vacation, too?"

"Me? I'm making up a grocery list, that's what I'm doing. You girls eat like lumberjacks!"

"Well, you know we're all going to be on diets when we get back, anyway," Chris said teasingly. "Just buy lots of lettuce."

The cook laughed and disappeared back into the pantry with a flash of his golden earrings.

Chris hesitated, then lifted her hair away from her face and took a deep breath. "Mrs. Thomas? Could I talk to you for a minute?" She threw a nervous glance at the pantry door, and Toby had no trouble hearing the word she did not say. Alone.

"Sure," she said, "why don't we go into my office? I want to open my present. This is very sweet of you."

In her office she put the gift down on her desk unopened and turned to Chris, a question burning on her lips. But before she could ask it, Chris blurted, "I wanted you to know I've started seeing a counselor. I had my first session last night, and tonight I'm going to a group therapy thing. I think it's going to help a lot."

"Oh, Chris," Toby said softly, "I'm so glad." She hugged her and then stood back. "I know it will help you. Your dad must be happy for you." And then, hoping she sounded casual enough, she added, "How is he?"

Chris frowned and cleared her throat. "That's the other thing I wanted to talk to you about."

But she looked at the floor, clearly uncomfortable about continuing until Toby, with her heart in her throat, prompted gently, "Yes?"

Then, all in a rush Chris said, "Did something, you know, happen between you and my dad? If I ask him, he'll just tell me it's none of my business, and I guess it isn't, but ever since Christmas he's been going around like this big black cloud, and I'm worried about him. I know he's really upset about something, and I was wondering...I was wondering if maybe you'd had a fight or something, and if you had, if it had anything to do with me." She finished in a whisper, breathless and flushed, her eyes bright with entreaty.

"Oh, Chris," Toby said, fighting to get the words past the constriction in her throat. "No, it doesn't have anything to do with you. Your father and I—" Her throat closed completely. She swallowed once or twice and whispered, "We ... have some things to work out."

"Oh," Chris said, "I see." And then she startled Toby by throwing her arms around her and saying fervently, "Mrs. Thomas, I just want you to know I hope everything does work out for you and my dad. I really, really hope that."

Hugging came easy to these girls, Toby knew, and they did a lot of it. But this was something different. Chris held on to her, trembling slightly, patting her back almost as if she were comforting her, and by the time she let go, Toby was struggling to hold back tears.

"Well," Chris said with a bright smile, wiping at her own eyes, "I guess I'd better be going. I hope you like the present. It sort of reminded me of you. I really love the earrings you gave me. Thanks. I guess I'll see you in a couple of days. Bye."

When she had gone, Toby tore the wrappings off her present and for a long time just sat there holding the little lacquered wooden box in her hands. The lid had a wild-flower design inlaid in lighter wood. After a while she lifted the lid and listened to the tinkling notes of "Scarborough Fair" while the tears ran unheeded down her cheeks.

"Did Chris leave?" she asked Malcolm a few minutes later as she wandered back into the kitchen.

"Yeah, she did. That's a young lady with troubles," the cook observed, giving Toby a piercing look. "Speaking of which—" he put one big finger under her chin and lifted it "—you look like you got a few yourself."

"Oh, well," Toby said with a little laugh, "I'm just being a little emotional. You know how holidays are."

"Yeah," Malcolm murmured, "I do. What was that Chris was sayin' about you not feeling well?"

"Oh, that." Toby shrugged away from his probing gaze. "It was nothing. Just a touch of the flu."

"Flu, huh? That wouldn't have anything to do with why you ate up three boxes of saltines and a whole jar of dill pickles over Christmas, all by yourself, would it?" Toby didn't answer. "Mrs. Thomas," Malcolm said in his soft, deep voice, "these troubles of yours—they man troubles?" His chuckle covered her silence. "Yeah, that's what I thought."

She turned to look at him, wanted to talk about it, needing a shoulder so badly, and found his eyes resting on her, calm, compassionate, knowing. She closed her eyes and wasn't very surprised to hear herself say, "Oh, Malcolm, I don't know what I'm going to do."

"Yeah," he murmured, "that's what I thought."

He listened, then, while she told him about the baby, muscular arms folded on massive chest, face impassive as a wooden effigy. And when she had finished he asked softly, "How do you feel about the kid's father? Do you love him?"

Toby got up off of the stool she'd been sitting on and walked away from him, rubbing at her arms. "It doesn't matter," she said with a lifting breath. "I know how he feels. He doesn't want to get married again, ever. And he doesn't want to be a father again, either. He offered to marry me, probably out of a sense of guilt or responsibility, but I know he'd only resent me, and I . . . couldn't stand that. I couldn't."

"Toby," Malcolm said patiently, "do you love the dude?"

"All right," she gulped. "All right, yes! But that doesn't—"

"Have you told him?"

"No! Of course not. If he knew, it would just make him feel that much more obligated to marry me. I'm not going to tell him, so don't even suggest it. I do have some pride."

"Pride don't buy Pampers," Malcolm observed dryly. "So you don't plan on marrying the papa. What do you plan on doing?"

"I'm keeping the baby," Toby said tightly.

"Ri-ight," said Malcolm. "And how long you figure on keeping this job?"

For a long time Toby just looked at him. Then she sank onto the stool and covered her face with her hands. "About as long as I can keep this a secret, I guess. Oh, God, what am I going to do? This job is my whole future. It's just about the only way I can get my degree, work and have a place to live. I could try to find work as a live-in maid or housekeeper, but even if I find a place that will let me keep my baby with me, how will I ever go to school? I don't even know if I'd be able to pay for a baby-sitter."

"If the kid's father was willing to marry you, I suspect he'll help you out."

"Oh, sure," Toby said bleakly, "he's planning to. And I guess I don't have any choice but to accept it. I'd never be able to pay the medical bills, otherwise." She sat up very straight, hugging herself. A cold wind seemed to be blowing through the kitchen. "But I won't let him support *me*, dammit. I can't. It would be as bad as marrying him, maybe worse. I just have to find some way to manage myself. I have to."

"You'll make it," Malcolm said quietly.

She whispered, "I'm scared, Malcolm."

"I know you are, baby. But you'll do okay."

His confidence warmed her enough so that she was able to rise, shrug and give him a crooked smile, but she was too shaky to concentrate anymore on kitchen inventory. A hopeless muddle of emotions, she went looking for the only solace she knew—her guitar.

As the kitchen door swung shut behind her, she heard Malcolm say softly, "Baby, I still think you should tell him."

## Chapter 12

On the last day of the year, a heat wave blew into Southern California on the wings of a dry Santa Ana. To Toby's great relief, by the next day the winds had departed. The heat, however, hung around. So once again, it seemed, the annual Rose Parade would be what Arthur had once called a commercial for the Pasadena Chamber of Commerce. After watching three and a half hours of that, she thought a good many northeasterners would probably hurl their snowshovels into the nearest drift and call a real-estate agent. Giddy Californians, on the other hand, would be heading for the beaches with their transistor radios.

Since Toby had very little tolerance for either sunshine or football, she walked down to the Village, found a drugstore that was open and bought every paperback and magazine she could find on baby and child care, from Benjamin Spock to Erma Bombeck to *Good Housekeeping*. Fortified with a fresh jar of dill pickles and a box of saltine crackers, she spent New Year's afternoon sitting cross-legged in the middle of her bed, reading flyleafs and chapter titles and poring over book jackets. She didn't actually read any of the books. She felt almost superstitious about it, as if too much acknowledgment on her part might make the miracle go away. As if it were a dream and if she tried to consciously involve herself in it, she would wake up.

A baby. Once it had been the most natural thing in the world to imagine herself a mother. A given, a part of growing up, like breasts and periods. Now it seemed a breathless, misty fantasy, a miracle, to think of a small fuzzy head bobbing beneath her chin, tiny fingers gripping her big one, gurgles and coos and luminous, drooling smiles, an impossible, beautiful, terrifying miracle. A baby. Her insides quailed at the thought.

For one thing, it just didn't seem real to her that there could be a whole new person growing inside her body. Her stomach was still so flat, for one thing, almost more now than usual because she'd been sick. And her breasts. No, wait, did her breasts feel just a little fuller? The nipples more sensitive? She put her hands over them and with her eyes closed, tried to imagine them heavy with milk. But it was impossible.

And she knew that it was neither the touch or thoughts of motherhood that made them grow hard and tight.

When the phone rang she thought about not answering it. Her legs were stiff from sitting in the same position too long and her feet were asleep. And there was the pickle jar to contend with. But in the end, swearing softly, she untangled her legs and dragged herself creaking and groaning off the bed to pick up the phone a split second before the answering machine did.

"We need to talk," a gravelly voice said without preamble.

Toby's stomach performed a maneuver she knew was physically impossible. Her hand grew slippery on the receiver. "Stony?"

"Yeah, it's me." There was a brief pause, and then a brusque, "How are you? Are you feeling okay?"

"Yes," she murmured, "I'm fine."

"Good. If you feel up to it, there are some things I need to talk to you about."

He seemed even more abrupt than usual. Toby could almost see his face, his brow lowering in a frown, care lines deepening around his mouth, eyes glittering like broken glass.... "All right," she said calmly, closing her eyes.

She heard the sound of an exhalation. "Any objections to dinner?"

"No," she said, "that would be fine. Where—"

"I'll pick you up in an hour."

"You don't have to do that. I can meet you somewhere, if you—"

"No." The word was clipped, final. "I'll pick you up. See you in about an hour." The line clicked and went dead.

Toby hung up the phone and only then realized that she was shaking. I won't cry, she said to herself. I won't cry.

One hour. Stony would be here in one hour. She had to take a bath, fix her hair, find something to wear! What should she wear? He hadn't told her where they'd be going. How could she concentrate when everything inside her was rattling around loose?

Dinner. It was just dinner, she told herself. Dinner and talking. And it was going to be torture to sit with him in his car or across a table from him, close enough to touch but separated by a chasm that made touching impossible. The chasm between them was like a gaping wound in her. Loving and being apart from someone was painful, but loving someone, being near him but not able to touch or even to tell him, that was sheer agony. How would she bear it?

She would have to learn to bear it, she thought bleakly, because this was what the rest of her life was going to be like. Stony was the father of her child, and since he wasn't the sort of man to abdicate responsibilities, he was always going to be there, on the periphery of her life but never really a part of it. She'd see him casually, perhaps, like tonight, to discuss the welfare of the child they shared, his face across a table, his voice on the telephone, his name on a check like salt in an open wound, making it impossible for her ever to forget what it was like to bury her face in the furry warmth of his chest and feel his heart knocking against her cheek, to breathe in his clean man smell and explore the varied textures of his skin with her lips and tongue, to feel his big hands on her, his arms holding her and his powerful body surging into her, then melting, dying a little, lying together afterward in such sweet lethargy.

Oh, Stony. Pain lanced through her. She doubled over, holding herself together with her arms crisscrossing her body. If this was what love was like, she thought wildly, she was glad she'd never had to go through it before. She wanted out. It hurt too much.

*Stony, please...as soon as possible, let me fall out of love with you.*

She must have been waiting for him, watching for him, Stony thought, because when he pulled into the driveway, she slipped out of the house and ran down the steps to meet him, as if she didn't want to be alone with him inside for even a moment. He supposed he couldn't really blame her for being uncomfortable with him, knowing how he felt about her and not being able to return his feelings, but it hurt just the same.

And it hurt to look at her, just as much as he remembered. Her hair was in a loose coil, but he could see that it wasn't going to stay contained for long. Dark, curly wisps were already playing like shadows over her temples and the pale, soft curve of her neck. She wore a cream-colored, loose-textured knit sweater with a V-neck that draped subtly over her breasts and left her throat and collarbones bare. Which was fine for the weather but rough on his resolve. He'd promised himself he wouldn't touch her, but everything about her cried out to be touched. He could see that she was going to test him to the limit.

"Excuse the truck," he said as he got out to open her door for her. "I don't like to leave my car in the lot when I'm gone."

"Gone?" she said, a little breathless from climbing into the cab. "You're . . . leaving?"

"Yeah, later tonight." He slammed her door, went around to his side and swung himself into the driver's seat, careful not to look at her again.

"Where are you going?" Her voice was very faint.

"Alaska," he said as he put the truck in gear and backed out of the driveway. "There's a freighter stuck in the ice I want to go take a look at." It wasn't the real reason he was going, of course. That freighter wasn't going anywhere, and ordinarily he'd have put it off at least until spring.

"I see," she said.

Stony risked a glance at her, but she was looking straight ahead through the windshield. Her profile was calm, remote; her hands were clasped together in her lap. "Don't worry," he said softly, "I've made sure you'll be taken care of."

Her head snapped around and she caught him with a look he couldn't read, but which, for some reason, felt like a slap in the face.

"Here—" He coughed uncomfortably, picked up the manila envelope that was lying on the seat between them and dropped it in her lap. He hadn't meant to do this until later, maybe after they'd eaten and talked a little. Gotten past the strangeness. He had a feeling he wasn't going to handle this very well.

"I've been doing a lot of thinking about this," he said gruffly, "and I think I've come up with a way to handle things that will be least awkward for everybody. Everything's in there. I think. I've had my lawyer draw up a trust. That's in case anything happens to me. And I've opened a checking account to handle your immediate expenses. You'll need to sign the signature cards and get them back to the bank as soon as possible. If you run out of money before I get back, just call Jake—Jake Riley, my assistant. And if there's any kind of emergency, too—you can call him day or night. The service will beep him. He always knows how to reach me." He took a deep breath. "Let's see, have I forgotten anything?"

Her face was turning away from him toward the window, so her words were muffled. "You don't have to do this."

Stony didn't try to answer that. After a while he cleared his throat and said, "I just think it's better this way, for both of us, don't you? A little less...awkward." And maybe, a little less painful, although he doubted it.

"Yes," she said in a tight, constricted voice, "of course. If that's what you want."

No, dammit, it wasn't what he wanted. The whole thing went against his grain, running away, tippy-toeing around like this. It was his nature to bulldoze his way through things, saying what he felt, letting his feelings show, going after what he wanted head-on, full steam. His impulse was to argue with her, tell her all the reasons why she should marry him even if she didn't love him. He had an idea he could change her mind if he went about it right. The one thing he was sure of in all of this was that the physical chemistry between them was real, or it had been, once upon a time. If it was still there, if he could just get her in his arms, kiss her until she couldn't think straight...

But he'd made up his mind he wasn't going to do that. He cared about her too damn much. He knew she'd already wasted twenty years of her life married to a man she didn't love. She deserved better than that. She deserved a chance for love and happiness. And as much as it was possible for him to do so, under the circumstances, he intended to stay out of her way and give her that chance.

They drove westward, into the year's first sunset. Stony reached over to adjust Toby's sunshade, trying not to be hurt by the way she stiffened and moved almost imperceptibly away from any possible physical contact—and then to cover it, shifted, coughed and said just a little too loudly, "How's Chris?"

His smile was twisted. "Oh, she's okay. Better, I think. Seems to be getting a lot out of her therapy sessions, especially that group thing. She's taking a self-defense class, too, and I think that's giving her back some of her self-confidence."

"Good," Toby said softly, "I'm so glad." And then after a moment, "Are you going to tell her about this?"

Stony looked at her in surprise. "I figured it was your call. But, I've got to tell you, I don't like keeping things from her. Especially something like this." He gave a soft ironic laugh and dragged his hand distractedly through his hair. "Do you know how many times Chris begged and pleaded with me for a baby brother or sister when she was little? If I don't tell her and she ever finds out she's got one, she'll never forgive me."

But, he reminded himself, it wouldn't be the first unforgivable thing he'd done to Chris, nor the first damning secret he'd kept from her.

"On the other hand," he said, frowning, "if I do tell her, she's probably going to drive us both crazy. She can be a terrible nag." And she wasn't ever going to understand why he didn't just marry Toby and bring her home where she belonged. She was still young enough to believe that falling in love meant automatic happiness, and what he was afraid of was that she would make things even more difficult for Toby. "Tell her if you think it's best," he said after a moment, "but if I were you, I think I'd wait awhile."

Long enough, he thought bleakly, gripping the steering wheel until his knuckles turned white, for Toby to find the man she was looking for, the one with whom she could finally fall head over heels in love.

Toby didn't eat much at dinner; her stomach was heaving and roiling like a school of porpoises. It was hard enough just being with Stony, his nearness a building torment, like an itch she couldn't scratch. But he had chosen a restaurant at the marina, and all she could think about was the last time she'd been there.

How serene it all seemed now, she thought as she watched the parade of pleasure boats coming into harbor, leaving behind them a pattern of overlapping wakes etched in silver on the purple water. How different from that strange wild night, with the rain lashing her face like spray, wind howling through rigging, masts clanking, boats bobbing gently on oily swells. The night she'd learned what the phrase "unbridled passion" really meant. Passion without restraint, giving without reservation, losing all sense of time and space and self. How would she ever forget that? And how would she ever learn to live without it again?

Looking back now, she wondered if that was the night she'd first known she loved him.

"You're not eating," Stony said softly. "Are you feeling all right?"

His eyes were resting gently on her, the look in them somber and brooding. Had he been remembering, too?

"I'm fine," she said. "I'm just not hungry."

He'd have given anything to know what she'd been thinking. There'd been something in her eyes, something he couldn't fathom. He shifted, indefinably disturbed. "Toby, are you sure you want to go through with this?" His stomach knotted, waiting for her answer.

"Oh yes," she said with quiet intensity, "I'm sure."

Stony nodded, took a deep breath and glanced at his watch. He said impulsively, "I've got time, would you like to go for a walk?"

"Yes, I'd like that."

While Toby excused herself to go to the restroom, Stony paid the check, then scooped up a handful of mints and wandered outside to wait for her. He was leaning on the dock railing, looking up at the night sky when she came to stand beside him.

"Nice night," he remarked, for want of something better to say. This would be the pattern of their conversations from now on, he realized; business and small talk, casual, polite, guarded.

"Yes," Toby said softly, "but you were right about the stars."

He made a small, surprised sound. It wasn't what he'd expected her to say.

"You told me once that city people don't know what stars are," she went on, looking beyond him, her voice remote and sad. A breeze picked up a tendril of her hair and laid it across her mouth. Unthinking, he reached out to pull it away, but found that her hand was there first. "I realized that you were right. We always lived in cities. But I do remember stars. I don't know where we were or why—I must have been very small—but I remember my father picking me up in his arms and showing me the Milky Way. Do you know, it's been years since I've seen the Milky Way."

"Best place to see stars is from a boat," Stony said gruffly, his hands curling with the urge to touch her. "You have to go way out, a long way from any land."

I'll show you the stars, he wanted to tell her. I'll give you the Milky Way. He'd take her down to Baja, and they'd lie on a beach with nothing over them but a warm breeze, her head on his shoulder, her cool hand tracing patterns over his belly, and he'd show her the stars. Big Bear and Little Bear and Orion.

He jammed his hand into his pants pocket and pulled out a small velvet box. "Here," he said hoarsely, thrusting it at her, "I guess this is as good a time as any to give you this." She looked blankly at him, so he added more gently, "Go ahead. It's just your Christmas present."

Her hands trembled slightly as she took the box from him. He saw her throat move as she opened it. He stood with hunched shoulders, watching her, feeling wary and exposed; and after a while, when she still hadn't moved or said a word, he cleared his throat and said, "They're star sapphires. I thought—"

"It's ... beautiful," she whispered. "Thank you."

"Here—" Stony took the necklace from her nerveless fingers and gently turned her. After a moment's hesitation she lifted her hair carefully out of the way and bowed her head, scarcely seeming to breathe as he fastened the clasp and settled the fine silver chain upon the softly draped bumps at the base of her neck. "There," he said gruffly, "now you'll always have stars."

Oh, how he wanted to put his mouth there, just where those wispy tendrils of hair stirred gently back and forth across her nape. He could taste her, feel her textures on his tongue. He felt the tickle of her hair on his face, smelled its wildflower fragrance as he bent toward her. Every muscle and tendon, every nerve and sinew in his body ached with the strain of resisting her.

"I haven't had a chance to thank you," he said abruptly, clearing his throat as he pulled his hands away from her. "For your Christmas present. That little bronze—it's beautiful. Where in the world did you find it?"

She turned, the sapphires shining against her skin and in her eyes. "Do you really like it?"

"Yeah," Stony said, "it reminds me of my dad."

She gave a funny, breathy laugh.

They began to walk slowly along the wharf. Toby shivered, and Stony asked if she was cold.

"A little," she said, shrugging. "I didn't think to bring a coat, it's been so hot today. Don't worry about it. I'm fine."

But he took off his jacket and put it over her shoulders, pulling and tugging it until he had it the way he wanted it, experiencing as he did so a poignant jolt of déjà vu. He'd done this before, he remembered, the first time he'd ever seen Toby. In his pickup, in the hospital parking lot, on a day when the possibility of falling in love had been the farthest thing from his mind. *I guess that's the way it happens,* he thought. *Love comes when you're least expecting it.*

"You look like you could use this," he muttered, wondering if she remembered.

*Is this what it's going to be like?* Toby thought as his body heat enveloped her, his warm scent as heady and nostalgic as brandy. *Remembering and remembering and remembering.*

He'd given her his jacket that very first morning. She'd been so confused, suddenly wrapped in that intimate warmth, surrounded by smells that were unfamiliar and yet strangely evocative, swamped by feelings so alien and inappropriate, under those circumstances, that they had shocked her. And later, when she had given the jacket back to him, there had been a sharp, cold sense of loss and an overpowering loneliness.

Had they somehow come round in a circle? She was no less confused now than she had been that morning. Her emotions were still in conflict with reason. You love him! they shrieked at her, like a tempest howling around her ears. *You love him!* Swallow your pride and tell him! Tell him you want to marry him even if he doesn't love you, tell him you'll take whatever he can give you, anything to keep him in your life! Don't let him go!

The small, frail craft of reason to which she clung in the midst of that emotional gale was a voice that said, No, never again. No more half portions. She wanted the whole thing or nothing at all. She wanted a real marriage, with caring and sharing, laughing and loving and warmth and friendship. She wouldn't settle for less, ever again. Not even if it meant . . .

"I guess we'd better be getting back," Stony said. "I have to meet Jake in an hour."

No. Oh, God, don't let him go!

"Oh yes, certainly," Toby said. "How long—" She choked; her throat felt as if it were bleeding. "How long will you be gone?"

"I don't know. A lot depends on weather conditions."

*Idiot! You love him. Tell him now!*

"Oh," she said calmly. "Yes, of course, it would."

"If I take the job, I'm looking at probably two or three months, barring interruptions for emergencies."

Toby swallowed and whispered, "Three months . . ."

"I haven't decided whether to bid on it or not," Stony said. Say the word, he pleaded silently. Say the words and I'll stay.

"Oh," she whispered, staring steadfastly at the center of his chest.

"That's why I want to take a look at it now." Look at me, he wanted to shout. Look into my eyes and tell me not to go.

"Well," she said on a quivering breath, "of course. I can understand why you need to do that."

This was nonsense. The only thing he wanted to do was pick her up in his arms, carry her to his boat, set it on a southwesterly course and make love to her until they hit Tahiti. The only thing in the world he wanted to look at was her face, flushed and dewy with desire, looking up at him from his pillows; her lips parting in a sigh, then softly smiling, her eyelashes drifting down like shadows. Her body, opening for him, warm and welcoming; a slow, sweet merging, poignant as a homecoming.

*Toby, for God's sake, if you can't say it, at least please do something! Touch me, reach out to me—the slightest move. Give me an excuse to touch you. Put your arms around me, give me a reason to stay.*

"Well," she said, her voice as distant and hollow as a whisper down an empty hallway, "I guess we'd better go."

But Stony didn't move and neither did she—when had they stopped walking? The silence seemed to go on and on, until she thought they might never move or speak again. As if they were caught forever in that moment, like butterflies in acrylic.

*Stony, I love you. Please don't go.*

*For God's sake, Toby, say something. Please ask me to stay.*

Somewhere a harbor buoy clanged; sailboat rigging creaked; footsteps sounded on the wooden wharf; voices drew near, then faded.

"Yes," Stony said, "I guess we'd better do that."

His face was in shadow, and for that Toby was grateful. She could never have endured looking at his wonderful, caring face—his battered nose, his mouth that smiled so beautifully, so tenderly, his soul-piercing eyes. At all costs, she must avoid those eyes. They saw too much and revealed too much. If he looked into her eyes, she thought, he must surely see the love written there. She wouldn't be able to hide it from him, any more than he would be able to hide the pity in his.

She could not abide pity.

*People handle what they have to.*

Strength poured into her from unknown wells, as it had that terrible day in the judge's office when she had first learned that she was penniless. I will make it, a quiet voice within her said. I—my baby and I—are going to be all right. Somehow.

Under the cover of Stony's jacket she touched the necklace he'd given her, feeling the hard, cold edges of the sapphires with her fingertips. Then she took the jacket from around her shoulders and handed it to him. "Thank you," she said, drawing herself up and straightening her shoulders, "but I don't need this anymore."

"Are you sure?" Stony asked, concern rasping in his voice.

"Yes," Toby said, "I'm fine now."

They walked back to the truck, slowly and without touching.


"Mrs. Thomas? May I—oh! I'm sorry, I didn't mean to disturb you."

"It's all right, Mindy," Toby said. "Come on in. I was just . . . resting."

She'd been hoping that lying down for a few minutes would make the dull ache in her lower back go away, but if anything, it seemed to be worse. As she sat up and slowly eased her feet down to the floor, she had to disguise a small involuntary gasp of pain by turning it into a yawn.

"Hmm, my goodness," she murmured, "I only meant to lie down for a minute or two. What is it, are the buses here?"

"Yes," Mindy said, "and people are starting to arrive. I've heard a couple of people asking for you. I thought you'd want to know."

"Yes, thank you, I'll be right there. Oh, and by the way," Toby added with a smile as the sorority president paused in the doorway, "you look absolutely terrific. That's a beautiful dress."

"Thanks!" Mindy's face blossomed. "I hope Brad thinks so. You look nice, too, Mrs. T. That blue looks really good on you. Well, gotta go. Hurry, we miss you!"

Toby held her smile firmly in place until the door had closed, then carefully stood up and refastened the waistband of her ice-blue silk charmeuse skirt. She probably could have left it unfastened—the long, loose matching jacket would serve to hide the gap. It was a matter of pride that she didn't. Pride and a refusal to face the fact that the days she had left to keep her secret—and her job—were numbered.

A rather painful trip to the bathroom did nothing to alleviate the pressure in her lower abdomen, a discomfort that had become chronic during the past couple of weeks. Why, she wondered, did so many of the changes in her body have to be unpleasant? She almost longed for the nausea; that, at least, had been an intermittent torment.

Right now, she ached all over, but especially in her lower back. All she wanted to do was crawl into her bed and sleep. Never had she felt less like playing the role of gracious hostess. But outside in the street she could hear the muted roar of the fleet of chartered buses that would transport the members of Gamma Pi Sorority and their escorts to the Beverly Hills highrise hotel that was to be the site of the annual Valentine's Day Sweethearts and Flowers cocktail party. And just beyond her door, the somewhat less muted roar produced by dozens of young couples as they gathered to board the waiting buses. Many of the girls would be Gee

Pis who didn't live in the house and who seldom got a chance to stop and say hello to its house director. They would expect Toby to be there. If she wasn't there, they would worry, and wonder, and ask questions about her health. And she couldn't have that.

So she rubbed her aching back one more time, patted her rebellious hair into place, shook down her skirt and stepped into her high-heeled pumps—good heavens, were they getting tight, too?—and went out to face the crowd, feeling anything but a model of maturity and style.

By the time the last bus had departed, she was feeling light-headed and dizzy and the pain in her back was worse. It was beginning to worry her. The word *miscarriage* kept flitting around in the back of her mind, even though, according to all the literature Dr. Morrisset's nurse had given her, the symptoms weren't right. She wasn't having any bleeding at all, for one thing, and the pain didn't feel like cramps. In any case, if she still felt this bad Monday, when she was scheduled for her regular prenatal checkup, she was certainly going to ask the doctor about it.

Meanwhile, she thought some Tylenol might help. She was on her way into the kitchen to see if she could find some in the first-aid supplies when she met Chris coming out with a glass of orange juice in her hand.

"Oh!" Chris said, looking startled, then flustered. "Mrs. Thomas..."

"Hi, Chris," Toby said warmly, and then, stating the obvious, "You're not going to the cocktail party."

Chris shook her head and smiled wryly. "No, I don't think I'm quite ready for that. My counselor says I shouldn't push it, so I'm not, but I don't know..." She gave a one shouldered shrug. "I don't think I ever will be ready for it— you know, the drinking and party scene."

"Well," Toby said, "frankly, I can't see anything wrong with that. Maybe it's just not your thing. It certainly isn't mine."

"Yeah," Chris said, "that's what my counselor said, too." She frowned suddenly. "Mrs. Thomas, are you okay? You don't look like you're feeling well."

"I feel terrible," Toby admitted ruefully. "I was just going to take some Tylenol and go to bed."

"Oh, yeah, that's a good idea. Well, if you need anything just call me, okay? I'll just be, you know—" she shrugged and lifted the orange-juice glass toward the ceiling "—in my room, reading. Hope you feel better."

"Me, too," Toby murmured as Chris continued on down the hall. She waited for a few moments, then took a breath and said, "Chris?"

The girl paused with one foot on the stairs. "Hmm?"

"How is . . . your dad? Have you heard from him?"

Chris looked uncomfortable. "Oh, yeah. he called me a couple of days ago. He's still in Alaska. He doesn't know when he's coming home."

"Oh," Toby said. "Well, I just wondered. Thanks."

"Sure." Chris hesitated, biting her lip as if there was something more she wanted to say, then murmured, "'Night, Mrs. Thomas," and began to climb the stairs.

Toby watched her until she was out of sight—a tall, slender girl in sweatshirt and jeans, tousled hair in her eyes, neither child nor woman, but something in between. How lonely she must be, Toby thought, isolated by the attack that robbed her of her innocence and self-confidence, and with Stony so far away... She remembered the way Chris had hugged her that day she'd brought her the music box. The way she'd held on. The longing to reach out to her, to comfort and protect her, was so powerful and poignant Toby wondered if it might be part of the physical and emotional changes taking place in her. Burgeoning maternalism.

But since the first of the year Chris had been avoiding her, not actively, just not seeking her out for advice and friendly conversation as she used to do, as so many of the other girls did. There were protective walls around her now, and Toby didn't know how to breach them. She went into the kitchen, feeling deflated and sad.

She found some painkiller capsules and took two with a few sips of water. After fighting off waves of nausea and dizziness, she made her way back to her room where she collapsed onto her bed, trembling and weak as a newborn kitten.

Something's wrong, she thought dimly. Something's terribly wrong with me.

Sometime later—she had no idea how much time had passed—she thought perhaps she ought to get up and take off her clothes and put on a nightgown. The attempt brought such waves of pain that it was all she could do not to scream. Later, she thought, clammy and panting. She'd do it later. In the morning. She'd call the doctor, first thing in the morning.

It wasn't the baby, she told herself. It couldn't be the baby. None of the books had mentioned anything like this. But if not the baby, then what?

She didn't sleep; the pain wouldn't let her. It seemed almost to have a life of its own, to have become an entity, an adversary she had to battle through the long, lonely night. Grimly she held it at bay, marking the slow progress of the night by the chiming of the parlor clock. Listening for sounds that would mean dawn was coming—the growl of a truck on a distant street, the roar of the first MTD bus going by, the slap, slap, slap of an early-morning jogger. The stealthy sounds Malcolm made, coming in at five o'clock to begin preparations for breakfast.

Malcolm. He was here, in the house, just down the hall in the kitchen. *He* could help her, if only she could reach him. But how? She couldn't move, couldn't get out of bed. If she called, it would wake the house. I won't do that, she vowed, clamping her lips together as the tears rolled into her hair. I won't lie here crying for help like a little baby.

Somehow, some way, she was standing up. She was walking, shuffling like an old, old woman toward the door. Clinging to it, clammy and trembling. The pain was unlike anything she'd ever imagined.

Incredible, she thought; am I dying? Is that what this is? How surprised everyone would be—she was supposed to be too young for this job!

She began to giggle. And then, realizing that she was becoming hysterical, she tried to bludgeon her mind back into sanity. *Don't be an idiot, you're not going to die. You're going to have a baby. You can't die now.*

Her hands were flat on the panels of a door, her forehead pressed against the wood. Winded, drenched with sweat, she rested, gathering the last of her strength. The pain was so intense it seemed almost to have sound, a voice, or was that only herself, crying? She pushed the door open.

"Malcolm," she gasped as she lurched into the kitchen, "please, I need . . . help."

# Chapter 13

Malcolm caught her just before her legs gave way. She screamed when he lifted her into his arms.

"Here, now, I got you...." The cook's deep, velvet voice soothed and calmed her. "What is it, the baby?"

She shook her head, gasping for breath. "I don't know. I don't think so. My back hurts. Something's wrong. I think I need a doctor."

"A hospital's more like it," Malcolm said. "You're burnin' up. Hang on, baby, we'll get you taken care of. Just take it easy now, you hear?" He kicked open the kitchen door, stuck his head—and Toby's—through it and bellowed, "Chris!" Toby stared at him in utter astonishment. It was the first time she'd ever heard the cook raise his voice. And why had he called Chris?

Several sleep-tousled heads were peering over the stair railing. Someone turned to shout into the upstairs hallway, "Go get Chris. Tell her Malcolm wants her in the kitchen." Yawning and bewildered, a few of the girls were making their way down the stairs. It was beginning to penetrate their sleep-fuddled minds that something was amiss: Why was their cook yelling at five o'clock in the morning, and why was he carrying their house director in his arms?

"Mrs. Thomas," bewildered voices said, "what's wrong? Are you okay?"

Toby closed her eyes. Explanations were beyond her capability.

"Mrs. Thomas has had an accident," Malcolm said in a tone that discouraged further questions. "I'm taking her to the med center, so you girls are on your own. If you're plannin' on eatin' breakfast this mornin', I suggest you get somebody appointed to KP duty right quick, you hear?" The chorus was dazed but affirming. "Atta girls," Malcolm said approvingly, pulling himself and Toby back into the kitchen. "How you doin'?" he asked her as the door swished shut, his voice once again a comforting murmur.

"Okay," Toby managed to whisper. She wanted to ask him again why he'd called for Chris, but before she could, the door swung open again and Chris burst into the kitchen in a way that reminded Toby wrenchingly of her father.

"Malcolm, what's wrong with Toby? Everybody's saying—oh, God, Mrs. Thomas, are you all right?"

I must look awful, Toby thought; Chris looked horrified. "I seem to have hurt my back," she heard herself say in a tight, airless voice. "Malcolm is taking me to the hospital."

"The hospital! Oh no—what can I—is there anything I can do?" She paused uncertainly, both hands pressed to her mouth, and then ventured, "Do you think . . . should I call my dad?"

There was a moment of dead silence. Malcolm looked at Toby, his eyebrows arched high in an unspoken question. Finally she nodded. She heard his quiet voice say, "Yeah, baby, I think you should do that. You go ahead while I run Mrs. Thomas over to the med center."

"Okay," Chris said breathlessly. "I'll call Jake—he'll know how to reach Dad. What shall I tell him?"

"Just tell him Toby's been taken to the hospital," Malcolm said patiently but firmly.

"No, wait," Toby croaked, "tell him—" But Chris was already gone. "He'll probably think it's the baby," she whispered to Malcolm as he carried her down the back steps.

"Yep, he probably will," the cook said enigmatically. And after a moment added, "And you don't know that it isn't."

A vast coldness filled her. "I can't lose this baby," she whispered. And then somewhere deep inside her, a flame ignited and began to burn strong and steady, driving back the cold. *I won't lose this baby.*

Malcolm chuckled softly and murmured, "Atta girl. Hold on, now."

Blinding pain wracked her as he shifted her, opened doors, lifted her, settled her on the back seat of his van. As he was backing out of the van, Toby clutched at his arms, holding him there while she fought nausea and encroaching darkness. There was something she had to ask him. "How—" she said, then stopped for breath. "How did you know?"

"That Chris's dad was the one?" Malcolm gave her one of his inscrutable smiles. "Oh, well, she confided a little, and you confided a little, and I can generally add two and two and come up three."

"But she doesn't—you didn't—"

"Naw," Malcolm drawled, "didn't tell her a thing. That's for you and her dad, know what I mean?"

"Yes," Toby whispered. She leaned back against the seat, exhausted and frightened. She was tired of being strong. She wanted to let someone else take over for a while. She was tired of being alone and in pain. She wanted someone to hold her and take care of her. She wanted Stony.

But Stony was in Alaska. Even if Chris did manage to get a message to him, he wouldn't come in off an ice floe and fly all the way home just to see how she was. And what if she did miscarry? He hadn't wanted the baby anyway.

"Hang on," Malcolm said softly as he climbed into the driver's seat, "we'll have you in that hospital in no time."

Toby closed her eyes, pressed her lips together and gave him a quick nod. But all she could think about was Stony and whether, if she lost the baby, he would be sorry...or glad.

Stony wasn't conscious of any sense of irony or déjà vu as he plowed through the doors of the medical center ER. He had only one thing on his mind.

"Toby Thomas," he barked at the receptionist, slapping his hands down on the counter. "She was brought in this morning. Can you tell me where she is? What's wrong with her?"

The receptionist, who had been staring at him with her mouth open, swallowed and murmured in an awed voice, "Just one moment, sir, I'll check for you." Tearing her eyes away from him, she began to type on a computer keyboard. *Thomas...Toby...* Stony waited, drumming impatiently on the countertop. "Yes, sir, she'd been admitted. If you—"

"Admitted! What for? What's the matter with her? What's her condition?"

"I'm sorry, sir, I don't have that information. You'll have to go to the main admitting desk. They will be able to help you. I'm sure."

"Oh, for—" Stony looked up at the ceiling and swore with quiet vehemence. Then he shook his head and gave a little snort of ironic laughter, because he could hear Chris's voice in the back of his mind, saying, "Daddy, please don't shout."

With as much patience as he could muster he apologized to the receptionist and tried to focus his mind on the directions she was giving him. But it was hard. For more than twelve hours now he'd been thinking the unthinkable and he'd about reached the end of his rope. He'd been hanging around Nome for days, trying to think of excuses not to go home, when he'd gotten Jake's call telling him Toby had been rushed to the hospital. It had to be the baby, of course. All the way home he'd thought about what it was going to do to Toby if she lost that baby and how much he wanted to be there with her if she did. He'd thought about other things, too, things that made his stomach knot and his eyes burn. And he'd realized that he didn't want Toby to lose the baby, any more than he wanted to lose Toby.

He'd never forgive himself if he was too late.

This time he was prepared for the startled look he got from the woman at the admitting desk. He'd caught a glimpse of his reflection in a darkened window on his way from the ER, and it was no wonder the receptionist there had seemed so shocked. For one thing, he was still wearing his parka, which was something you didn't see every day in L.A. With his bloodshot eyes, skin that had been pretty well strafed by arctic winds and six weeks' growth of hair and beard, he figured he must look like a Yukon prospector heading for town on a Saturday night. With that in mind, he made a valiant effort to appear calm and nonthreatening.

"Thomas?" the admitting receptionist said, consulting her computer with deliberation. "Hmm, are you a member of the family?"

"Yes," Stony grated between clenched teeth. The receptionist didn't look as if she wanted to challenge him.

"Room 314, third floor," she murmured, pointing beyond him. "You can take the elevator or the stairs."

"Thanks," Stony said, then hesitated and turned back, steeling himself. "Can you tell me what her condition is, please?"

"She's listed as stable."

"Stable?" Stony exploded, unexpectedly shaken. "What the hell is that supposed to mean?" The word was probably meant to be reassuring, but he found it to be very much the opposite. For Toby to be "stable" now, implied that at some point she had not been, which made this present state seem to him very precarious and fragile.

"I'm sorry, sir," the receptionist said severely, "I don't have that information. You'll have to ask the nurse on duty." She pointed again, in a manner that reminded Stony of his third-grade teacher. "Third floor."

Stony took the stairs. Hospital elevators were always slow as molasses, and besides, if he didn't burn up some of his nervous energy, he was going to explode. The stairwell door opened into a waiting area directly across from a nurse's station, which seemed to be a busy place at that hour. Ignoring the occupants of the waiting room and sidestepping nurses, volunteers and dinner carts, Stony strode up to the counter and panted, "Toby Thomas, Room 314—where is it?"

"I'm sorry," the nurse said with maddening calm, after consulting a list on the counter, "Mrs. Thomas can't be disturbed. She's sleeping. If you'd care to wait—"

"No, dammit, I don't care to wait!" Remembering where he was, he tried to keep his voice down and only succeeded in sounding like someone unloading a dumptruck load of gravel. "Look, miss," he said tersely, "as you might guess from looking at me, I've come a helluva long way to find out how that lady is in there. Now, for God's sake, somebody tell me! Is she all right? What about the baby? Is the baby all right?"

"Daddy?" It was Chris's voice, coming from the waiting area behind him. "Oh, Daddy, I'm so glad you're here. What—"

Stony gave her a quick glance and held out his hand to forestall her while all his attention stayed focused on the nurse, an Oriental woman with a scrubbed face and compassionate eyes. He didn't blink and he didn't breathe, waiting for an answer.

"Are you her husband?" the nurse asked, eyeing him with a certain wariness.

"Not yet," Stony growled, "but I intend to be. Just tell me, dammit, did she lose the baby?"

"Baby?" Chris's voice was a bewildered whisper.

"Not so far," the nurse said gently. "The doctors have been very concerned, and she is being monitored very closely, but as of now, they are optimistic about the pregnancy."

Stony closed his eyes and felt himself slowly deflate. From behind him came an incredulous squeak. "Pregnancy?"

"Optimistic," Stony said slowly, as the nurse's words sorted themselves out in his mind. "Then it wasn't a miscarriage?"

"M-miscarriage?" That was Chris again, but he couldn't think about her now.

"Oh, no," the nurse said. "No, Mrs. Thomas has a severe kidney infection, which can cause premature labor and miscarriage, but as I say, the doctors are optimistic that they were able to catch it in time. I really can't tell you much more, Mr.—"

"Brand. Stony Brand."

"Mr. Brand. You really should speak to the doctor. He can answer your questions about Mrs. Thomas's condition. If you'd like, I will call him for you."

"Mrs. Thomas—is going to have a baby?"

"Uh, yeah, sure, I'd like that," Stony said to the nurse, "but later, huh? Later." He threw a distracted look over his shoulder at his daughter. She was standing there staring at him, and right behind her was Jake Riley. Jake had his hands on Chris's shoulders, and she was hanging on to one of them as if it were the only thing holding her up. There was another man there, too, a huge black man with gold earrings and arms like tree limbs.

Stony turned back to the nurse and rasped, "When can I see her?"

"Well," the nurse said, "as I told you, she's asleep."

Stony held up his hands. "Look," he said very, very softly, "I just want to see her. Please."

The nurse relented. "Well, all right, but just for a—"

"Dad?"

Stony pivoted and found himself facing a stranger. Not his little girl, but a grown woman. A very hurt and angry woman.

"Toby's going to have a baby, and you...didn't tell me?" The last part was a disbelieving whisper.

The look in Chris's eyes gave him a cold, sick feeling in his stomach, but he couldn't for the life of him think what to do about it. He was shell-shocked and reeling from the emotional bombardment he'd been under the last few hours; being a father was, at the moment, utterly beyond him. Finally he lifted his hands helplessly, growled, "Jake, take care of her, will you?" and strode off down the hall.

At Room 314 he paused, took a deep breath and pushed open the door.

He thought later that he should have been prepared for it but he wasn't. He saw Toby lying there, propped on the pillows, her face so pale and still, with tubes connecting her to various IVs and monitors—and just like that, nineteen years were erased and he was back there again in that other hospital room, with another still, white face, this one obscured by a plastic mask, the hair on the pillows brown, not black, with the hiss and sigh of the respirator, the tiny, rhythmic blip of a line on a screen, and then the silence, and the line going straight and flat.

Ice-cold and drenched with sweat, he managed to claw the door open and slip through it into the hallway. For a moment he stood there leaning against it, but then he thought it would be embarrassing as hell if they found him passed out cold on the floor, so he sat down, put his head back, closed his eyes and sucked in air like a drowning man.

"It's tough," a soft voice said, "seein' somebody you love like that."

Opening his eyes, Stony saw a white object hovering at eye level. A foam cup. The smell of coffee drifted to his nostrils. "Who're you?" he muttered, frowning as his eyes focused on a muscular brown arm and followed it upward.

"Name's Malcolm. Friend of Toby's. Here—looks like you could use this."

"Yeah?" Stony accepted the cup, squinting with one eye closed and finally recognizing the man from the waiting room. He was thinking that Toby had some strange friends. This one looked like something out of the *Arabian Nights*.

Malcolm chuckled as if he'd read the thought. "I cook at the house. I'm the one that brought her in."

Stony nodded, sipped scalding coffee and muttered, "Thanks." After a moment he said, "How's Chris?" The thought of Chris made his stomach go cold and hollow all over again. She was never going to forgive him for not telling her about the baby. *Never.*

"She's okay," Malcolm said, jerking his head toward the waiting room. "Jake's with her. Nice guy."

"Yeah," Stony grunted, "the best." He started to get up, then took the hand Malcolm offered him and made use of it.

"Going back in?" Malcolm asked.

"Yeah," Stony said, "I am. Thanks for the coffee."

"Sure. And after that?"

"What?"

"When she's better," Malcolm said. "You going to go off and leave her again?"

Stony got very still. He looked at Malcolm, and Malcolm looked back at him, two strong men taking each other's measure.

"She's scared," Malcolm said softly, drawing the word out. "She doesn't know how she's going to live."

Stony snorted. "She can't be too scared. I told her I'd marry her. She turned me down."

"Her husband left her without a bean," Malcolm said conversationally. "Did you know that?"

"No," Stony said, and paused while he played it over in his mind, remembering the questions he'd never been able to ask her. But then she'd bought him that expensive little bronze. He gave an impatient wave of his hand, "I didn't know that. But it doesn't matter. I told her I'd take care of her."

Malcolm shook his head. "She's got a lot of pride. She won't take charity, or pity."

"Pity!" Stony exploded, "Is that what you think this is? You think I'd come tearing all the way down here from Alaska for pity?"

"Oh," said Malcolm mildly, "so you do love her?"

"Of course I love her!"

"She know that?"

"Well, she sure as hell should. I told you, I asked her to marry me!"

"Uh-uh," Malcolm said, shaking his head, "that's two different things. Two different things." He touched the sleeve of Stony's parka, then held up his hand, as if commanding him to listen. "Think about it, man."

Toby had been so sure she'd heard Stony's voice. She'd been dreaming, of course, but it had sounded so real, as if it were right outside the door. Awake now, even though she knew it had been a dream, she kept straining her ears, lis-

tening for it. But all she heard were the hospital sounds—
anonymous voices, doors opening and closing, footsteps,
ambiguous clanks and rattles and a bewildering variety of
bells and buzzers.

A hospital. She'd never thought she'd be happy to be in
one. That's what happened to you when you were really
sick, she supposed; so sick you were happy to relinquish
control to someone who would take care of you and make
the pain go away. It wasn't completely gone, of course, but
she did feel better. A lot better. Her fever seemed to be gone,
too. She wondered whether she ought to let someone know;
they might want to take her temperature again. She was
reaching for the hand buzzer when the door opened and
Stony walked in.

It's the drugs, she thought. Something they'd given her
was making her have these strange, realistic dreams.

"Hi," he said, "how are you feeling?"

It was Stony's voice, gravelly as ever. Afraid to answer,
afraid of shattering the illusion, she watched him come
closer, sit down beside her bed. Wonderingly she reached
out a hand to touch his face, ignoring the pinch and tug of
the IV needle in the back of her hand.

"You're real," she said.

He made a strange sound, not quite a laugh. "Yeah, I'm
real."

She touched his beard with her fingertips and whispered,
"You grew it back."

"Told you I would." He took her hand in both of his and
turned it carefully, staring intently at the needle and the
white crisscross of tape that held it in place.

Only then remembering how he'd left her, she removed
her hand from his grasp, the joy of seeing him dissolving
into a thousand memory fragments, dangerous and painful
as broken glass. She took a quick breath. "When did you
get back?"

"Just now," he said, smiling wryly, "can't you tell?"

"Yeah." She laughed a little as she fully took in his appearance, letting her eyes touch his windswept hair and frostburned skin. His tired, red-rimmed eyes. "I guess you could probably take your coat off now." And then as what he'd said made its way into her consciousness, not laughing at all she said, "Just . . . now?"

"Yeah," Stony said. His gaze wandered restlessly over her, taking in the wires and tubes. "Sorry I couldn't get here sooner. I had a little trouble getting a flight from Nome to Anchorage."

"You mean you came . . . for me?" She could only whisper, staring at him, not daring to believe.

His eyes jerked back to hers, startled, almost angry. "Of course I came! What, did you think I wouldn't? Geez, Toby, I thought—" He stood up suddenly and turned his back to her, his movements jerky with controlled violence. His hand covered his face, muffling his words. "I thought . . . you'd lost the baby."

"Well," she said steadily, not looking at him, "I didn't." Inside she was trembling, the tension so terrible she couldn't breathe.

"I know." She heard the sigh of an exhalation, and then, incredibly, a barely audible, "Thank God."

She couldn't have heard that. He couldn't have meant it.

Toby slowly swiveled her head, the tension screaming inside her. "What?"

His shoulders lifted; he spun erratically back to her. "I said, 'Thank God.' I'm glad the baby's all right."

"I didn't think you'd care." One tear escaped from the corner of Toby's eye and ran unnoticed into her hair.

"Didn't think I'd care!" He started toward her, anger burning in his eyes. Finding himself impeded by his parka, he shrugged it off and threw it onto the foot of the bed. "Of course I care, what the hell kind of man do you think I am?"

"I thought...you didn't want it." Another tear followed the first; and then another, impossible to ignore now, but too late to stop.

"I didn't at first. And frankly—" He blew out air and dragged his hand through his hair, leaving it even wilder than before. "Frankly, it scares the hell out of me to think about becoming a father again. All that heartache and worry—God, the worry! But geez, Toby, it's my child. Our child. And I—" He stopped, his face changing in a way that filled her with wonder so intense it was almost fear.

"What?"

Instead of answering, he leaned over her, intercepting her tears with gentle fingers. In a strange, broken voice he said, "Please don't cry."

"You what," she demanded, slapping away his hands, belligerent about her tears now that they had been acknowledged.

Stony straightened abruptly, an expression on his face she'd never seen before. Uncertainty, vulnerability, wariness...fear.

"You told me I'd always know where I stand with you," Toby said accusingly, her heart beating at a pace that would have alarmed the hospital staff. She sniffed and mopped futilely at her nose with the back of her hand. "But I don't know what any of this means. I don't know why you're here or—"

"It means I love you," Stony shouted, throwing his arms out, narrowly missing a plastic water pitcher and risking the wrath of the night duty nurse. He lowered his voice. "Dammit, why do you think I'm here?"

Toby just stared at him. Joy and wonder burst inside her without diminishing her tears one iota, like the sun breaking through clouds in the middle of a deluge. "You...love me?"

"Of course I love you—you know that!"

"How could I know that? You never told me!"

Stony threw up his arms in total exasperation. "Well, I told you I wanted to marry you, didn't I?"

"Yes," Toby sobbed, "but only because I was pregnant."

"Because you were— All right, that had something to do with it at the time. But Toby—" He put his hands on her pillows, one on each side of her head, and leaned on them "—I told you I thought there was only one reason for getting married, don't you remember? I thought you understood that. When I told you I wanted to marry you—"

"It's not the same thing! I thought—"

"Toby," Stony said with tenderness and wonder, "you're shouting."

But she was on complete emotional overload now, sobbing, able to see him only through a wavering shimmer of tears. "I don't understand anything. I don't even understand why I'm doing this."

"You're pregnant," Stony said, smiling, staunching the flow of her tears with his hands. "The only thing you have to understand is this." He leaned down and gently kissed her, stifling a distraught little squeak.

She held so very still, breath suspended, mouth soft and tremulous and wet with tears. He kissed her as if she would break, trembling all up through his arms and deep inside his chest. He kissed her as if it were the first time he'd ever kissed, and clung to it as if it would be his last. Until he felt her body relax and her warm sigh bathe his lips.

"Stony..." He felt her fingers touch his face, and drawing back a little, encountered a look of such wonder it stopped his breath. "Do you...really love me?"

"Oh yeah," he whispered. "It took me a while to admit it, but I really do. And does all this—" he brushed his hand across her drenched cheek. "Does this mean you love me, too?" He spoke jauntily, but there was a space inside him that waited aching and empty for her to fill it with the right words.

Fresh tears warmed his fingers, and the words came. "Yes. Oh, yes. I do love you."

Stony closed his eyes and let the warmth pour into him. But he couldn't help asking, out of the residue of pain and loneliness, "Toby, why didn't you tell me? It would have saved us both a hell of a lot of grief."

"Oh, I couldn't," she said, looking tearfully appalled. "I didn't want you to feel sorry for me. I have some pride."

"Too damn much," Stony growled. "Sorry for you? I'd like to wring your neck! I just spent six weeks freezing my butt off on an ice floe, thinking about you, worrying about you, while you were down here worrying yourself sick about your damn job—" He cut off her protest by putting his hand over her mouth. "Hush—Malcolm told me. And that's another thing you should have told me. I thought you were working at that housemother's job because you liked it."

"I do like it. I just can't stay there now that I'm—"

"Hush," Stony said, silencing her this time with his mouth. "It doesn't matter. We'll get married. Maybe you'll like that, too."

"No, Stony." She pulled away from him to look into his eyes. "I know how you feel about getting married again and being a father again. There's not much I can do about the fatherhood thing, but you don't have to marry me. Ssh." Now it was she who laid a hand across his mouth. "Let me say this. Stony, I love you. And . . . I can't believe you love me, but I'm so very glad you do." The tears were flowing again; would they ever stop? She wiped her cheeks and went on, haltingly, "But I know how afraid you are of marriage, afraid to try again because it didn't work for you the first time. And I don't . . . want to marry you unless you're sure. Really sure. Because I meant what I said—I want it right this time. It has to be right for *both* of us."

Stony sat back slowly, rubbing his eyes. "I'm not going to lie to you." His voice sounded strained and tired. "It scares me to death to think about marrying again. And it's not because I don't love you. In fact, it's loving you so much that scares me."

Toby whispered, "I don't understand."

"Toby, I'll have to leave you sometimes. Times when I won't want to leave and you won't want me to go. And I'll have to go anyway, with no way of knowing for how long. And whatever happens, the problems and emergencies, you'll have to handle them by yourself. I just ... don't want that for you."

"I've always managed," Toby said staunchly. "I can handle what I have to."

"You'll be lonely."

"I'll have the baby," she said, trying to erase the loneliness in his eyes with her smile. "And Chris."

"Chris." A spasm of inexplicable pain lashed across his face. He covered his eyes with his hand. "God, Toby, I don't know what I'd do if something happened to you because of me."

"Stony." Frightened, she reached for his hand, ignoring the twinges of pain in her back, "nothing's going to happen to me. And because of you? What on earth makes you even think such a thing? You could never hurt anyone."

He gave a harsh laugh, a terrible sound. "God, how I wish that were true, but it isn't." With a sudden, almost desperate movement he caught her hand and held on to it so tightly it hurt. His face was mask of anguish. With devastating simplicity, he said, "I caused my wife's death."

"That's ridiculous," Toby said with conviction.

"No." He shook his head, the look in his eyes that of a man clinging to the edge of a precipice. "I killed her. I might just as well have shot her." He gave another of those tortured laughs. "Believe me, if there were some way to absolve myself of the blame, I'd do it. This isn't something I've enjoyed carrying around with me." He dropped his face into his hands. "Needless to say, Chris doesn't know. I don't know what I'd do if she ever found out."

"Please," Toby whispered brokenly. "Tell me."

She held his hands while he talked, the pain inside her—his pain—more terrible than anything she'd ever experienced, holding him as if she were the only thing keeping him from falling off that precipice.

"She was pregnant," Stony said, his voice flat and tired. "You know that. She was pretty close to her due date when I got an emergency call. I don't remember what it was, now, but I know I felt I had to go. I didn't even hesitate. My dad had just died the year before and I was still trying to prove to everybody, myself included, that I could handle things by myself. Anyway, I went, knowing I probably wouldn't make it back in time to be there when the baby was born. Lynn was brave about it, but I could tell she didn't want me to go. She was scared, I suppose. It was our first baby...."

He paused for a long time, looking down at his hands and Toby's, before he finally took a deep breath and went on. "There was a storm. The power was out and the phones were dead. She was in labor, with no way to call for help, so she decided she'd drive herself to the hospital. I don't know what happened—maybe she had a contraction while she was driving, maybe she just lost control in the rain—but anyway, she swerved into oncoming traffic. Hit an Edison Company truck head-on."

"Oh...God."

Stony let go of her and leaned forward, hands clasped between his knees, staring at nothing. "They kept her alive on machines," he said in a soft, empty voice, "because of the baby. They were able to save Chris—she was born by C section. By the time I got there, there wasn't anything left for me to do but give my permission to unplug the machines. So that's what I did." He closed his eyes and drew in a deep, shuddering breath. "Chris doesn't know. I never could tell her. I don't know what I'd do if she ever found out."

The silence seemed to vibrate, like a rubber band stretched to the breaking point. The thing that snapped it was small; a sniff. And then a single, quivering sob.

Stony became as rigid as his name. Toby's horrified gaze swept past him to where Chris stood in the doorway, both hands pressed to her mouth, her eyes shimmering with tears.

"Chris." It was a breath on Stony's lips, nothing more. His body seemed to sag.

Neither of them had heard the door open. So intently had they focused on each other, the world might have ended just outside the room and they wouldn't have noticed. Now, for Stony it must have seemed as though it had.

"Daddy?" Chris came toward them like a sleepwalker, her voice high and tremulous, like a child's.

Stony sat absolutely still, his eyes reaching desperately for Toby's, clinging to them. The look in them was one she'd seen before. She hadn't really understood it then, but she did now. A parent's dread, the fear of losing a child. So strong was her empathy that her hand curled protectively over the slight swell of her abdomen and the wires that recorded the tiny, fluttering heartbeat there.

"Daddy?" Chris said again, touching the back of Stony's chair. "Is it true?"

He turned his head toward her, anguish in his face and voice. "Chris—"

And suddenly she was on her knees beside her father, her arms around his neck, sobbing and whispering over and over, "Oh, Daddy, I'm so sorry. I'm so sorry."

For an instant Stony resisted her, still locked in his icy shell of dread, too stunned to understand. Then the floodgates broke and warmth flowed through him again; impulses raced along his nerves. Dazed and shaking, he wrapped his arms around his daughter while his eyes sought Toby's over her head. Through a shimmering fog he saw her mouth the words, "I love you."

And he thought again of miracles, as he had once on a spring morning in November.

"Ooh, wait," Toby said, "here comes another one. Feel that?" She placed Stony's hand on her stomach and they watched together, fascinated, while a mild "practice" contraction hardened the muscles of her great, distended belly, and then relaxed.

"I don't think Jenny liked that much," Stony said.

Toby caught her breath in surprise as the contraction suddenly moved around into her lower back and down into her pelvis. She didn't think Stony noticed. He was too busy watching the large bulge that had appeared on one side of her abdomen. She decided not to tell him just yet.

"That's Jason," she said. "Jenny's over here." She pointed to a smaller lump on the other side.

Stony leaned over to plant a tender kiss on the bulge. "All right, Jason," he said in a loud voice, "this is your father speaking. Be good now and don't crowd your sister. Just be patient, you'll be out of there in a few weeks."

"That tickles," Toby said, giggling. "What are you doing?"

"Teaching them my voice. Don't laugh," he protested, looking sheepish. "You've been playing the guitar for them."

"That's different. It soothes them. You get them all excited."

"Hmm," Stony said smugly, nuzzling. "What about you? Do I get you all excited?"

"Go away," she grumbled, pushing at him. "I know all I am to you is a great big baby factory. A great big, swollen, ugly—"

"Watch it," he growled, cutting off her litany with a kiss, "you're talking about the woman I love."

There was a discreet knock at the door. Chris called through it, "Dad, it's Jake. He wants to talk to you."

"Damn," Stony muttered, then raised his voice to call back, "Okay, I've got it," as he reached for the telephone.

"Not the phone, Dad. He's here."

"Here? Why's he coming over instead of just calling me?" Stony said to Toby in a puzzled undertone. "He's been doing that a lot lately, have you noticed?" To Chris he shouted, "Okay, I'll be right there," as he gave Toby's stomach one last kiss and pulled her nightgown down over it. "Stay there. I'll go see what he wants."

"It's time I got up anyway," Toby murmured. "Go ahead, I'll get dressed and be down in a minute."

She had to hide her smile from Stony. It was perfectly obvious to her why her husband's young assistant had begun finding every possible excuse to come to the house, especially during the summer months, when Chris was likely to be there. But fathers were reputed to be obtuse about such things and possibly even resistant. It was probably best to let Stony figure things out for himself in due course or let Chris do the telling, Toby thought as she rolled onto her side and began the awkward maneuvers required to lever her cumbersome body out of bed.

As she stood up, another "practice" contraction gripped her. She had to sit back down and wait for it to pass. She had another one in the bathroom while she was brushing her teeth and another on the way down the stairs. With the last one she found that if she breathed the way she'd been taught in Lamaze class, it felt a little better.

Stony, Jake and Chris were standing in the living room, quietly talking, their faces somber. When Toby came in the room, Stony lifted his head and shot her a look that stopped her breath. It was a look of pure anguish.

"Bad news?" she said as she went to stand beside him, keeping her voice breathy and light.

Stony's arm came around her; she felt the tension in it. "There's been a ferry disaster in Hong Kong," he said softly. "Capsized and sunk. There's a possibility of trapped survivors. I'm going to have to go."

Waves of love rippled through her. She slipped her arm around her husband's waist and leaned against him, hoping he could feel them, too. "It's all right," she said, "I understand." *It's not the same, Stony. Darling, I promise, it's not going to happen again.*

"Toby, I—"

"It's all right," she said, smiling up at him and then at the two young people holding hands unnoticed near the fireplace. "Chris is here. I'll be fine."

Chris looked at Jake, then at Stony. "Dad," she began.

Stony let his breath out in a gust and dragged a hand distractedly through his hair. "It shouldn't be for long. And you're not due for another three weeks, but dammit, Toby, I promised— What's the matter?"

It was a bad time for another contraction. "Oops," Toby said in a small voice, and gave up trying to hide it.

"Another contraction?" Stony asked incredulously. Toby nodded. "You mean, real ones?"

"Yes," she gasped, "I think so."

"But—you're not due for three weeks! It's early."

"The doctor said with twins it probably would be. Anyway ready or not . . ."

Stony lifted her into his arms, swearing violently. "Dammit, I won't go."

"Daddy," Chris said, "Jake can go."

"I can't leave you—I won't. Ah, dammit!"

"Daddy!"

Jake cleared his throat. "Look, Stony—"

Stony turned to look at them both. He saw his daughter's face, shining and eager, the way she used to look as a little girl when she was all excited about something. He saw her hand, holding tightly to Jake's. And Jake Riley, just looking at him with that steady-as-a-rock way of his that had impressed him so much the first time he'd seen him.

"Let Jake go," Chris said.

"Jake?" Stony said with dawning realization. "What about it—can you handle this?"

Jake nodded. "Absolutely."

"Okay, man," Stony said, shifting Toby to hold out his hand, "it's yours."

"Thanks," Jake grinned, shook Stony's hand and gave Toby a little salute. "I'm on my way."

Chris was grinning, too, so happy it made Stony's throat ache to look at her. Swamped with conflicting emotions, he looked down at Toby and found that she was smiling at him, the love in her eyes like sunshine on a rainy day.

"It's going to be all right," she whispered. "It's different now. You have Jake and I have Chris."

"Yeah," he growled, "and pretty soon here, we're going to have twins. I've got to get you to the hospital, Mrs. Brand! Coming, Chris?"

"I'll meet you guys at the hospital, okay? I'm going to drive Jake to the airport. Bye—" She gave Stony a quick kiss on the cheek, caught Toby's hand and give it a squeeze, said breathlessly, "See you soon, Mom," and was gone.

"Driving Jake to the airport?" Stony exploded in the silent aftermath, feeling as if he'd just been hit by a rogue wave. "How in the hell did that happen?

"Oh, the usual way, I imagine," Toby murmured, touching his face with loving fingers. "Do you mind? I mean, are you happy?"

"Happy?" Stony repeated, feeling dazed and overwhelmed. "Of course I'm happy. I guess it's just . . . a surprise."

Toby gave him a sweet, sleepy smile. "I think," she whispered as he kissed her, "that love almost always is."

\* \* \* \* \*

## *Silhouette Intimate Moments*®

# COMING NEXT MONTH

## #325 ACCUSED—Beverly Sommers

Anne Larkin was assigned to defend her former law professor, Jack Quintana, on a murder charge. Jack was innocent, but Anne was guilty—guilty of falling in love with her client. When the verdict was handed down, would it be life without parole—in each other's arms?

## #326 SUTTER'S WIFE—Lee Magner

When Alex Sutter and Sarah Dunning met, the air crackled with electricity. If only they could find a way to merge their lives.... Could a cynical, semiretired intelligence agent who was accustomed to a no-strings-attached lifestyle and an independent, settled young woman find permanent happiness together?

## #327 BLACK HORSE ISLAND—
## Dee Holmes

Keely Lockwood was stuck between a rock and a hard place. She was determined to fulfill her father's lifelong dream to work with troubled boys, but she got more than she bargained for when she hired Jed Corey. Could she mix business with pleasure and succeed at both?

## #328 A PERILOUS EDEN—
## Heather Graham Pozzessere

What do you do when the man you've fallen in love with may be a traitor to your country? That question haunts Amber Larkspur when she finds herself held hostage in a terrorist plot. Suddenly she has to trust Michael Adams, not only with her heart but with her life.

## AVAILABLE THIS MONTH:

**#321 SPECIAL GIFTS**
Anne Stuart

**#322 LOVE AND OTHER SURPRISES**
Kathleen Creighton

**#323 STRANGERS NO MORE**
Naomi Horton

**#324 CASE DISMISSED**
Linda Shaw

At long last, the books you've been waiting for
by one of America's top romance authors!

# DIANA PALMER
## DUETS

Ten years ago Diana Palmer published her very first
romances. Powerful and dramatic, these gripping tales
of love are everything you have come to expect from
Diana Palmer.

In March, some of these titles will be available again in
DIANA PALMER DUETS—a special three-book collec-
tion. Each book will have two wonderful stories plus an
introduction by the author. You won't want to miss them!

**Book 1**
**SWEET ENEMY**
**LOVE ON TRIAL**

**Book 2**
**STORM OVER THE LAKE**
**TO LOVE AND CHERISH**

**Book 3**
**IF WINTER COMES**
**NOW AND FOREVER**

 *Silhouette Books*®

DP-1